Eleven Miles South of Half Moon Bay

Bill Sullivan

Writers Club Press
San Jose New York Lincoln Shanghai

Eleven Miles South of Half Moon Bay

Published by Writers Club Press
an imprint of iUniverse.com, Inc.

For information address:
iUniverse.com, Inc.
620 North 48th Street
Suite 201
Lincoln, NE 68504-3467
www.iuniverse.com

ISBN: 0-595-09827-4

Printed in the United States of America

Dedication

This book is dedicated to Bruce Michael Stevenson—
the greatest cousin a guy could ever have.

Contents

Foreword

The day that I met Bill Sullivan I knew that there was something special about him. But more than that, there was an exquisite loneliness borne in his heart that needed expression. We seemed to be drawn together in a way that I could not describe at the time, but I believe now that it was the unquenchable desire to share our innermost souls with each other. And share we did.

When I heard about Bruce Stevenson and how he died, I wanted and needed to know more. He played such an important part in my soon-to-be husband's life. My desire was to know Bruce as Bill had known him.

Years later, as Bill was completing his manuscript, he asked me to read through it and give him my honest opinion of how his story made me feel. When I started reading *Eleven Miles South of Half Moon Bay*, I absolutely could not put it down. The words so touched my heart and talked to me so vividly, that I was sure that I could actually feel Bruce's presence. I laughed at his boyhood shenanigans and agonized with his inability to "fit in." I remember thinking that he was so different from me in so many ways, yet so endearing to my heart. I knew instinctively why Bill had loved him.

The motorcycle trips were so emotional that I longed to be a part of them. Sadly, as Bruce left for California to find some peace in his soul, I found my own heart breaking. "Not now, please don't let them be separated," I thought. "I have just met you…don't leave yet!"

I cannot put into words the utter sadness I felt that day on the beach when Bruce ran towards the sea to help in the rescue of another human brother. I can say, however, that I felt my husband's pain and agony as if I had lived through it with him. The funeral service on the same beach months later proved to be a small bandage hiding a very large wound. It was not until Bill found the stamped piece of metal that had once been held in Bruce's hand and now, by some miracle, had been slipped into Bill's hand, that he found some measure of guiltless acknowledgement.

This wonderful tribute to you, now, Prince of Tides, is complete. Our son, Bruce Michael Sullivan, carries on your legacy—and your memory will ever live.

And so, Rest in Peace, Bruce Michael Stevenson. I am honored to have made your acquaintance. And am so very honored to have married your cousin, the love of my life.

Donna Sullivan

Preface

There was never any doubt that this book would be written and published. It was simply a matter of when. I have been compelled to write *Eleven Miles South of Half Moon Bay* as surely as I am compelled to breathe. One can only imagine the anxiety I have suffered in holding my literary breath for three full decades! Indeed, April 5, 2000—the day my manuscript was submitted for publication—marked exactly thirty years since the event that altered the course of my life. How glorious it is to breathe!

Lest the reader should question whether the story portrayed within the following pages is true—it is—as true as mortal memory can faithfully attest. While a reasonable amount of research has gone into the verification of certain facts, and interviews have been conducted with those having firsthand knowledge of many of the events described herein; the fact remains that the primary fountain of recollection that waters this work is my own. Only the dialogue has been desalinated in deference to decency and the protection of the innocent.

Introduction

Coming of age in the sixties was an adventure. At least it was in the no-frills neighborhood where my cousin, Bruce, and I survived it—barely—in southwestern Ohio. That neighborhood was a tiny sliver in the middle of Mad River Township, a narrow strip bordered by Springfield Pike and Northcliff Drive on the north, the old trolley levee on the south, Glendean Avenue on the east, and Planters Avenue on west.

Whenever the boys in our neighborhood crossed those boundaries on foot, particularly the eastern and southern borders, we learned to be vigilant. Our neighbor to the east was Harshman Homes, a World War II military barracks development converted into low-rent housing. To the south was "the plat," a hodgepodge of tiny homes, many only shacks thrown together with the wood of salvaged crates, and in some cases nothing more than a retired streetcar with its wheels removed. Although we had many friends in these areas, there were always other youthful residents who seemed to delight in tormenting those they considered trespassers.

At various times when passing through these areas I experienced the adventure of being surrounded by a gang of twenty roving punks seething for a fight, being shot with BB guns, and being threatened for my life with broken bottles. It could be said without hyperbole that the boys in our neighborhood were afforded an excellent educational opportunity at an early age: the opportunity to learn how to fight, how to run, and equally important, when to do which.

One thing that the boys in our neighborhood took seriously was the game of marbles. Some lads, myself for instance, took it a bit too earnestly. My goal was to acquire a treasure of a thousand marbles, and I could have cared less whose marbles I had to win, or how, to achieve it.

Every marble player had a favorite "shooter," the marble he propelled with a flip of his thumb in the hope of smacking another marble out of the "pot," thus claiming it as his own. Over time, though, a good shooter would become marred and chipped from its frequent bashes against other marbles. Bruce was like a well used shooter, marred and chipped from frequent bashes against his neighbors.

One need not look below the surface to discover my cousin's imperfections, for his character flaws were clearly visible to the naked eye. He made no attempt to hide them. Unlike the marble masses, uniformly round and flawlessly common, differing only in circumference and in the pretty colors they wore to impress their neighbors, Bruce was a rare and magical marble. But alas, a magical marble is slippery and ever so difficult to grasp. For those privileged few, however, who were permitted or compelled to gaze beneath the surface, there was the rare prize of profound allegiance.

Tragically, like a magical marble, Bruce was slippery. One day he was here; the next he was gone. On April 5, 1970, at age 22, he joined in a rescue effort at the beach on a Sunday afternoon and slipped into the sea—forever—sacrificing his life for a total stranger. His body was never found.

No death before or since has affected me the way Bruce's did. My book is a monument to him and a cathartic grieving for myself. It is Bruce's story, my story, and the story of others who are inseparably connected to my beloved cousin. It is the story of everyone who has ever lost a loved one and pondered why. It is the story of conflict and bonding between young men coming of age in the sixties. It is the story of spiritual awakening.

Come with me back to a time that rocked the world. Dare to return to the mind bending days of Vietnam, Easy Rider and Woodstock. Experience the turbulence of adolescence in mid-America during a tempest of social change. Join the boys of Mad River Township as they swim naked at the YMCA and resolve blood feuds among themselves. Struggle with these lads in neighborhood battles, as they unwittingly prepare for a battle some of them will soon be facing in another neighborhood—a neighborhood in Southeast Asia.

Feel the exhilaration of freedom blowing in the faces of three cousins as they gallop their two-wheeled ponies across the land. Shiver with them on the cold planks of their park table bunks. Grieve with two at the incomprehensible loss of the third. Join one on his aching quest for meaning from the madness.

Become a witness to youthful visions of loved ones lost. Make the incredible journey from the back yards of Mad River Township to the pounding surf of North Pescadero Beach—*Eleven Miles South of Half Moon Bay.*

1

Fence Lizards

The decade of the fifties refused to die quietly. 1959 saw Fidel Castro conquer Cuba, denying communist ties. Charles de Gaulle took office as President of the Fifth Republic of France. Cecil B. DeMille, Frank Lloyd Wright and Ethel Barrymore all departed the mortal plane of performance. Able and Baker, two American sponsored monkeys, traveled 1700 miles in space and were recovered in the Atlantic. Ingemar Johansson defeated Floyd Patterson for the heavyweight championship of the world. Buddy Holly, J.P. "Big Bopper" Richardson and Richie Valens died in a small plane crash near Mason City, Iowa. Vice President Richard Nixon publicly debated Soviet Premier Nikita Khrushchev in Moscow over the relative merits of capitalism versus communism. The immensely popular television program, *$64,000 Question*, was revealed to be a fraud. Ford discontinued the Edsel, and Charlton Heston starred in the movie, *Ben Hur*.

Indeed, the Stream of Life coursed powerfully over the Promised Land of America. Springing from Her source in the mighty Harbor of Liberty; pounding without apology across the ageless Alleghenies; rushing, with neither pause nor notice, through the humble Ohio Township of Mad River; and raging toward her destiny in California's Golden Surf—*Eleven*

Miles South of Half Moon Bay. None of this, however, seemed of much consequence to the budding boys of Mad River Township: certainly not to the Stevenson boys, Bobby and his younger brother Bruce; their cousin, Billy Sullivan; nor the Stevensons' next door neighbor, Ronny Martineau.

It is strange how two youngsters, next door neighbors and the children of sociable parents, could become such bitter enemies when there were so many opportunities for friendship. Maybe the strong competition during the boys' cub scouting years between Den Three, led by Virginia "Ginny" Stevenson, and Den Four, led by Mary Martineau, had something to do with it. Den Three's yell, for example: "One, two, three. Who are we? We are Den Three!" never quite measured up to Den Four's: "Stand them on their head. Stand them on their feet. Our Den Four just can't be beat!"

Perhaps there was unspoken friction between the two den mothers themselves, which friction was reflected in Bruce's actions. Whatever his motivation, Bruce seemed intent on upstaging Ronny at every opportunity and provoking him for no apparent cause. Everyone knew there was no love lost between Bruce Stevenson and Ronny Martineau.

It was common for the Stevensons and the Martineaus to vacation together during the summer. Singularly uncommon, though, was the fact that Billy Sullivan was invited to go with them this year for a long Memorial Day weekend in Kentucky. The tallest and most massive of the four boys, Billy had been hearing from both his cousins and also from Ronny for the past three years how wonderful it was down there. Even Bruce and Ronny could agree when they were telling wonderful tales about Kentucky: Tales about sleeping in the old school bus that served as a cabin. Tales about fishing in a lake that held monstrous big catfish—big enough to bite off a man's leg. Tales about water skiing behind a speeding boat. Tales about swinging from a rope tied to a tree limb on a cliff edge and dropping into the deep water below. Tales about chasing elusive lizards.

It was this last item—elusive lizards—that intrigued Billy the most. None of the boys had yet been able to catch one, and Billy wanted to be the first.

"If Mother and Daddy let Billy go with us this year," Bruce, the youngest and smallest of the four boys, had said prior to the invitation, "I know he'll catch one of them lizards."

"If anyone can do it, Billy can," Ronny, the skinny lad with neatly combed brown hair and lots of nervous energy, had agreed. "But I'll have to see it to believe it."

Billy's critter catching skill was well known in the neighborhood. He had, in a sense, made a living catching small aquatic creatures. During the summer months he often helped his dad catch minnows from Mad River, Bear Creek, or Wolf Creek by the five-gallon pails full. Their catch was then sold for live bait to anglers who patronized Trader's Haven, the family hunting and fishing store. Later, as Billy matured physically, the pails grew to eight gallons.

Billy's dad always paid him for his work. More important than the money he earned, though, catching minnows with his dad afforded Billy the opportunity to catch frogs, turtles and snakes. During the summer months he always kept a menagerie of such in tanks, tubs and cages. Billy's critters made him the envy of every boy in the neighborhood. Sometimes he sold a specimen or two, hating to let them go, to other boys or to their parents who came to Trader's Haven looking for just such items. But he had seldom seen in the wild, and had never captured, a lizard.

Reptiles and amphibians were not Billy's only areas of expertise. He also possessed far and away the niftiest insect collection in the neighborhood. In fact, he pursued and captured specimens of every species of insect that flew, crept or crawled within his reach, dispatched them in killing jars, then mounted them on long thin pins stuck in cardboard. He spent hours painstakingly spreading and fixing the wings of beautiful butterflies and marvelous moths for drying. His cousins and buddies admired his skill and persistence.

Billy, though, was never satisfied with his collection, nor ever could be. For even if he perfected his skills to the point where he could mount the perfect specimen of *Hyalophora cecropia* without so much as smudging a single delicate scale, there would still be umpteen zillion species left to pursue. He had yet to learn that the only place where he could truly appreciate the animate wonders of Mother Nature was in her own living laboratory—not some museum showcase.

When Billy was actually invited to go with his cousins to Lake Cumberland, and his parents gave their permission, he was ecstatic. In his mind he determined that when the opportunity came to test his lizard catching skill—he would be ready.

In fact, the first morning after they arrived at the Stevensons' wooded lots near Burnside, Kentucky, Billy slipped away from the group and disappeared for half an hour. When he reappeared his pale-blue eyes, set deep beneath the brow of his suntanned face, were intense. His dark hair, cut flattop fashion, seemed to bristle with pride. "Look what I got," he bragged to his companions.

The skinny brown creature was just six inches long including its slender tail. Referring to his paperback field guide of North American reptiles and amphibians, Billy positively identified it as *Sceloporus undulatus*, a fence lizard, by its deep blue throat.

"Way to go buddy!" Ronny said, beaming and patting Billy on the back when he returned to camp with his prize. "I knew you would catch one of those darn lizards for us."

"That isn't what you said a couple of weeks ago!" Bruce snarled, his perpetually disheveled hair flopping in the breeze like dry grass, and his light brown eyes glaring through the dark framed glasses he had only recently been condemned to wear.

Ronny's normally sunny countenance became suddenly serious. His oversize dark eyebrows seemed to pucker slightly from their natural flared smoothness over his large, expressive blue eyes.

"It is so!" he snapped. "You don't know anything anyway."

"I know what you said! You said you wouldn't believe Billy could catch a lizard until you saw it," Bruce declared.

"Why don't you mind your own business!" Ronny was shouting now. "I had confidence in Billy all along!"

"Sonny!" shrieked a familiar voice, Mary Martineau's voice. "You stop that arguing right now. We didn't bring you boys all the way down here to cause trouble."

Ronny did not have to be told something by his mother twice. She would not hesitate to whip him with a belt if she thought he deserved it. Not that the other boys' mothers would hesitate to warm their hides on occasion. Daphne Sullivan, like Mary Martineau, was partial to the belt. Ginny Stevenson, though, preferred using a buggy whip, intended for stubborn horses. Either way, leather to backside left an indelible impression.

Bruce made a taunting face at Ronny, obviously trying to provoke him further, hoping to see Ronny get whipped. Ronny glared at his antagonist but would not take the bait. From the look on his face one could easily conclude that he was aching to break his self-imposed rule against cursing.

"How did you catch that thing," Bobby interrupted, the blonde hair on top of his narrow head appearing more wavy than usual in the late May humidity. "Let's see if we can catch some more."

"Yeah," Ronny quickly agreed, breaking the tension with Bruce, "show us how you did it."

The heavily wooded area was literally teeming with fence lizards, and Billy was happy to demonstrate his technique. "Look over there," he said, pointing, "see the lizard on that log."

"There's two of them," Bobby observed.

"Oh yeah, there is two of them," Billy agreed on second look. "Here Bruce, hold this one for me."

Bruce extended his hand as cautiously as if the wriggling reptile were a rattlesnake, and a deliberate exchange was completed.

"You guys stand right here," Billy ordered, "and don't move. You gotta move real slow and easy till you get within grabbing range." As he began to move indirectly toward his skittish quarry, it soon became apparent that "real slow" was an understatement. It took him five painfully slow minutes to reach the end of the log opposite where the lazy lizards laid sunning themselves. Then he stood motionless for a one-minute eternity, waiting for his prey to stop tilting their heads and rolling their eyes in his direction.

At last Billy began his final stalking, easing forward with the rapidity of a sloth. When within arm's reach, his motion barely perceptible, his knees began to bend. From his kneeling position he eased his right hand tediously toward its target. Then, without warning, the hand exploded in a blur of motion, like the strike of a mongoose on the throat of a cobra.

Two spindly, scaled bodies moved even quicker, scampering away from danger, and leaving Billy's hand grasping rotting bark.

"Man!" yelled Bobby. "Did you see those things take off?"

"Yeah I saw 'em," Ronny answered, "but Billy almost had 'em. They just barely got away."

"Well you can't catch all of them," Billy said truthfully. "But that's the way you do it. It took me three tries to catch the first one."

Later that afternoon Billy was introduced to water skiing for the first time. To say he was not very good at it would be an overstatement—he was pathetic. Still, he enjoyed it, except waiting for the return of the towline after each fall. It was during these moments—as he hung suspended by a life vest in a hundred feet of ominous black water, his toes dangling down as if live bait for some prehistoric denizen of the deep to devour—that his imagination engaged involuntarily. As he waited for the speedboat to circle around and return the towline to his hands, his thoughts drifted back to a similar summer day two years previous....

Billy had been invited to spend the Fourth of July holiday with his cousins at Crystal Lake. Aunt Ginny's mother, Mrs. Garity, owned a cottage there. The Martineaus were invited as well. The boys played in the water while the adults relaxed in the sun on the sandy beach. A raft, anchored in deep water, was the boys' big attraction. Bobby and Ronny were able to swim to it without a struggle, but neither Bruce nor Billy was an accomplished swimmer. They could, at best, stay afloat for a short time by dog paddling.

The dog paddlers found a way around their obstacle, though, a bicycle inner tube. It had just enough buoyancy to support one of them at a time, and they took turns laying across it and kicking themselves out to the raft. Billy went first, then tossed the inner tube back to Bruce.

All was well until the boys decided to go to shore for a snack. There was disagreement as to who was going to use the inner tube first. Bobby had already swum to shore with Ronny right behind, and neither Bruce nor Billy wanted to be left on the raft alone. Finally, Billy reluctantly agreed to let his little cousin, ten months his junior, go first.

Bruce launched himself in a kicking frenzy, churning a geyser. By the time he was in waist-deep water, however, the raft was out of Bruce's throwing range. Not that Bruce failed to try, but his toss was several yards short and off line as well.

Billy could have gotten help from one of the adults, but was embarrassed to call for it. He had told Aunt Ginny he knew how to swim. Maybe he could dog paddle to the tube. Then again, maybe he could not!

He perched on the edge of the raft, took a deep breath, and sprang toward the tube with all his might. The momentum of his dive, combined with two or three underwater strokes, carried him halfway to his goal. Popping to the surface he caught his breath, spotted the tube and began to paddle like a panicked poodle.

Unfortunately, Billy's best effort was not enough. The wind was blowing the tube away from him, and he ended up ten feet short. He could not dog paddle any further. Maybe he could touch bottom. He tried but could not. He struggled back to the surface, coughing and gagging. He was frantic. He kicked and paddled for all he was worth, but only sputtered on the surface like a stranded moth. His energy was rapidly depleting.

Billy sank a second time. Again he struggled to the surface, fighting for his life. He had swallowed water where it was not supposed to go, and was having trouble breathing. He would not last long. If he went down again it would surely be all over for him. Then, just at the moment when he was about to sink into oblivion, to give up his mortal flesh for a new watery existence at the cool bottom of Crystal Lake, something, some powerful force, snatched him by the hair of his head and dragged him to safety. It was Aunt Ginny....

"Ya' gotta keep your legs stiff!" Ronny shouted over the hum of the speedboat's idling motor. Billy's thoughts snapped back to the present. He checked the ties of his life jacket. Even Aunt Ginny could not save him if he sank to the bottom of Lake Cumberland.

The next day the boys explored a cave where they stuffed their pockets with tiny fossils of the type they called "cave man screws, nuts and bolts." Here, too, in the cool blackness, they discovered pretty orange and black salamanders hiding under stones immersed in the cold spring creek that flowed from the cavern. Yet despite the treasures they found in this ever dark, nether world, Bruce and Ronny had another confrontation.

"Come on you guys, we better get back. We were only supposed to be gone for an hour, and we've already been here longer than that," Ronny correctly reminded his companions.

Seemingly incapable of allowing an opportunity to torture his natural foe pass, Bruce snapped, "What's the matter? Are you afraid of the dark?"

"You're the one who's afraid of the dark, not me," Ronny snarled. "I just don't wanna get in trouble. You don't care if you get in trouble. You don't care about anything. I'm leaving right now. You guys can do what ya' want."

"We probably should be getting back before Mother gets all bent out of shape," Bobby offered.

"Yeah," said Billy, "but I sure would like to find one or two more salamanders. One more would make four; then we could all have one. It would be nice to have an extra one too, just in case one dies."

"Okay," Bobby agreed, "let's look for fifteen more minutes then get out of here."

"I gotta go," Ronny said, and turned toward the mouth of the cave.

"See ya' later Martineau Fartino," Bruce taunted. Yet even this lowest of blows could not provoke Ronny further. As he stomped his way toward the mouth of the cave, the clatter of his heavy footfalls on loose rock echoed like the clopping of horseshoes on cobblestone.

By the end of their vacation, the red metal cooler the boys had permission to use to retain their collection of reptiles and amphibians was stocked with six lizards, three of which had been caught by Billy. There were also three salamanders, three toads, and one small king snake. To Ronny, Bobby and Bruce this was an amazing accomplishment, seeing as how none of them had brought so much as a dung beetle home from Kentucky before.

Yet despite his blatant pride in his cousin's success at catching critters, Bruce undoubtedly felt excluded from the celebration. He was, after all, the only one of the four boys whose combination of slow hands and rapidly depleted patience prevented him from capturing a single lizard. The other boys did not even have to point it out to him. It was painfully obvious.

Though Bruce compensated for his own lack of success by vaunting Billy's in Ronny's face, the victory must have been hollow.

2

Pass the Ammunition

Two weeks after the Cumberland vacation, Billy's dad and "Cricky" Creekmore, the old gentleman who worked part-time at Trader's Haven, butchered turtles. Surely God never created a tougher creature to slaughter and butcher than *Chelydra serpentina*, the snapping turtle. The accepted method of dispatching the cantankerous reptiles was decapitation.

The neighborhood boys were fascinated by both the creatures and by the butchering process. Even after a turtle had been beheaded for several hours it continued to respond exactly as if it were alive. The carcass would fight and writhe against its butcher, its long, sharp claws tearing at that butcher until its last limb was dismembered.

Yet to the boys, the severed head was even more fantastic. Its powerful jaws continued to snap at sticks, cautiously placed within their grasp, for many hours after slaughter. Bruce seemed to enjoy getting his fingers tantalizingly close to the disgusting danger.

"Get away from there!" Billy's dad boomed when he noticed Bruce's fingers perilously close to the huge head just severed from a thirty-pound snapper. "What's the matter with you? Do you want to get your finger snapped off?"

Bruce reflexively jerked his hand away and scowled in his Uncle Bill's direction. He did not talk back, however, not even a mutter under his breath. He knew better.

Bill Sullivan Sr. was not tall, just 5'9", but he was stockily built, volatile tempered and iron-willed. A meaningful stare from the intense brown eyes of this former World War II marine, the dense black hair on his Popeye forearms bristling, was enough to silence any kid in the neighborhood—even Bruce.

Yet something more than disembodied, snapping heads excited the boys and attracted them to the annual slaughter of turtles. That something was the availability of turtle eggs. "Save the eggs for me," Billy said, as his dad and Cricky set to their day's labor.

Save them they did. By mid afternoon, when all twenty-two turtles had been butchered and the meat packaged for the freezer, there was a five gallon pail nearly half full of eggs. What is more, they were not hatching eggs—they were throwing eggs.

Each summer adult female snapping turtles lay their eggs and bury them in the sand or soft ground where they incubate from the heat of the sun. A fully developed snapping turtle egg looks and feels identical to a white Ping-Pong ball, only a bit smaller.

Depending on the time of year his dad butchered turtles and how far north the turtles had been caught, the eggs of a dispatched female were found in various stages of development. If they were fully developed, Billy enjoyed burying them in the ground and allowing them to hatch. Premature eggs like this batch, however, were something else again. Perfectly spherical in shape, about the size of a "half-pint" marble, and consisting solely of yolk covered with a tough transparent membrane: they were perfect for throwing. One could drop one of these babies onto a hard smooth surface from a height of two feet and it would bounce. Yet throw one with significant velocity and it would splatter on contact with just about anything solid—a body for instance.

"Turtle egg fight!" Billy exclaimed when he saw the extraordinary supply of ammunition. "Let's get everybody together and have a battle."

"I'll go get Ronny," Bobby volunteered. "You two go get William and George. We'll meet back here as soon as we can."

"Okay, hurry," Billy responded, and Bobby ran. Billy and Bruce, meanwhile, climbed over the picket fence into the Schulkes' back yard and called for William and George.

The rules for a turtle egg fight were simple: choose up sides, set boundaries, divide the ammunition and commence firing. Turtle eggs generally did not hurt when they hit; they just made a sloppy yellow mess.

"Let Bobby and Billy choose sides," Ronny suggested when the guys were assembled. Bobby was the oldest of the group and Billy the largest.

"First choose," Bobby, ever the opportunist, proclaimed without hesitation.

"No, let's flip for first choose," Billy countered.

"I called it," Bobby protested.

"*Changes!*" called Billy. "I 'finny' we flip for it. No changes."

Though "calls" were most specifically associated with the game of marbles, they were an important part of all the boys' competitive activities.

"I think Billy is right," Ronny interjected. "You should flip for it. That's fair."

"Oh all right," Bobby conceded. "Does anybody have a coin?"

Ronny had a nickel. "Bobby call it," he said, as he sent it spinning into the air with a flick of his thumb.

"Heads!" Bobby shouted. The nickel landed on the ground with its Indian head gazing back at the boys.

"Two out of three!" Billy declared.

"No way, I won fair and square," Bobby said truthfully.

"Come on chicken, let's go two out of three," Billy repeated. There it was, the ultimate insult at his disposal to shame his older cousin into acquiescence.

"Uh-uh!" Bobby was unmoved.

"Bobby's right," Ronny declared. "Let's get started."

"Yeah, come on and let's get started," George added. "It's getting late and me and my little brother have to be home at five-thirty for supper."

"Hurry up and choose then," Billy said poutingly.

"I'll take Ronny," Bobby obliged. Ronny was fast, a good choice.

"I got George," Billy announced. A predictable choice, seeing as how George was tied with Ronny for fastest kid in the neighborhood.

"William," said Bobby, passing over his own younger brother.

"Okay then," said Billy, "Bruce, you're on our side."

Bruce wore his typical sullen expression. He was the slowest kid in the neighborhood, and he had the weakest throwing arm. He was accustomed to being chosen last for neighborhood games. He did not have to like it. Bruce, though, had ways of offsetting his lack of athletic skill. What he lacked in physical prowess, he compensated for with audacity and cunning.

With the formalities of choosing sides out of the way, the friends and relatives on opposing teams became mortal enemies. Half an hour later, great gobs of yellow goo clung like snot to the boys' jeans, their naked upper bodies, their faces and their hair. Unconsciously, Billy scratched his head behind his right ear and discovered a crusted wad of goop.

Another half an hour later the battle was over, the ammunition exhausted. The mortal enemies were friends and relatives again, busy bathing in the gushing flow of Grandmother Stevenson's water hose.

Snapping turtle eggs may have been the most unusual ammunition employed in the neighborhood during the summer of 1959, but certainly not the most dangerous. Shortly before the Fourth of July the boys secured a supply of miniature pyrotechnics. One afternoon the Stevenson brothers and their cousin walked across Springfield Pike to the little pond behind Saint Mark's Church. There, against their parents' instructions, the mischievous boys played with firecrackers.

Bruce lit a firecracker and tossed it into the pond. It sank. The boys waited expectantly, but nothing happened. "I thought you said these things would go off under water," he snarled at his older brother.

"I said cherry bombs will explode under water," Bobby corrected.

"What's a cherry bomb?" Billy asked.

"It's just a real powerful, round firecracker," Bobby explained. "They sound like a cannon when they go off."

"Oh," said Billy, pulling an object out of a back pocket of his jeans. That object was his homemade slingshot. It was fashioned from a forked stick for a handle; two slices of bicycle inner tube for propulsion (one attached to each tine of the fork); a patch of soft leather connecting the two loose ends of inner tube (creating a pouch to cradle a projectile); and nylon cord tying the apparatus together.

Billy loaded his weapon's pouch with a firecracker and pulled back, aiming skyward. "Light it for me," he said, and Bobby obliged.

When the fuse began to spark and crackle Billy released his grip on the pouch. Instantly the black rubber inner tubing contracted, launching the firecracker high above the pond. Soon, though, the missile's inertia was overcome by gravity, and tumbling downward, it gently rippled the surface of the pond and disappeared. There was only momentary disappointment, then glee, as the firecracker exploded just beneath the surface. The water boiled, and the hydro-dampened explosion sounded as if a thirty-pound carp had savagely sucked a floating mulberry from the surface.

"Let me shoot one. Let me shoot one," Bruce begged.

"No let me," Bobby implored.

"Keep your pants on!" Billy growled. "I want to shoot another one, then Bobby, then Bruce." Bobby grinned and Bruce glared, but the issue was settled.

After several rounds of taking turns shooting firecrackers into the air, Bobby had a bright idea. "Let's drop a firecracker in here and throw it in the pond," he said, referring to a glass peanut butter jar some litterbug had tossed on the ground.

"That would be too dangerous," Billy objected.

"No it won't," Bobby insisted. "I'll throw it way out in the pond."

"Yeah, come on Billy," Bruce interjected, "It'll be fun."

"You guys are crazy," Billy proclaimed, even as he pulled a firecracker, sporting a skin of red and white paper on its cardboard casing, from his pocket. "Hold the jar, and I'll drop a firecracker in it," he instructed.

Bobby picked up the empty jar, holding it by the lip of its lidless mouth. He held it in his hand and posed as a shortstop drawn back to make a hard throw to first base.

Billy attempted to light his miniature explosive. He was tense, and his hands were unsteady.

Boom! Billy jumped backward and threw up his arms to shield his face. Incredibly, his two cousins were laughing wildly. Slowly it registered that he was the butt of Bruce's twisted humor. As he had been in total concentration, attempting to light a firecracker and drop it cleanly in the jar, Bruce had lighted another and tossed it at his feet. Bobby had been a mute accomplice to his brother's prank.

Seeing Billy continue to cringe, even after it was obvious what had occurred, seemed to strike his companions as exceptionally hilarious. They continued to howl like hounds after a treed raccoon. They howled, that is, until another firecracker exploded—the one Billy had dropped into the jar, unnoticed by either of his conniving cousins, just as Bruce's joke had erupted.

Bruce's eyes resembled two photographer's lenses set to overexposure. Bobby was Simple Simon's twin. His eyes bulged in their sockets like two big Ohio buckeyes. His mouth gaped to nearly match one of the holes in Stevensons' old outhouse. It was amazing he had not choked on his own guffaw.

Billy glanced at Bobby's throwing hand, expecting to see a charred and mangled mess. It was not. By some miracle Bobby was relatively unscathed, receiving only a few minor cuts on his hand and forearm. No one else was injured. Surely they had been protected by the patron saint of idiots.

Later in the summer, lacking both turtle eggs and firecrackers, the boys found a new source of projectiles: apples. As a supplier of ammunition, they had never seen anything to compare to Grandmother Stevenson's apple tree. Year after year it produced bushels of hard green apples averaging about two inches in diameter, perfect for throwing.

Of course those apples were sometimes used for something other than throwing. Occasionally one of the neighborhood boys would eat a few and get a bellyache. Also, Billy spent many hours beneath that tree playing solitary home run derby, pretending to be Frank Robinson or Wally Post, and using apples for baseballs. The true purpose for those apples, though—God's intended purpose—was throwing.

There were several neighborhood apple skirmishes that season, but only one of particular note, only one which would have made Johnny Appleseed reconsider the day he introduced apples to Ohio. That battle started pretty much the same as the turtle egg war. "Hey Billy," Bobby said one early August afternoon, "you want to have an apple fight?"

"Sounds good to me," Billy agreed. "Let's see who we can round up."

Soon a rowdy crew of boys was assembled, sides were chosen (with Bruce and Billy ending up on opposing teams), and the neighborhood scoured for steel trash can lids. These lids were essential for deployment as shields. In fact, Billy's gratification at the solid crunch of an incoming apple, as it smashed against his well positioned shield, was only surpassed by his gratification at the thump and accompanying yelp as one of his own projectiles slipped past an opponent's defense and struck him in the ribs.

The ground beneath the oversized and eternally unpruned apple tree was littered with apples, mostly wormy. The sweet, tangy scent of cider filled the air. Bees and wasps, drunken with the wine of fermenting apples, hummed the hum of a neighborhood bar on Friday night. The tree's long, stringy branches slouched under their remarkable burden of apple clusters. The teams collected bushel baskets full of ammunition, and the battle raged for two hours.

Billy had a strong arm, and did not mind taking a hit to score one in return. He enjoyed the challenge of long range missile launching, though, almost as much as the thrill of close-in, face-to-face apple bashing.

Bruce, in contrast, was sneaky. He tended to try to flank his opponent inconspicuously, wait until his target was occupied with another combatant, then charge in and whack the enemy a good one at close range. Pop off two or three quick surprise shots—then run—that was Bruce's style.

Bruce succeeded in ambushing his cousin early in the battle. His first shot caught Billy squarely in his left thigh. Even though Bruce's throwing arm was highly suspect, from a distance of only fifteen feet, and throwing with all his might, his well placed missile delivered a serious flash of pain.

Billy reacted reflexively, dropping the shield from his left hand and grasping at his wound. Between the hobbling effect of his aching thigh and trying to dodge Bruce's second shot, which nearly caught him in the head, Billy slipped and landed on his butt. Then, adding insult to Billy's embarrassing predicament, George Schulke connected with a wicked shot, solidly to his neck.

Bruce was already running before Billy, tears in his eyes from pain and rage, could struggle to his feet.

"I'm sorry, man," George yelled, apparently with genuine alarm. "I didn't mean to hit you in the neck."

Billy's only answer was a rocket shot that crashed into George's shield with a resounding clang, leaving a deep depression where it struck. George ran too.

Billy turned his attention to his cousin, who was now at a relatively safe distance, and fired two cannon shots in his direction anyway. One of them missed cleanly, and Bruce easily blocked the other one with his shield, laughing his taunting laugh as he did so.

Half an hour passed before Billy received the opportunity he craved, the opportunity to exact his revenge. But when his cousin made the mistake of trying his flanking strategy a second time, exact it he did. Though Billy did not seem to be paying attention to his cousin lurking in the periphery of his vision, he was. When Bruce charged this time, Billy was ready. He fired a vicious shot that streaked past the ear of his would-be attacker.

Bruce dropped to the ground like a sack of apples and hunkered behind his shield. Billy's second shot crashed into that shield like a Bob Feller fastball. Bruce did not budge. Billy knew his quarry would be looking for an opportunity to run, but would not want to expose his back. He counted silently to five; then fired hard, aiming just above Bruce's firmly clasped trash can lid. Both his timing and his aim were perfect.

Bruce peeked over his shield just as the accelerating apple arrived with a solid *chonk*! The missile and Bruce's head proved a fundamental law of physics: two objects cannot occupy the same space at the same time. Applesauce splattered like a piece of fruit blasted with a Galagher patented "Sledgeomatic."

"Oh! Oh! Oh!" Bruce screamed as he grabbed his forehead, crumpled backwards and started to cry. A temporary truce was called. The Schulke boys ran over to see if Bruce was okay. In a matter of moments Bruce had a lump on his forehead about the same size as the apple that delivered it.

Bobby and Billy took advantage of the truce to restock their ammunition. Ronny stood at a distance and watched Bruce writhing on the ground. It was impossible to tell from his appearance whether he was mourning the misfortune of a neighbor or celebrating the calamity of an enemy.

When Bruce's sobbing finally reduced to sniveling, Billy walked over to where he sat on the ground. If there was one thing Billy despised, it was sniveling. "Come on and get up *sissy*; you aren't hurt," he chastised callously.

Bruce did get up, and after sulking for a few minutes, the battle resumed.

When at last the boys' energy waned and a cease-fire was called, the battlefield was widely and densely strewn with bruised and broken apples. The boys were also bruised and exhausted. Their shoulders ached from too much throwing, and they reeked of a brew of apple juice and perspiration. Adding insult to injury, the boys were required by indignant parents to clear the battlefield of spent ammunition. An hour of forced labor accumulated five steel trashcans full of apples.

One might think that such a monumental struggle would have cured the boys of wanting to throw things at one another, of wanting to make war, at least for a time. It did not. Later the same week the boys spent their allowances on small, penny apiece balloons at Cloyd and Lottie's Market. The ensuing water balloon fight was classic. That fall, after the first hard frost, the boys engaged in horse-weed spear fights. Fortunately no one lost an eye. Of course winter brought the inevitable snowball fights.

Little did the roughneck lads realize how well they were training themselves, as were boys in other neighborhoods across America, for potential deployment to another kind of battle, in a far away land of which they had never heard. Nor did they suspect that in a few short years boys from all across the continent would be employing their combat skills in a neighborhood called Vietnam.

They could not foresee that some of their friends and classmates would soon be drenched, not with the juice of broken apples, but with the blood of their own broken bodies; and crusted, not with the slop of splattered yolks, but with the goo of their own splattered guts.

3

Bittersweet

One day near the end of summer, Billy and his cousins walked naked from the locker room into the swimming pool area at the Dayton YMCA. Not that it was their idea to swim naked. It was the longstanding and strictly enforced rule of the institution itself. If a boy wanted to swim in the YMCA pool he was required to leave his clothing—all of it—in the locker room.

One concerned lad had asked at the new member orientation the previous spring, when told about weekly family nights, whether boys had to swim naked then too.

"If you want to swim naked in front of his mother," the almighty administrator replied, pointing with a manicured finger toward another peasant boy, "then be my guest."

The group enjoyed a laugh at the red-faced lad's expense, and the potentate's comment stopped anyone else from expressing concerns about swimming naked. Anyone else, that is, except for one bespectacled youngster. "Probably why we have to swim naked," Bruce said loud enough for the other boys sitting at his table to hear, "is because that guy likes looking at boys' butts."

The new round of snickering caught the administrator's attention. "If someone has something to say, say it loud enough for everybody to hear," he said in his condescending tone.

Bruce wasted no time in taking him up on his offer. "If you have to pee when you're swimming, are you allowed to go in the pool?" he asked. Nor did he flinch at the aristocrat's glare.

"You are an impudent lad, aren't you?" the administrator derided.

"A what?" Bruce asked with unfeigned ignorance.

"Arrogant, audacious, brazen, presumptuous!"

"I can't help it if my mother raised me that way," Bruce came back in his most surly tone. He obviously had no notion of what this learned adult was talking about except that it was not complimentary.

Bobby and Billy buried their faces in their arms on the table, trying not to draw attention in their direction as they convulsed with laughter. Billy even held his breath, trying to gain control. He was filled to bursting with an intense and conflicting combination of admiration and chagrin. He did not think about it at the time, but those two clashing emotions were fast becoming the hallmark of his relationship with his younger cousin. The bittersweet tension between those two emotions always triggered the hint of a third, as yet unnamed emotion.

The lord of the manor obviously had not counted on having to contend with Bruce Stevenson. He quickly discerned, however, that it was better to ignore Bruce than to engage him.

All that was water down the overflow now, though. The boys had been swimming naked for several months and were resigned to it.

"What's that on your hand," the pool honcho quizzed Bruce. It was his responsibility to deny access to urchins afflicted with contagious skin disorders.

"Snake bites," Bruce reported proudly, "and the red stuff is Mercurochrome." He had found a way to compensate for his lack of quick hands and patience, a way to compensate for his failure to catch a Kentucky lizard. He had tackled creatures too hostile to turn and flee when they could strike and bite.

The supervisor stared in dumb disbelief. "That's right," Billy spoke out, "he got bit twice on a field trip with the Museum of Natural History to catch snakes. But they weren't poisonous." Secretly Billy wished it were him who was wearing the wounds, though there is no way he would have been so careless or so brash as to allow himself to be bitten—*twice*!

The cousins swam and played tag with other boys. They dove from the diving board and jumped from the high platform, being careful not to rupture themselves on entry. They tossed hockey pucks into the pool and competed to see who could retrieve them from the bottom. After two hours they were water logged to the point of blue lips and puckered skin.

"Let's play Ping-Pong," Bobby suggested, even before they were dried and dressed. He knew he could win most of the games, but was not noted for being a good sport when he failed. In fact, he had been reprimanded only the week before—not to mention being fined the replacement cost—for breaking a paddle in a fit of temper, after losing to Bruce. Fortunately, when Bobby had thrown his paddle at his brother, Bruce had ducked.

This week, Bobby won the first game against his cousin and the second against his brother. The third game, however, by some strange quirk of atmospheric interference or other, was lost to Billy. Having last week's fine fresh in his mind, and knowing his cousin's volatile temper, Bobby did not repeat his former mistake of throwing his paddle. Instead he just whacked the paddle flat against the table, making a sharp cracking sound like the report of a rifle. Unfortunately, he also broke another paddle. So much for Bobby's Ping-Pong privileges at the Dayton YMCA.

After Bobby got his butt chewed out by the recreation room director, the boys walked over to the Greyhound bus station on Perry Street.

There they spent their spare nickels and dimes playing the pinball machines. Bruce invested fifty cents in another kind of machine, making himself a good luck charm. Billy envied his cousin, punching the machine's control buttons. The boys watched through the machine's window as the precursor to robot aided manufacturing worked its magic, stamping the characters Bruce selected into a thin, inch and three eighths diameter aluminum disk.

Soon the disk was in Bruce's eager hands. "Let *me* see it! Let *me* see it!" Bobby and Billy chattered simultaneously, like the Saturday morning cartoon magpies, Heckle and Jeckle. When it was his turn, Billy admired Bruce's creation as if it were a rare coin hidden away by some relative years before and newly discovered, or as if it bore an inspired inscription of invaluable future portent.

The center section of the disk formed a star defined by five small crescents cut clear through the metal. On one side, the center section was embossed with a four-leaf clover, on the other an American flag. The outer circumference of the disk was embossed with a ring of dots, like periods. A quarter inch inside the first ring of dots was another, the two rings forming the borders between which Bruce's message appeared on the clover leaf side: "BRUCE STEVESON GOOD LUCK 11."

Then Billy noticed the flaw, noticed that Bruce had misspelled his own last name, omitting a letter. The imperfection troubled him. He would not want to own a good luck charm with any misspelling, let alone a misspelling of his name. Yet the defect did not seem to bother Bruce at all.

Billy handed the charm back to his cousin, who cheerfully slipped a tiny beaded chain through one of its crescent cutouts, the one just below "OD LU," and attached two keys. Billy was puzzled. He had yet to recognize that his cousin's self-image was flawed, and therefore, his expectation of perfection in all else was diminished. Perhaps Bruce even found solace in the imperfections of things and people around him. Perhaps their shortcomings made his own perceived failings more tolerable. Neither had Billy yet learned that some blemishes—with time—become cherished.

"We better get going," Bobby suggested after forty-five minutes of goofing off, "we're supposed to be home in an hour."

The boys had blown most of their money, and now could not afford to take the Greyhound coach. Instead they walked over to Third Street and caught a City Transit bus. The ride home on the yellow, electric-powered trolley bus was typical. The boys sat in the rear, and Bruce acted rowdy. As they began to ascend Third Street hill, however, Bruce arose without a word and moved toward the front door. His companions glanced at each other quizzically, then followed.

The cousins generally exited via the rear door so as not to have to pass by the driver, who was sure to be annoyed with them. Why was Bruce inviting a lecture from the driver? "You boys will have to sit down while the bus is moving," the driver warned them firmly but not unkindly. The boys obeyed.

Minutes later the bus reached the loop at the top of the hill and stopped. As soon as two new passengers entered and paid their fares, the boys exited—Bobby, followed by Billy and then Bruce. Just as Billy stepped from the last step to the ground he heard a retching sound behind him and turned to identify its source. Bruce was holding his abdomen, bent over a saucer-sized puddle of glistening vomit. Despite having shown no previous signs of illness or discomfort, apparently Bruce had just deposited his lunch on the floor of the bus right next to its driver.

"Oh I'm sorry sir," Bruce said, oddly apologetic. "Do you have anything I can clean that up with?"

"That's okay son," the driver responded, half-smiling and half-grimacing. "I'll clean it up. Are you okay?" he asked, grabbing a napkin and reaching for the chunky mess.

"I'm just fine," Bruce responded, suddenly sporting an impish grin. Then, beating the driver to the draw, he reached down and snatched up his pile of rubber puke. Leaping from the bus, Bruce turned and held the mess up for the butt of his joke to see, and forced a taunting giggle.

Bobby and Billy almost peed their pants from laughing so hard, though at the same time Billy was so embarrassed he wanted to vanish like dirt from a TV detergent commercial. A part of him admired the antics of his rebellious cousin; another part cringed. There was that bittersweet tension again, and a shadow of something more. Fortunately, even the driver had to laugh. On a roll now, Bruce reached in a pocket and produced a wad of plastic dog poop as well.

The good humor generated by the incident lasted the boys most of the three-mile walk home. It would have lasted the whole way, except they decided to cut through "the plat" on Fairpark Avenue instead of taking Smithville all the way to Springfield Pike. "Let's not cut through the plat; we would probably get into it with the 'plat rats,'" Billy complained.

"It's a lot faster going through the plat," Bobby countered. "Besides, I know most of the plat rats."

"Yeah, I know them too!" Billy argued. "That's why I don't want to cut through there."

Bruce did not seem to care which way they went, and in the end Bobby had his way. The boys saved themselves half a mile of walking. They also encountered Robert, Roger and Norman "Tootie" Fuller, along with friends, at the intersection of Fairpark Avenue and Byesville Boulevard. The plat rats were taking turns pushing each other on a homemade cart.

For no apparent reason there was instant friction between the two groups of boys. Maybe Billy started it with a smart aleck remark about the Fuller's jalopy. Maybe Tootie or Bruce started it with an obscene gesture. Or maybe it was just because they lived on opposite sides of the old traction line levy. Whatever the reason, there was very nearly a fight and probably would have been if it had not been for the challenge.

"If you guys think you're jalopy is so hot," Billy dared them, "why don't you bring it over by my house and race against our jalopy." The Fuller boys accepted.

A Jalopy was a group project and a source of neighborhood pride among the boys. The "Pink Flash," Billy's neighborhood's latest model, was solidly built. Its heavy, two-by-ten chassis; its axles made of half inch steel rods fastened to two-by-fours with heavy staples; its ball bearing wheels fitted snugly on their axles; and its front axle securely fastened to the chassis with a five eighths inch diameter bolt as a pivot point for easy steering, all combined to set the flash apart from the boys' original effort, three years previous. That original jalopy had been built from rickety old one-by-four fence rails, barely held together with rusty nails. The wheels, fastened to the axle rails with spikes, had tilted and wobbled at precarious angles and threatened to disengage at any moment. Steering had been non-existent.

What a sour note had been sounded when Uncle Tom Stevenson had refused his nephews' proud offer to take little cousin Tommy for a ride. But that was history.

Billy and his cousins hurried home and rounded up some neighborhood push-power. Eric, the youngest Stevenson brother, had legs too short to steer properly; so Bruce, as the next lightest candidate, claimed the honors.

It was agreed that both crews would consist of a driver and four pushers. The drag strip was laid out along the one block length North Garden Avenue, beginning at the levy and ending forty feet short of Northcliff Drive. The last forty feet of North Garden was reserved as a buffer to allow the racers to stop before being run over by cars turning into the Trader's Haven parking lot.

The Fuller team won the first heat by default when one of Bruce's cylinders tripped over a hammer that bounced out of the Pink Flash's rear mounted tool tin. Bruce's team won the second heat, also by default, when the Fuller jalopy lost a wheel. By the time the third and final heat started there was open animosity on both sides.

"I told you…you're jalopy…wasn't so hot!" Billy gasped between breaths when the Flash barely nosed out its competitor across the finish line.

"Well at least we're not *sissies* like you guys," Roger countered.

"What do you mean—*sissies*?" Billy demanded, clenching his fists.

"At least our jalopy isn't pink like yours. Only sissies would paint their jalopy pink," Roger taunted, clenching his own fists.

"We only painted it pink because Mr. Lewis gave us the paint for free, *pantywaist*!" Billy fired back. "If there's any sissies around here it's you and your sissified brothers. Why don't you take your sissy-mobile and skip away home?"

"That does it!" Roger proclaimed, as though declaring war.

"Hit him! Hit him!" shouted Tootie.

"Punch him in his big fat mouth," added Robert, the oldest of the Fuller brothers.

"Yeah, hit me if ya' got the nerve for it," Billy derided. Roger obliged.

Billy largely blocked the roundhouse swing but still absorbed a glancing blow to the forehead. Then he hit his opponent back, landing his punch squarely on Roger's cheek. Enraged, Roger began swinging wildly, roundhouse-style. Billy blocked most of the blows with his forearms until Roger grew weary. Then he threw two more punches of his own. One of them caught Roger on his nose and the sequence of wild punching recycled.

The battle raged for fifteen minutes, by which time both combatants were bruised, bloody and exhausted. The Fullers and their pals swaggered back toward the plat, pulling their jalopy with a rope, cursing and threatening all the way.

Billy's buddies stood their ground, cursing and scoffing, with newfound courage. Apparently they were all impressed with Billy's success in battling Roger Fuller in a contest of inter-neighborhood gladiators.

After all, none of the Fuller boys were pushovers, and Roger was the most aggressive of them all. While Billy was taller, Roger was a year older and heavier muscled.

Above all others, Bruce's admiration for his cousin was evident. It was evident, too, that his admiration was unadulterated, not intermingled with embarrassment as Billy's had been for him just two hours earlier. In some inexplicable way, Bruce's unconditional acceptance of his cousin's behavior made Billy feel somehow responsible for, and to, his little cousin. Once again Billy experienced a bittersweet tension and just a pinch of the unnamed emotion.

That weekend, the Stevenson brothers, Ronny Martineau and Billy Sullivan all went camping with their Boy Scout troop at Kiser Lake. Bobby and Billy could not wait to go fishing. Ronny and some of the other boys were anxious to hit the swimming beach. Bruce, however, the youngest scout in Troop 334, had another pressing concern: an opportunity for profit. Friday evening after the tents were pitched, Bruce reached into his pack, like a magician's hat, and produced bags of cookies and candy.

"All right! Look what Bruce brought for us!" Darryl Jewell, Patrol Leader of the Moose Patrol, exclaimed. "You *are* going to share, aren't you?"

"Sure I am," Bruce agreed. "You can have all the marshmallow cookies you want for a nickel apiece. Chocolate candy is ten cents apiece."

Billy did a quick mental calculation. At that rate Bruce would take in more than two and one half times the thirty-nine cents a package he had paid for Zephyr marshmallow cookies on sale at the Liberal Market. Not to mention the 30 extra King Korn Premium Stamps he had received. Billy did not even try to calculate the profit margin on the Maud Mullers Milk Chocolate Chunks Bruce had purchased on sale at the Arcade Food Market for ninety-eight cents a pound.

Darryl hesitated for a moment, as if taken aback. "Oh…uh…okay," he stammered. "I'll take ten cents worth of cookies." The market was open.

Billy stood by and observed in awe as his little cousin fleeced their fellow scouts. As he watched he struggled within himself. On one hand he admired Bruce's shrewdness and assertiveness in pursuing a ruthless profit. The act appealed deeply to his personal sense of avarice. Yet Billy would not have—could not have—done it. He did not have the nerve to look his fellow scouts in the eye while taking advantage of them. Not that he was less willing than his cousin to fleece the sheep; he was simply unwilling to reveal that fact to the flock. He even felt uncomfortable appearing overly friendly with Bruce, for fear of guilt by association. Once again he felt the familiar bittersweet contest between admiration and chagrin within his heart, and then the nagging pangs of the unnamed emotion.

To make matters worse, Bruce shared his treats with Billy for free.

4

Martineau's Marbles

"I'll draw the 'pot,'" Bruce declared, surveying the ground through his specs. It was the first Saturday morning of the new school year, and four boys were standing in their favorite spot to play marbles: the hard, smooth ground beside the south end of the "old" Stevenson's Animal Hospital, the "old office."

The old office had been built by Grandfather Stevenson, and he had practiced veterinary medicine there until his death in 1947. Then Bobby and Bruce's dad, Dr. Robert Louis Stevenson Jr., had practiced the same profession there until the "new" Stevenson's Animal Hospital, the "new office," was finished in 1957. Now the old office served as Billy's home while the contractor's crew worked to finish the Sullivans' new two bedroom house at 1011 North Garden Avenue, just thirty yards to the southeast.

The rest of the boys watched Bruce, just embarking on his second attempt at the fifth grade, pick up a stick and draw an eccentric ring in the dry September dirt.

"That's not big enough," Billy complained before the dust had settled. To prove his point he smudged out the line of demarcation with the sole of his shoe. "Give me the stick, man," he ordered.

Bruce's face would have made Medusa's mother cringe. His mouth contorted into a snarl; his ample forehead wrinkled up like the face of a Chinese Shar-pei, and his straight, light-brown hair, recently clipped for school, bristled like the hair on the back of one of his dad's coon hounds. His brown eyes flashed black through their glassy windows. Nevertheless, Bruce complied, surrendering the stick to his seventh grade cousin.

Billy drew a new ring, a most excellent ring. It was larger and more circular than its predecessor. Nonetheless, it still was not good enough. Employing his foot again as an eraser, Billy wiped away more than ninety degrees of arc and redrew it. He still was not satisfied, but it would have to do.

Bobby, showing no mind to his cousin's perfectionist tendencies, had already drawn the "lag line." Each player would soon toss a marble, while standing behind the just completed ring, or "pot," toward the lag line. The relative distance each player's marble landed from the line would determine the sequence in which he would take his turn to "shoot."

"Last lags," called Bobby.

"I'm going first," Bruce declared, showing no regard for the conventions of marble calling. With a sullen scowl he took his mark behind the edge of the pot farthest from the lag line.

"I got second to last," called Ronny.

"I got next to last," called Billy simultaneously.

"I called it first," Ronny proclaimed.

"Uh-uh, I did," Billy protested.

"O.K. then, let's ask Bobby," Ronny appealed to his eighth grade classmate.

"I'm keeping my nose out of it," Bobby announced without hesitation. The best marble shooter of the bunch, Bobby just wanted to get on with the game.

"Let's ask Bruce then." That remark from Ronny took everyone by surprise. Bruce's face scrunched up, if possible, even more than it had when Billy smudged out his ring. Bobby's eyes rolled back in his head and his face formed a Simple Simon grin. His ears seemed to stick out from the sides of his thin face as if he were about to go airborne.

Billy broke the long moment's tension. "It doesn't matter anyway. You called second to last; I called next to last. That means I go after you."

"You're crazy! Next to last and second to last are the same thing," Ronny countered fervently.

"*You're* the crazy one!" Billy shouted, his steel-blue eyes radiating fire. "It goes last, first to last—that's the same as next to last—and *then* comes second to last."

"You always have to have things your own way!" Ronny proclaimed without exaggeration.

Maybe it was because he was an only child, the pride and joy of Bill Sullivan and Daphne Stevenson Sullivan. Maybe he learned his stubbornness from his dad. Maybe he was simply born strong-willed. Whatever the explanation, there was no denying that Billy wanted things his own way.

"Billy's right," Bobby finally intervened, temporarily defusing a volatile situation. It did not take much to start a fight in Mad River Township in 1959, and a fight would not help Bobby win a few marbles.

"Oh all right, he can have thirds," Ronny relented. "I'll take seconds." Even in compliance, however, it was clear to all that Ronny had not submitted. Though the boys could not have expressed how they knew so, they knew. Ronny's referring to Billy in the third person and his use of the terms "seconds" and "thirds" instead of "next to last" or "second to last" composed a proclamation of defiance.

"Let's play 'fives,'" Ronny suggested.

Still scowling, Bruce slammed five marbles into the center of the pot. "There's my 'bait,'" he declared.

"Let's play 'tens,'" Billy countered.

“I don’t want to play tens,” Ronny complained.

“*Chicken*!” Billy snapped back.

“I’m not chicken; I just don’t want to play tens,” Ronny insisted. “You always have to win anyways. If you won’t play fives then I’m going home.”

“Aw, go on home then ya’ chicken,” Bruce interjected, his brooding anger with his cousin dissipating in an instant when the opportunity arose to antagonize his dearest enemy.

Ronny’s face flushed redder than a newborn baby’s butt. His countenance seethed hostility and his eyes radiated soul deep animosity. In a single-digit moment his calculating nature was overpowered by sheer rage, finding expression in an obscene gesture.

Bruce fired back with the standard quip, “Is that your age or your I.Q.?”

Ronny’s left foot plopped down in the middle of the pot, and his right hand, already clenched tightly into a fist, pulled back in preparation for launch. Billy stepped quickly between the two adversaries, his arms stiff at his sides, his fists clenched. His eyes glared a steely-blue stare down at Ronny from his five foot ten inch height. “If you want to hit somebody, why don’t you hit me?” He sneered into Ronny’s face.

“You think you’re real big don’t ya’!” Ronny screamed. Distended veins, like two overblown bicycle inner tubes, bulged above his temples. His nostrils flared as a bird dog scenting the wind.

The truth caused a twinge in Billy’s conscience. He knew all too well he could beat up any boy in the neighborhood within two years of his own age. He had already proved it. Though Ronny was seven months older, Billy was bigger and stronger. “Oh all right then,” he conceded. “Let’s just play fives if you’re gonna whine about it.” He reached in his pocket and dropped five marbles into the pot.

“I’m not playing with you guys—you creeps!” Ronny raged. Apparently he did not like being accused of whining even if it was true. “Here, if you want my marbles so bad you can have ’em,” he shouted, tossing several marbles into the high grass and weeds behind the playing area. "I'm not gonna waste my Saturday on you idiots!"

"See ya' later Martineau *Fartino*!" Bruce called after him.

Bruce and Billy watched Ronny march stiffly and swiftly between the "ammunition tree" and Grandmother Stevenson's white, two-story frame house. Watched him stomp across the gravel parking lot that served both the office and Trader's Haven, "the store." Watched the little puffs of dust raising and settling in the wake of his stomping, scuffing feet.

Bobby, though, wasted no time watching. Instead he went straight to the task of searching for Ronny's discarded marbles. He had already salvaged two of them before his companions noticed.

"Those go in the pot," Billy insisted, as he and Bruce joined in the treasure hunt.

"I found them," Bobby argued, citing his standard philosophy: "losers weepers, finders keepers!"

"No! They go in the pot. That's fair." Billy was emphatic.

"Yeah, that's fair," Bruce agreed.

"Hey look, man, a 'crystal'!" Billy announced suddenly. Now he had found a prize in the grass. "I bet Ronny didn't know he threw this one away."

"Let me see it," Bobby said eagerly.

Billy tossed it toward his older cousin, but the younger one snatched it out of the air and, squinting behind his specs, eyeballed it against the sky. "That's a nice crystal, man," Bruce declared, "not too many bubbles in it and no chips neither."

"Let me see it!" Bobby demanded. He was not noted for patience.

"Aw, hold your horses," Bruce replied in his usual surly tone. After taking an unnecessarily long time to examine it, he tossed it to his brother without even looking in his direction. The glassy globe caught Bobby by surprise and thumped him in his forehead.

"Hey you little twerp! I ought to knock the crap out of you," Bobby growled.

"Yeah, if you could," Bruce snarled back.

"Hey, this is a nice 'cleary,'" Bobby observed, quickly changing the subject.

"What do you mean *cleary*?" Billy asked in a mocking tone.

"You know, a *cleary*, a marble you can see through," Bobby answered.

"Oh, you mean a *crystal*!" Billy said emphatically.

"Yeah," Bruce agreed, "you mean crystal."

"Well, in the eighth grade they call them clearies," Bobby defended himself.

"Well in the seventh grade we call them crystals, because that's what they are," Billy declared. "I know you've been in the eighth grade for two weeks now, and you probably forgot."

Two greenish-hazel marbles rolled around in Bobby's eye sockets while his face played Simple Simon. Meanwhile his fingers dropped the disputed transparent sphere discreetly into the pot. Billy immediately snatched it out.

"Hey man, that goes in the pot," Bobby objected.

"Losers weepers, finders keepers," Billy mocked, and stuffed the marble into his pocket.

"Get out of the way!" Bruce demanded, "I'm trying to lag."

Bobby stepped aside, and Bruce tossed his marble. It stopped six inches short of the lag line. "Good lag," Bobby offered.

"Yeah, but not good enough," Billy added as he took his place behind the pot. He leaned forward and stretched toward the lag line as far as his long arms would allow. His white T-shirt pulled up from his low hanging blue jeans, revealing a dark patch of lower back. When he tossed his marble it stopped short of the line, two inches inside of Bruce's.

"Luck!" Bruce snarled.

Bobby took his place behind the pot. "If you go past the line, you lose," Billy announced.

"Uh-uh!" Bobby disagreed.

"Yes you do, I called it," Billy insisted.

"You have to call it before the first man lags or else it doesn't count!" Bobby argued. He spoke with such authority—the authority associated with two more years of worldly experience than one's youthful rival—Billy actually conceded. Bobby's marble stopped within an inch of the line. "I get to break," he announced, stating the obvious.

"No 'fudging,'" called Bruce.

"No 'knuckles down,'" called Bobby.

Calls determined orthodoxy for the religion of marbles. Calls established the rules by which religionists of varying persuasions could fellowship together for a time in interdenominational ecstasy.

"No 'half-pints' or 'boulders' for shooters," called Bruce. Using an oversized marble for a shooter was an advantage because the extra mass made it easier to knock other marbles out of the pot, thus making them the property of the player who was shooting.

"No 'pot grabs,'" called Billy, thus declaring it illegal for a player to call "pot grabs" at an advantageous moment and snatch a handful of marbles from the pot. "Hey, do you guys want to play 'money ball'? I've got a 'peewee honey bee' on me that we can use."

Billy liked playing money ball. He always seemed to find a way to knock the designated money ball out of the pot, thus winning all that remained. The strategy had served him well in his relentless and ongoing campaign to acquire a collection of a thousand marbles. The distinctive yellow and black pattern and diminutive size of his peewee honeybee made it an excellent choice for the assignment.

"It's okay with me," Bobby agreed; though, with his skill he certainly did not need to rely on a lucky shot to win some marbles.

"I ain't gonna play money ball," Bruce declared, settling the issue. If one wanted Bruce's marbles he would have to extract them from him one by one, like a veterinarian pulling tusks out of a young boar.

Bobby knelt down to shoot. He pulled his shooter out of his pocket and gripped it between the knuckle of his left thumb and the tip of his index finger. It was a slightly oversized white "cat's eye," clear with a twist of white in the center. He lined up his shot with the eye of a surveyor.

Bruce interrupted his brother's concentration, yelling, "Wait a minute, I called no half-pints."

"This isn't a half-pint, it's only a 'quarter-pint,'" Bobby refuted.

"What do you mean a quarter-pint?" Billy demanded.

"It's one of these," Bobby explained, handing his shooter to his cousin. "See, it's between the size of a regular marble and a half-pint." He reached in his pocket, produced a handful of colorful glass orbs, and selected two. "See what I mean," he said, handing both a half-pint and a regular sized marble to Billy.

Billy scrutinized the marbles as adoringly as a miser counting his money. "Guess he's right," he finally admitted, extending his fist clutching the three marbles toward Bruce.

"Aw, who cares?" Bruce growled, refusing to take the marbles. "Go ahead and use your stinking half-pint."

Bobby made his Simple Simon face again, and two bloodshot half-pints rolled back in his head. Billy handed the three marbles back to Bobby, who put the two non-shooters back in his pocket. Then he knelt again, aimed his quarter-pint white cat's eye, and fired.

Crack! Bobby's shooter collided squarely with the tightly packed cluster of fifteen marbles, dislodging several from the pack. One flew completely out of the pot, so exquisitely drawn in the dirt. What is more, his shooter "stuck" in the pot, entitling him to another shot.

"You fudged, that doesn't count," Billy protested.

"I did not!" Bobby declared.

"You did too, didn't he Bruce?" Billy appealed.

"Yeah. I saw his hand move forward," Bruce testified.

"It's not fudging if you do it on the break as long as your hand doesn't cross the line," Bobby contended.

"You didn't call that," Bruce countered.

"Yeah, you have to call it *before* you shoot," Billy agreed.

"Oh all right then," Bobby acquiesced, "if you guys are gonna cry about it, I'll shoot over. And I'm calling fudges don't count on the break if you don't cross the line."

Billy repacked the marbles precisely in the center of the pot. Bobby knelt for the third time and took aim, his face a composite portrait of determination, exasperation and goofiness. The tension was so thick it threatened to explode. Then, in the exact moment before he released his shooter, it did. Bobby ripped of a tremendous blast of flatulence, convulsing his opponents in laughter. Neither of them saw his release clearly enough to accuse him of fudging, but somehow he managed to impart exceptional velocity to his shooter.

Crack! Marbles went "sputnik." Bruce and Billy's laughter stopped as suddenly as it began, jaws hung slack. Bobby was a perfect portrait of Simple Simon. "I don't believe it! How many did you get?" Bruce asked in astonishment.

"Forget the marbles," Billy quipped, "how did you manage to conjure up that evil power? Captain Gas-Master, that was *magnificent*!" The three boys rolled in the dirt and literally laughed until they cried. Then Bobby cut another one.

When the laughing and the gassing finally subsided, Bruce and Billy were faced with the cold hard reality that Bobby had recaptured all of his bait with a single gas powered shot. It was the first time any of them had seen five marbles knocked out of the pot on the break.

To make matters worse, Bobby's shooter was stuck in the pot. He knelt in preparation for his second shot. Splat! Two more marbles were dismissed from the pot and still the shooter stuck. Somebody was out two marbles.

Bobby shot again. This time, mercifully, one of the two marbles to roll out of the pot was Bobby's shooter, and it was Billy's turn—but eight of the original fifteen marbles now belonged to Bobby!

Just as Billy prepared to take his first shot, a door opened in the light-blue, cinder block building, ninety feet to his left. Billy's Aunt Ginny stuck her head out the back door of the new office and hollered, "Bobby…Bruce…come on…it's time to eat!"

Bobby did not hesitate. "You guys can have what's left in the pot," he said. "I'm gonna go eat lunch."

Bruce bent down and snatched five marbles out of the pot, saying, "I'm taking my bait back; I gotta go." Then, turning quickly, he tried to walk away.

Just as quickly, Billy grabbed his upper arm, preventing his escape. "Hey man, you can't take those marbles," he insisted. "That's my bait too. Besides, it's my shot."

"I gotta go right now or I'll get in trouble," Bruce argued.

"Okay then, leave the marbles here and we'll finish the game after you eat," Billy suggested.

Bruce jerked his arm suddenly, freed himself and tried to run away. His slow-chugging feet, however, were not quick enough. Billy tackled him and wrestled him onto his back.

"Billy, you get off of him!" Panic raced down Billy's spine at Aunt Ginny's shrill command. He glanced up, saw her dark eyes flashing black lightning at him from the back steps of the office. Saw Bobby brush past her on his way to lunch.

Billy, however, was not ready to concede five marbles. Instead of letting Bruce up, he seized the hand that still clutched the marbles and bent it backward at the wrist. "Oh! Oh! Oh!" Bruce yelped like a just docked puppy, as though he were either about to expire from pain, or as though he wanted to be sure his mother could hear his sufferings. Yet he did not open his hand.

"Billy, you let him go right now!" It was Aunt Ginny again. Billy glanced up long enough to see her stocky figure marching in her herky-jerky shuffle across Grandmother's back yard directly toward him. His mind was working at light speed now. He was already in trouble; there was no turning back. Bruce had tried to cheat him; moreover, he wanted those marbles. He knew what he had to do.

This time he bent back hard on Bruce's hand. He knew the resulting scream was for real. Bruce's knotted fingers unraveled, and Billy stripped their treasure like five pearls from an oyster. He scrambled to untangle himself from Bruce before Aunt Ginny closed to within striking distance.

Bruce did not cooperate. Instead he sat upright, grabbed Billy's white T-shirt and spat in his face. As furious as he was, Billy realized that he had to make his escape. In one final effort, he broke free of Bruce's grasp and simultaneously kneed him in the privates. Pausing only long enough to snatch the last two marbles from the perfect pot, he dashed inside his house, the old office, and locked the door. He did not look back as Aunt Ginny shouted after him, "I'm gonna talk to your father about this. Then he can take care of you."

Inside, Billy ran through the combination kitchen and living room, formerly Uncle Bob's examination room, into his tiny bedroom. He barely noticed the scent of medication that lingered from the years the room had served as Uncle Bob's drug room. Yet it was enough to trigger a curious memory. It was the recollection of Uncle Bob—tall, slender, and raspy voiced—handing him a tiny object and saying, "Here you go Billy; put this under your pillow tonight and see what you can get for it."

It was a common occurrence for the boys in the neighborhood to find a quarter, or even a fifty-cent-piece, under their pillows in the morning on such occasions. The incident Billy recalled was no exception. He remembered waking the next morning and digging under his pillow with anticipation. Sure enough, as if by magic, the object he had placed under his pillow had been mysteriously exchanged during the night for not one, but two shiny quarters. It was amazing to ponder.

Kids in other neighborhoods could only rely on their own deciduous teeth for such miracles, but Billy and the other lucky boys in his neighborhood were occasionally recipients of these other magical objects—bobbed off puppy dog tails. For a fleeting instant he felt empathy for the donors of those objects. Yet that empathy was quickly swallowed up in the magical power of possession. He curled up on his bed like an undocked puppy. In the darkness of his den he felt secure. He counted the glass jewels in his hand just to make sure. Indeed there were seven, his bait plus two extras.

Then Billy remembered Martineau's crystal, pulled it out of his pocket and admired it. He held it in a shaft of light streaming through the gap between the curtains in his window, focusing a bright spot on his faded-blue bedspread. He imagined the glass globe to be a universe and each tiny bubble within to be a miniature world with millions of inhabitants the size of atoms. In their microscopic worlds one of Billy's seconds might be an eon, with vast civilizations rising and falling. With regret he finally removed the crystal universe from its place in the sun, imagining that a great cataclysm would ensue, and all its inhabitants would perish.

Billy knew he would "get yelled at" by his dad that evening. He knew, too, he would have to steer clear of Aunt Ginny for a few days. He also knew he would have to get even with Bruce for spitting in his face, which would likely bring more condemnation upon his head from his elders. On top of everything else, Billy was mildly plagued by his *own* conscience. Nonetheless, in his scheme of reckoning—it was worth it.

On Monday morning following the marble altercation, the neighborhood boys assembled in front of the newly painted yellow home at 4812 Northcliff Drive. In a few minutes Bus Number 3 would appear and haul them away for another day of forced labor at the local penal institution. They had all been sentenced to a minimum of five years, grades four through eight, at Mad River Elementary.

"I wish we still rode Bus 7 like last year," William Schulke, a sixth grader with a burr haircut, complained. "That old pile of junk used to break down at least once a week, and we always had to wait for them to get another bus to pick us up."

"Yeah, that was cool last year when we would get to school late all the time," Bruce agreed.

"Hey, I wonder where Ronny is," George Schulke interjected. "If he doesn't get out here he's going to miss the bus." George and Ronny were eighth grade pals, and George sometimes helped Ronny with his paper route.

"Well he'll just have to walk to school then, won't he?" Bruce said with a hint of glee. "A five mile hike won't hurt him none. Besides, he thinks he's cool because the bus stops in front of *his* house and *he* doesn't have to come out until the last minute."

Just then Ronny stepped through the door and onto the front porch of the little one-and-a-half-story home. Unlike his older sister, Jeanie, who had left her room in the house's finished attic a mess before she departed in a rush for high school earlier in the morning; Ronny had made his bed and tidied his own room before leaving. His toy collector-cars were all parked neatly on their shelves. His model airplanes were all suspended, at precisely the correct angles, by strings from his bedroom ceiling. Ronny—with his cleaned and pressed shirt, neatly combed hair, and beaming smile—could have been a poster boy for the All American Eighth Grader Contest.

"Hey Martineau Fartino," Bruce taunted, as if the sheen from Ronny's halo pained his sub-par eyes, "have you lost any marbles lately?"

This time, however, Ronny was ready for his antagonist. Instead of becoming flustered, he strode confidently, purposefully toward the coming into adolescence assemblage like a politician toward a podium. Staring Bruce dead in the face, he drawled, "What do you want to know for? Do you need to borrow some...*Stinkinson*?"

Billy and the Schulke boys started to laugh as only youngsters can when one of their own has been wounded. Bobby also laughed his high pitched, horsy laugh and rubbed the palms of his hands together vigorously, but only for a brief moment. Then the grin on his face faded into the perplexed realization that "Stinkinson" was his name too.

It was generally thought to be impossible to embarrass Bruce, but apparently Ronny had succeeded in doing just that. Bruce's face would have surely flushed red, except it was instantly contorted into a knot so tight as to squeeze all blood out of his facial capillaries. Molten hatred glared from behind his spectacles.

Yet Ronny was not finished. "What are you laughing at…*Smellivan*?" he demanded, turning away from Bruce and facing Billy. Billy felt his own face flush like a ten cent pay-toilet. Instantly the hounds were on him: William and George laughing like hyenas, Bobby braying and rubbing his hands together as if it were thirty degrees instead of sixty, Bruce laughing his goading baboon laugh loudest of all, and Ronny standing there sneering like a jackal.

Never before had Billy recognized the power in a name, but he would not forget. Never again would he say "Fartino" in Ronny's presence. Bruce, though, was a cat of another color.

Later, when the incident was rehearsed and laughed about among neighborhood kids, Ronny's stock took a temporary rise. Even Bruce demonstrated a certain new respect for his perpetual adversary. Still, Bruce's theory was that Ronny had not come up with the names on his own, insisting that "he probably had help from Jeanie."

5

Atonement

The bloody climax to the feud between Bruce and Ronny would not come for another year—but come it did. The boys were playing basketball, using the rim mounted to the front of the Stevensons' detached garage. It was a warm, early autumn evening, and dusk was falling. As usual, Bruce and Ronny argued. It was nothing serious, a simple disagreement about who fouled whom. Angry words were exchanged. Uncharacteristically, Bruce stormed inside his house.

The more common occurrence would have been for Bruce and Ronny to come to blows, with Ronny ending up with a bloody nose. It was Ronny's misfortune to be subject to nosebleeds at the slightest pounding and Bruce's perverse glee to exploit the condition. The new method to Bruce's madness, however, was soon apparent. Moments after he disappeared inside the back door he reappeared in the window at the southwest corner of the house, directly opposite the basketball hoop. He was standing in the bedroom shared by his younger brother and his sister, Eric and Louise.

Safe behind his casement window shield of hard steel and heavy glass, Bruce began to work his devilment. Making faces and hand gestures that communicated as clearly as words possibly could have, he drove his victim to the brink of temporary insanity. Ronny approached, no, *charged* the window, threatening with gestures to punch Bruce's face which was pressed against the glass in a taunting grimace.

"Oooh! I'm scared," Bruce said in pantomime. Then he cranked open the window just a crack as if to verbalize another insult. Instead, he spit in Ronny's face.

To the utter astonishment of the other boys, Ronny leapt from the brink and went berserk. In a driving lunge he drove both fists through wildly shattering glass. Billy felt sick to his stomach as he witnessed thick streams of deep red blood gushing from the gashes in Ronny's arms. Ronny stood there looking through glazed eyes at the gored limbs extended in front of him as if he could not believe they were his own. Even Bruce's eyes registered horror before he ran to find a hiding place.

Ronny stumbled next door to his own home, where his father was busy laying tile on a bedroom floor. Splashes of deep crimson quickly marred the new surface. Fred Martineau was aghast. "Oh my God! What happened to you?" he shouted.

Mary was using the family car, so Fred quickly borrowed the Stevensons' 1958 Dodge. Ed "Bus" Tarter, the Martineaus' next door neighbor on the west and a volunteer fire fighter, jumped in the car as well to navigate. Ronny was rushed to Miami Valley Hospital, where—sixty stitches and two pints of blood later—he recovered. Mary arrived at the hospital just in time to hear her son exclaim to the treating intern, "You must be really rich being a doctor in a place like this."

By some miracle his dreadful brush with disaster did not prevent Ronny from future participation in athletic activity. Nevertheless, he will carry with him to the grave wicked scars bearing mute and haunting witness to a horrible moment of youthful indiscretion. Remarkably, though, Ronny did not seem to hold a grudge against Bruce after his gory ordeal. In fact, as if some sort of blood atonement had passed between them, their relationship became more peaceful after the terrible incident. A few months later Ronny's curiosity and quick wits would save Bruce's life.

The season following Ronny's injury soon yielded to winter and winter slid toward spring. Then, as if the god of mischievous boys and winter pranks had decided to reward his faithful followers, a heavy snowfall forced the cancellation of school. Furthermore, as if that god had not already provided sufficient recompense to his perpetually naughty followers, the temperature began to rise, rendering the eight-inch blanket of snow perfect for packing snowballs.

Early afternoon found Billy and his cousins paying homage to their snow-blowing benefactor in one of the most disobedient and dangerous rites of all—throwing snowballs at cars. Of course the lads did not think of their activity as dangerous. To them it was simply a game. Even the youngest Stevenson brother, nine-year-old acolyte, Eric, and the youngest Miller brother, Danny, were permitted to participate.

Making matters even more wonderful, Ginny Stevenson was scheduled that afternoon to work at the office. That left the boys to fend on their own. Making matters perfect, an uninhabited house was suspended on columns of cinder blocks over a hole in the ground in the previously vacant lot next to the Stevensons' home. That house had been moved into position above its four-foot deep crawlspace before its block foundation had been laid. Apparently the Millers, who owned the intended rental home, had been anxious to get the house moved but ran out of time to complete the foundation before cold weather arrived. Its close proximity to the street made the hole with a house suspended over it an excellent fort for bombarding unsuspecting motorists driving up and down Northcliff Drive.

The boys should have taken a clue when certain of their targets began driving through their shooting gallery for the second time. But enthralled as they were in the frenzy of snowball worship, they did not. It took something less subtle to strike fear into the hearts of these fanatics. It took the local police authority!

"Don't you boys know it's dangerous to throw snowballs at cars?" Constable Williams demanded of his three captured culprits in his most authoritative tone.

"We weren't throwing them very hard," Bruce said creatively, "so we wouldn't break any windows."

"Yeah," Billy added, "and we didn't throw at any cars with their windows down."

Red Williams nearly laughed at that one. Then *Constable* Williams lectured the boys severely. "I'm going to have to make a report on this," he advised when he finally reached the end of his tongue-lashing. "You boys will probably have to come up to the village court."

Fear shot through Billy as electricity shoots through the body of a fool with his finger stuck in a light socket when somebody flips the switch. He was positive his dad would kill him.

The constable pulled a pad and pencil from his pocket. "What's your name?" he asked, looking at Bobby.

"Robert Stevenson," Bobby answered, hanging his head.

Red Williams' blue eyes twinkled. "Are you Doc Stevenson's boys?" he asked, "the president of the Mad River Board of Education?" Bobby and Bruce admitted their relationship, and Billy confessed to being their cousin. Red chuckled outright. "Well I'm going over to the animal hospital and have a talk with him right now. I'll let him take care of you," he said.

Did that mean that the court thing was off? Billy certainly hoped so, but he was still scared. Bruce's obvious lack of concern over "being in trouble" bolstered Billy's confidence only slightly.

No sooner had the constable retraced his tracks through the snow back to the road than the three older boys heard Eric and Danny pleading, "Get us out of here!" Their inability to climb out of the hole, due to their diminutive size, had delayed the younger boys' first brush with civil authority.

By Saturday the fear of retribution, if there had been any, had long since fled from Bruce's thoughts. He was in search of a new adventure, a new game. The one he invented was even more dangerous than throwing snowballs at passing cars. He took advantage of the warm spell to complete the project in his parents' garage. Using scraps of wood he found there, Bruce built a tiny but heavy raft, about four-foot square. Determined to launch it in the pond behind St. Mark's Church, he loaded his raft onto a makeshift cart and pulled it a block up Northcliff, a block along Glendean, across Springfield Pike, and through the church's gravel parking lot to the high bank overlooking the pond. Ronny and the Miller boys (William, Eugene and Danny) tagged along, fascinated.

The little pond had one small pool of open water above a spring but was, for the most part, still ice covered. Undaunted, Bruce dragged his raft onto the ice and slid it to the open water. It floated. More boldly than a group of boys snowballing cars on a winter day, and more foolishly than three cousins playing with firecrackers in July, Bruce stepped onto his raft. Though the ice had not given way under his weight—the raft immediately did. He was instantly floundering in icy waters much deeper than his own height. He struggled frantically but unsuccessfully to pull himself back upon the slippery ice. For ten torpid seconds Martineau and the Millers watched in frozen shock. Then Ronny dashed into action, grabbing a fallen tree limb. Laying down and sliding his body onto the ice, he extended the twelve-foot limb to Bruce's grasp. Exerting the last of the energy that was rapidly being sucked from his body by the frigid water, Bruce clung to the limb and was pulled to safety—this time.

6

Confession

Time marched into its blurry transition with eternity as relentlessly as a troop of boy scouts hiking toward a rendezvous with the unknown. Billy, meanwhile, marched inexorably into the blurry transition of adolescence. Gradually, almost imperceptibly, the "y" on the end of his name faded and disappeared. Just as gradually Billy became ever more aware of his unnamed emotion toward Bruce. Instinctively he avoided confronting it. Yet there eventually came a time—*Billy* could not have identified the exact moment or even the year—when he confessed to himself and named the unnamed. *Bill* labeled it *guilt*!

Of course a substantial load of guilt was common for adolescents in those days. Parents and teachers, in particular, were adept at administering large doses of it to the lazy, the disrespectful and especially to the rebellious. Most of it was well deserved.

What Bill experienced, though, went beyond normal adolescent guilt. He felt somehow responsible for his cousin, as if some unseen hand had tapped him to shepherd his black sheep cousin and would, at some unknowable time in the future, hold him accountable.

In later years, whenever Bill thought of his cousin he experienced a certain measure of guilt. He remembered names: Odus Brown, Buddy

Butcher and others. Those names were forever associated in his mind with having failed in his responsibility to Bruce, of having failed to go all the way to the wall with his cousin without regard for consequences and without regard for who was right and who was wrong.

Bill remembered, for example, the summer day when Bruce and he had sat in the glider on the Stevensons' front porch with his Red Ryder BB gun as their companion. *Sput!* went the spring-powered Red Ryder in Bill's hands. *Ping!* came the reply, as his BB struck the black iron cauldron that served as a shelter for homeless petunias.

Sput! went the Red Ryder again, now in Bruce's hands. *Thack!* came the response, as his BB hit a telephone pole. *Sput!* went the Red Ryder. *Thud!* came the report, as Bill's BB placed a dent in the Stevensons' mailbox.

Just then two other youngsters entered the scene, riding their bicycles, as unsuspecting as two moving targets at a sideshow shooting gallery. "Bet you can't knock one of them off their bike," Bill said impulsively, not really meaning it.

Sput! went the Red Ryder. *Smack!* came the sound of Bruce's BB striking its target in the side. "*Ouch!*" yelped the target. Odus "Junior" Brown, meet Bruce Stevenson!

Odus hit his bicycle's brakes and skidded to a stop. "Hey man! What did you guys shoot me for?" he shouted.

"I didn't shoot you, he did," Bill answered in a sarcastic tone, conveniently avoiding the fact that the shooting had been his suggestion.

"You better get out of here before I shoot you again," Bruce threatened.

Odus took him at his word and pedaled back in the direction from which he had come. His companion, Danny Street, was close behind.

"I didn't think you would really shoot him," Bill said, watching Odus ride away. "If he tells on us, we're in big trouble."

"You dared me to," Bruce answered nonchalantly, apparently unconcerned about the imagined consequences of adult authority. His mother would not be home to cook dinner after her shift at the office for at least two hours. Two hours of unhindered liberty between his misdeeds and any threat of punishment was no threat at all to Bruce. It was not adult authority, however, which determined the immediate consequences of Bruce's action. It was the law of the jungle.

Half an hour after the incident Bruce and Bill were inside the house playing rummy at the kitchen table. Alarmed by the sound of angry voices, they rose simultaneously and looked out the back window. To their dismay, crossing the lot behind the Millers' rental house (now firmly established on it cinder block foundation) and heading toward the Stevensons' house was Odus Brown. Junior, however, was not alone. Marching with him were his older brothers, Lynn and Larry, as were Danny Street and the three oldest Fuller boys. This could get ugly.

Reluctantly, Bruce and Bill stepped out the back door. Bobby, who had just come home, followed them. "What do you guys want?" he asked the plat rats, not unpleasantly.

"I want your brother," Odus answered.

"Bruce? What do you want with him? He ain't worth nothing," Bobby quipped.

"He wants to whip his butt for shooting him with a BB gun," Roger Fuller replied in place of Odus.

All of a sudden Bruce showed signs of beginning to be concerned about consequences. "Aw, man, it was just an accident!" he snarled.

"If it was an accident why didn't you apologize?" Robert Fuller wanted to know.

"Yeah! And why did you threaten to shoot him again?" Larry Brown added.

"I didn't say I was going to shoot him again," Bruce lied.

"You did so!" Odus yelled.

"You're crazy," Bruce snapped. "It wasn't even my idea to shoot at you in the first place."

"Then whose idea was it?" Roger demanded.

"It was Bill's idea," Bruce answered.

Bill flushed intensely. He was ashamed. He was friendly with Larry Brown and Danny Street at school and had nothing against any of the Browns. "I was only kidding," he mumbled apologetically.

"It wasn't a very funny joke, was it?" snapped Robert Fuller.

The truthful glare in Robert's eyes pierced Bill to the quick. Surely the flames of hell could be no more discomforting than was the heat he was feeling at the moment.

"All I want to do is fight Bruce by myself," Odus interrupted, breaking the tension.

Bill felt a great sense of relief. He had been in more than his fair share of fights in his short life, but he did not like fighting when he knew he was in the wrong.

"I don't want to fight," Bruce responded. "You guys can fight if you want too. I'm going in the house." Then, turning hatefully, he took a quick step toward his back door.

"You're not going anywhere until this thing is settled," insisted Larry, grabbing Bruce firmly by the upper arm.

"Get your hands off me!" Bruce barked. His eyes radiated hate as glowing embers radiate infrared. His upper lip curled into the snarl of a rabid mongrel. "If he wants to fight, I'll fight," he growled, throwing his glasses on the ground and charging Odus with a wild swing.

The fight was intense, though Odus, who was taller and had quicker hands, had the advantage. The combatants alternately punched, kicked, tackled and gouged one another, encouraged in their brutal acts by their respective cheering sections. Bobby and Bill were, however, more subdued than was the more numerous Fuller/Brown alliance.

For a time the two gladiators were on their feet swinging at one another with the fervor of two rookies swinging at baseballs in spring training. Odus swung often and accurately, settling for the cumulative effect of many crisply hit singles and doubles. Bruce swung less often, but always with all the power he could muster. He seldom connected squarely, but was clearly gambling for a home run.

Then Bruce employed a new tactic, kicking Odus in the groin. Infuriated, Odus sprang in retaliation. His strike—black hair flared as a hood, dark cobra-eyes locked on his adversary—took Bruce at the knees. Instantly they were tangled on the ground, two cords in the same knot, writhing and hissing like two mating snakes.

"Bite him in the privates," Bobby advised his brother.

Soon the antagonists broke free from their serpentine embrace and scrambled back on their feet. Their clothing was grass stained and torn. Red welts on their faces glistened with perspiration. The cycle of punching and pounding repeated itself. Then, without warning, Bruce said simply, "I quit!" Apparently he had endured enough consequences for the moment.

The faces of the plat rats beamed with exultation. Bill and Bobby hung their heads like geese with broken necks. Odus radiated confidence and positively reinforced expectation. "You can't quit," he said, "until you say you're sorry."

Bruce hesitated, scowling, an uncomfortably long moment. Bill recognized the look in his cousin's eyes. It was the same look he had witnessed when they had been cub scouts and Bruce had been teased and embarrassed by the other boys because he could not memorize the Cub Scout Oath. The tension in the air was thick as sand in the Sahara.

Don't do it! Bill screamed in his mind. *Don't say you're sorry. Not after you've gone this far, don't do it!* If Bruce could hear Bill's thoughts, however, he ignored them. Instead, he choked out a barely audible, "I'm sorry," and turned away. Trying not to let the other boys see his tears, he hurried, slump-shouldered, into the house. His butt had been whipped.

Bill hated that Bruce lost the fight. Yet he was not concerned so much for Bruce as for himself. He hated anything that gave the plat rats an excuse to gloat, an invitation to mock and taunt. Not that the Browns or Danny Street were guilty of such, but some of the Fullers and other plat rats certainly were.

Furthermore, Bill was ashamed of himself for starting the whole incident with a foolish remark. He was especially ashamed at his own willingness to allow Bruce to absorb the brunt of Odus Brown's anger. Even though he knew Bruce was in the wrong, Bill felt disloyal to the depths of his soul for not joining in the fracas. That day added a ton of guilt to his already heavy burden.

Bill also remembered another day, actually an evening, during his freshman year at Walter E. Stebbins High School, when his load of guilt had been increased again. It was half time of the varsity basketball game. Buddy Butcher, his black hair slicked straight back, walked up to Bill and without so much as a salutation demanded, "Hey man, is Bruce Stevenson your cousin?"

Buddy and Bill were not friends. In fact, they barely tolerated one another. "Yeah!" Bill replied. "What of it?"

Buddy got right to the point: "Bruce was over there messing with a friend of mine, and I told him to leave my friend alone or I was going to kick his backside. He said if I messed with him that you're gonna beat me up. Is that right?"

By rights, by the law of the jungle, Bill should not have said another word. He should have just busted Buddy up side his big greasy head with a heavy fist. He should have pounded him into a bloody pulp, or taken a pounding himself. He should have pounded him without regard for who was morally right or wrong. Without regard for the fact that he resented Bruce's invoking his name. Without regard for the consequences of fighting at a school activity or maybe having to fight one or more of Buddy's buddies. Without regard for anything except that Buddy, *the punk*, Butcher was in his face threatening his cousin. That *should* have been enough, but it was not.

"No, that isn't right," Bill answered. "If somebody is picking on Bruce I might help him out, but if he starts something, I'm not jumping in it. I know how Bruce is, man." What Bill *did not* say was that he knew how Buddy Butcher was too.

No matter that Bill knew the law-giving adult authorities—the teachers and administrators—would approve his words, he felt disloyal. He felt guilty. Because in his heart he knew his words were not based on any respect for either the lawgivers or their law: it was based on expedience.

Bruce and Bill grew apart over the next few years. That segregated growth came mainly because Bill entered high school two years ahead of his cousin and, quite naturally, nurtured a different group of friends than did Bruce. Bill received good grades, participated successfully in school sports, and was reasonably popular. His garden of friends reflected that popularity: roses, daffodils and tulips.

Bruce, whose roots were buried in less fertile soil, received generally poor grades, was unsuccessful in school sports, and was typically categorized as a hood. His ragged plot of friends reflected those circumstances: dandelions, thistles and briars—at least from the perspectives of those who considered themselves roses, daffodils and tulips.

It was among the undesirable, uncultivated plants where Bruce received acceptance and approval. Bill felt uneasy claiming his cousin, *the weed*, to his friends, *the bouquet*. Not that Bill was a domesticated seed himself; in fact, one of his high school nicknames was "Wild Man." Yet, in comparison to his cousin, he should have better been known as "Mild Man."

Sadly, during those years the two cousins who had been as close as brothers found relatively few occasions in which to associate. Friday night, February 19, 1965, however, was one of those occasions. On that night, during Bill's senior year, he accepted yet another brick onto his still growing load of guilt.

Bruce, Bill, and Bill Schmidt—Bill's counterpart at defensive tackle on the opposite side of Stebbins High School's defensive football line—decided to attend a basketball game together. When the three young men arrived at Fairmont East High School, however, they discovered that they had only enough money between them for two to get into the game.

Standing in the lobby outside the gymnasium, they discussed their situation and decided to flip coins three ways. The odd man would give up his money so the other two could enter the game. The loser could get in for free at half time. Bruce lost and paid his debt, having a single dime left to his name.

Another young man, unknown to the three gamblers and surely no more than a sophomore, observed the wagering and approached. "Anybody want to flip for a dime?" he asked boldly.

Before Bill's mind could assimilate and process the request, Bruce had already accepted it. "Yeah, I'll flip with ya," he snarled. Both young men flipped their dimes spinning into the air, caught them with one hand, and smacked them down on the backside of the other. "I'm like you," Bruce declared. Both boys raised their hands from their dimes, revealing two heads. Not waiting for the other youngster to pay his debt, Bruce snatched his dime from his hand with a scowl. "Wanna go again?" he challenged.

Schmidt watched and laughed the hearty laugh that matched his lineman's body. His black eyes sparkled as if he wished he could spare a dime to join the gambling. Bill, though, had other thoughts. His mind flashed back two and a half years to another time and another dime....

It was a July afternoon in the air-conditioned lobby of the Lowe's theater in downtown Dayton. Bill and his cousins had just finished watching Burt Lancaster star in *The Bird Man of Alcatraz.*

On their way out of the theater Bruce tried to purchase a soft drink from a vending machine with a penny he had previously filed down to the approximate size of a dime. He dropped the dime/penny into the coin slot several times. Each time the machine rejected his misshapen offering. Bruce did not respond gently. Each time the machine refused to perform its primary function, he pounded the coin return with his fist.

Suddenly, and seemingly out of nowhere, an attendant appeared and snatched the coin from the change return after Bruce's last attempt. "Let me see that," he demanded. Then, after scrutinizing the coin he declared, "No wonder it won't work! This isn't a dime, it's a penny."

"It looked like a dime to me!" Bruce snapped, turning and heading directly for the exit.

"Wait a minute," the attendant demanded, "I want to talk to you.

"Keep the stinking penny!" Bruce yelled back, disappearing out the door like a canary or a convict fleeing his cage....

Bill's consciousness flashed back to the present.

"Okay," the kid agreed, "let's go again."

"I'm like you again," Bruce declared, as the betters repeated the flipping process. This time when they raised their hands, though, Bruce had heads and the kid had tails. But before the kid could react, Bruce pivoted without a word and stomped quickly away.

"Hey buddy, you owe me a dime!" the kid protested.

Bruce stopped in his tracks, turned back and glared into his accuser's eyes. "Get your face away from me kid!" he snarled, then turned and disappeared into the crowd.

At half time Bruce found his companions, and they watched Stebbins complete a 63-41 victory. *Big deal!* Bill thought to himself. He had not gone out for the team his senior year after a falling out with Coach Jim, *the jerk*, Morgan the year before. At least the game provided something to do on a winter Friday night.

Afterward the trio filed out of the gymnasium with the rest of the crowd. Back in the lobby where they had so recently gambled they again encountered the plucky, unknown kid. But this time he was not alone. "He's the one!" the kid announced to his companion, pointing a skinny finger at Bruce.

The companion—who looked to be in his mid twenties, nearly six feet tall and 200 pounds of body builder muscle—strode up to Bruce. "Did you cheat this kid out of a dime?" he demanded.

"I won the punk's money fair and square!" Bruce growled, with such bravado that an unwitting bystander might easily have anticipated that his 5'8", 135-pound, bespectacled body was about to physically confront his hulking interrogator.

The muscle man answered directly and ominously. "Either you pay him what you owe him, or you and I are going to have trouble."

Bruce stood alone for an interminable moment, glowering silently at his antagonist. Part of Bill wanted to come to his cousin's defense despite the fact that he knew Bruce deserved what he was getting. Part of him—the part of him that admired his unpretentiously rebellious cousin, instead of being embarrassed by him—wanted to step forward and say, "How about having a little trouble with me? How about if I beat a few knots on your head to match the rest of your big, bad, lumpy body?"

Instead Bill kept his mouth shut. He hid the part of himself that was socially unacceptable. Not that he had any intention of trying to correct it; he just concealed it. On the reverse side of the dime, Bruce did not, *could not*, conceal his faults.

Despite his success in athletics and academics, though, Bill knew he was no better than Bruce, only more gifted. He knew that he did not have to resort to such drastic behavior as allowing himself to be bitten by snakes or shooting a stranger with a BB gun to gain social acceptance and approval. This secret knowledge—the knowledge that his motivation for behaving more civilly than his rowdy cousin was not so much attributable to some superior morality as it was to social pressure and self-interest—caused Bill to feel seriously guilty.

Bill stood and watched, feeling cowardly and impotent. He watched as Bruce's eyes moistened and seethed the hostility born only of unutterable loneliness. The hostility born of perpetually being last chosen for neighborhood games. The hostility born of failure, both academic and athletic, and the associated taunts of cruel peers. The hostility born of being labeled a punk and a loser. The hostility born of being branded a social pariah. He watched Bruce's countenance grow darker and blacker until it matched the hateful and pitiful expression that had come upon him just before he apologized to Odus Brown a few years before.

Bruce reached in his pocket and slammed the disputed dime on the floor. It bounced and skidded across the hard surface like a fisherman's top water plug across the surface of his favorite pond. The unknown kid was after it like a hunger crazed bass. "Why don't you let him fight his own battles?" Bruce snarled, and scuffed his feet out the door.

Bill was relieved that the muscleman let Bruce pass, but that did not reduce his burden of guilt by so much as an ounce.

Then there was the night two weeks later when Bruce and Bill arrived with different groups at the same party, neither of them having driven. Bill decided to leave the party early to visit the Stage Door coffeehouse. There he hoped to run into his girl friend, with whom he was spatting. Unfortunately, Bill could not find anyone willing to leave the party and drive him downtown. And though the party house was near a city bus line, he had no money for bus fare. In desperation, he went to his cousin, explained his situation and asked for a loan.

Bruce reached in a pocket and produced his billfold. It contained two bills, a five and a ten. *Good old Bruce*, Bill thought, *he's going to loan me five dollars.* Bruce hesitated only a moment, then handed a bill to his cousin—*the ten.*

"I can't take this," Bill objected. He was genuinely touched by his cousin's generosity.

"It's okay man," Bruce insisted. "You might need it."

"Thanks man," Bill said earnestly, "I'll see you later." Reinforced with the power of wealth, Bill found his coat and walked to the door. Then, as he reached for the doorknob, he heard a voice over the clamor of the occasion.

"Wait up till I find my jacket," the voice said. "I'm going with you." The voice's owner disappeared into another room for a minute, then reappeared with his jacket in hand. "I can't let you go down there by yourself," Bruce said simply.

As they rode downtown together that night on one of the yellow City Transit busses, as they had so many times before, Bill felt closer to his cousin than he had for a long time. He knew he could count on Bruce when times got tough. He knew his cousin would come to his rescue when others would not. He knew Bruce would go all the way to the wall with him, without embarrassment and without selfish considerations. Bill also knew his own loyalty was not equal to his cousin's. He felt guilty.

They did not find Bill's girlfriend at the Stage Door. Neither did they find anything else of interest. The few people they talked to seemed smug and aloof or just plain weird. The young men did not stay long, but by the time they left the last bus had completed its daily schedule. It was either call a cab or else walk the five miles back to the party through the cold winter night. They decided to save the bucks.

Walking through the crisp air led to periods of brisk conversation interspersed with periods of quiet contemplation. During those quiet moments they were accompanied only by the sounds of their feet on the sidewalk and the billowing clouds of steam pumping from their lungs. The cold air seemed to clarify Bill's thinking, as if his life's experience were a distilled drop of dew temporarily frozen into a single, multifaceted crystal for his review and contemplation. Again he felt guilty because of his lack of loyalty to his cousin. He tried to assuage his conscience by calling up memories wherein Bruce had been less than loyal to him.

There was the time, for example, that the two of them had played poker in Stevensons' garage with Ronnie Fultz and Tojo. Bill lost twenty dollars in that game, a small fortune. Tojo, whom Bill had never met before and never saw again, was the big winner. Later, after Tojo was long gone, Bill learned he had been cheating. Both Fultz and Bruce had observed it, but had said nothing.

"Why didn't you guys say something?" Bill demanded, receiving nothing more than an excuse for an excuse. Yet Bruce was not really to blame. It had been Fultz who invited Tojo to the game, and Fultz was Bill's con artist friend, not Bruce's. Bruce simply did not want to get in the middle of a bad situation.

Moreover, Bill got even with *Fultz* for that offense shortly after the fact. One night when Fultz pulled several loose bills out of his white jeans to pay for his fast food order in the Red Barn restaurant, Bill noticed one of those bills fall to the floor. A furtive glance around the premises revealed that no one other than Bill—especially not the usually hawkeyed Fultz—seemed to notice.

Bill, his heart racing, tried to appear casual as he stepped on the bill and covered it with his big foot. Then, after glancing around again, he bent down, pretended to fiddle with his pants leg and palmed the bill—a ten-dollar bill. The way Bill figured it, Fultz had just anted up his fair share.

Then there was the time Bruce had come literally within an inch of inflicting a potentially mortal wound on his cousin. Bill ran inside the Stevensons' house and locked the screen door behind him to avoid Bruce's wrath. Thinking himself safe, he stood just inside the door and watched. Bill was not prepared, however, for his cousin's next move. Resembling a wild-eyed pole-vaulter running down the ramp before going airborne, Bruce charged the door with a metal clothes prop.

Fortunately, Bill reacted by falling backward just as the sharp tip of the prop pierced the screen and jutted directly toward his naked throat. Had he remained flatfooted he would have been seriously wounded. As it happened, he received only a minor scratch as the wicked instrument scraped the side of his neck.

Bill could not really blame his cousin for that attack though. Bruce had deserved to be angry. The two of them had been fighting, rolling on the ground. Bill's reaction to rolling in dog poop and having Bruce laugh at his predicament had not been genteel. Upon coming to the awful realization that he was hopelessly smeared with the stinking, slimy, yellow-streaked stool, Bill had grabbed a handful and squished it on Bruce's head. Even as he recalled the experience Bill had to smile inwardly.

Then Bill remembered the day, half a decade previous, when his cousin had tried to cheat him out of a handful of marbles. He recalled his anger when Bruce had employed his favorite tactic of spitting in his face. Yet that did not wash. After all, had Bruce not far more than made up for that incident? Of course he had. He made up for it time and again by continuing to play marbles with his cousin, who was obsessively pursuing the one thousand marble plateau as eagerly as a contestant on the popular television game show pursuing the *Sixty-four Thousand Dollar Question*. All the while Bruce had known, like the television program, that the winner was rigged.

There was no escaping it. There was no avoiding it. There was no denying it. Bill was deeply aware of a self-imposed, perhaps even divinely imposed, responsibility to his cousin—and he had not lived up to it. His conscience was seared with the hot iron of guilt.

7

From the Halls of Stebbins To the Barracks of Fort Knox

Bill was not alone in his conflicting emotions toward Bruce. Another young man became similarly confused. That young man was none other than Odus "Junior" Brown.

Bruce and Odus had been mortal enemies after the BB gun incident until one day in the fall of 1963. Though Bruce was a year older, they were both high school freshmen. Hazing of hapless freshmen was common at Stebbins High, though school authorities tried to prevent it, and the favorite locations for senior bullies to ply their trade were the student restrooms.

In general, freshmen boys tried to avoid those facilities: to enter only when nature commanded, and to exit immediately after achieving relief. Odus, however, had an overriding reason for spending extra time in the restrooms—he craved nicotine. Accordingly, one fateful September afternoon between fifth and sixth periods, Odus walked into one of those restrooms to sneak a smoke. Before he could light up, however, he was accosted by two menacing seniors. One of them "drained his radiator" on the floor. The other one dropped a penny in the urine.

"Get down on your knees and push that penny across the floor with your nose, punk!" one of the seniors commanded.

Odus was powerless and he knew it. How could one lowly freshman resist two surly seniors? His brain was a hive of crazy, buzzing alternatives: Scream! Beg! Bribe! Attack! He was desperate. Then, at the very moment Odus felt the last particle of hope escape from his freshman soul, at the very moment he abandoned himself to a fate worse than a whipping—he heard the ranting voice of salvation:

"Hit him Brown, hit him!" came as words from a burning bush to the ears of Odus.

Stark amazement pounced on the commanding senior's face at the same moment Bruce Stevenson pounced on his back. Both clung to their victim like ugly monkeys. Odus could not believe his eyes. The individual in all the world whose guts he hated most, save one, had rescued him from the brink of disaster—worse—from mortal humiliation. His enemy had assailed his would-be assailant.

Despite Bruce's admonition, Odus did not strike the suddenly not so bold senior. Instead he grabbed the warrior turned "wuss" by the front of his shirt, and, when Bruce released his death grip from the startled young man's throat, slammed him into the wall. Meanwhile, the other senior, the floor-wetter, slipped swiftly and silently out the door, abandoning his push-a-penny pal to two hostile freshmen.

As soon as the facility was emancipated from the would-be oppressors of the freshman class, Bruce offered Odus a Lucky Strike. "Thanks, man," Odus said, accepting the cigarette. "I mean thanks for saving my butt."

"That's okay, man; I owed you one," Bruce answered.

Still, as he sucked in a long drag of noxious smoke into his lungs, Odus was confused. He was not sure what his new role was with Bruce, but it was clear they were no longer bitter enemies. In his estimation Bruce had more than atoned for his former sin.

As if to further complicate matters, the gods of school administration had ordained—through the miracle of class scheduling—that the destinies of Bruce and Odus were bound to intertwine. They soon discovered they had something in common, the inclination to rebel in the face of authority. As time passed, the young men's relationship was gradually redefined. By sleight of hand, by smoke and mirrors, with a pinch of subtlety here and a dash of subterfuge there, and mostly by the skin of their teeth, Bruce and Odus survived their freshman year. What is more, by the end of that school year they had clearly become rowdy pals.

In November of 1963 Odus joined the school wrestling team and worked hard to succeed. One Saturday he and some teammates caught the shuttle bus from the Page Manor military housing area to the Hilltop Gym on Wright-Patterson Air Force Base. During their workout the area was hit with a severe winter storm, and their return shuttle ride never materialized. Their only option was to hitchhike.

Odus walked the last couple of miles from the Parkmoor restaurant on Airway Road, down the railroad tracks between Overlook Homes and the undeveloped government property. Though he shivered involuntarily as he walked, he hardly noticed the cold wind biting at him. He had more pressing matters on his mind.

The difficult trek home meant Odus arrived at his house later than the ten o'clock curfew levied by his father. This was the father after whom Odus was named. This was the father who had been convicted of manslaughter in regard to the death of his first wife. This was the father who seemed to enjoy totally dominating, even degrading his entire family.

Please let the old man be in bed, Junior thought to himself. He gulped a shallow breath of frigid air and peeked through the living room window of the cinder block house at 4518 Derwent Drive. The old man was sitting in his chair chewing on a big cigar, drinking whiskey—and waiting!

Junior shuddered from near hypothermia as he exhaled a white cloud of breath and hope. His choice was simple: enter and take a brutal beating, or stay outside and freeze to death. His face was so numb with cold he could barely form words, not that it would have mattered. His dad was in no mood to listen to explanations.

The beating, whipping and stomping that followed was merciless. "You're going to cry if I have to beat you to death, you ungrateful piece of crap!" old man Brown screamed when Junior absorbed his wicked punishment stoically. Yet Junior *refused* to cry. Perhaps there was some value to being frozen numb. He would not give the man he had come to hate the satisfaction of seeing his tears—even if it cost him his life.

At last Mr. Brown gave up, perhaps as much from exhaustion as for any other reason. Junior limped into the bedroom he shared with two brothers and two sisters. "Why didn't you cry?" Lynn asked. "If you would have cried he would have left you alone."

"I'll never let him make me cry again," Junior mumbled through fat, bloody lips. "If you guys will help me, we can go in there and kick the crap out of him right now."

Junior's plea was met with hung heads and silence. There was no way his siblings wanted any part of such nonsense. They wanted to live to see another morning.

Junior made a vow to himself at that moment: when the time was right, he was leaving home. He would not take his dad's beatings any longer.

At the end of the school year, June of 1964, Junior determined the time was right. He packed a suitcase and slipped it out a bedroom window. "Just where are *you* going?" his mother inquired, spotting him in the act.

"I can't take it anymore," he answered simply. "I'm leaving." Then he was gone—a fifteen-year-old vagabond on foot. When he reached Springfield Street, though, instead of heading west toward Dayton, he turned east. In a matter of minutes he had walked the several blocks to his buddy's house.

"What's going on?" Bruce wanted to know, observing the baggage.

"I left home. I can't take any more beatings from my old man," Odus blurted from the verge of tears. "I'm taking off for my granny's in Kentucky for awhile. Then I'm heading down to Florida."

Odus had stopped to say goodbye to his buddy and to muster wind for his sails. Yet lurking down in the shadowy hold of his heart—where hopes one fears to hope are harbored—he cargoed a fantasy. His words were barely audible, the hint of a whisper: "You want to come with me?"

Bruce's response was a short, sweet puff of sea breeze: "Wait a minute while I pack some stuff."

Odus did not know whether to cry or shout. Bruce had not even hesitated. Where else in the world could a forsaken youth have discovered a friend so true? Where else in all the world could Odus have found a kindred spirit, literally willing to leave his home behind on a moment's notice, and pursue a twelve hundred mile Odyssey into the unknown? It was as if Bruce had instantly comprehended the depth of his pal's suffering by some means surpassing language and responded in a manner transcending logic.

Bruce was in possession of an expensive set of machinist's precision measuring instruments obtained by some ill gotten means. Pawning it without a second thought, he received enough cash for two bus tickets to Harlan, Kentucky. Then, without so much as a goodbye, the duo was gone.

The little town of Harlan was the seat of Harlan County. Originally named Mount Pleasant, it was renamed to honor Major Silas Harlan who was killed while leading his command at the Battle of Blue Licks, August 19, 1782. Nestled between Big and Little Black Mountains, at the confluence of the three forks of the upper Cumberland River, and on top of a prehistoric Indian burial ground, Harlan was the coal capital of Kentucky. Coal, however, was not the only substance of value that poured out of the green hills surrounding Harlan. There was moonshine too.

The runaways stayed with Odus's granny for two weeks. She and her kin, who were splashed around the county like paint on an old drop cloth, accepted Bruce as one of their own. Granny fed and looked after the boys as well as her meager means would permit. The boys, in turn, spent their days leisurely among the hills and hollows, stills and creek bottoms of Harlan County.

The runaways knew they could not continue to mooch off Granny indefinitely. Odus also knew that sooner or later his dad would find him if he stayed in Kentucky too long. On the day the boys told Granny goodbye, she dug deep into her pockets and gave them each a precious dollar. It was all she had.

The lads hitchhiked to Knoxville, Tennessee and located the bus station. There they were approached by a couple of perverts of the slimy sort: the sort who lurks around bus stations in the hope of seducing young boys into their sordid business. These boys, however, were not easily manipulated. They eagerly accepted the perverts' invitation to come to their apartment, ostensibly to play poker. Cheating at cards was Bruce's specialty. The runaways spent the perverts' money on bus tickets south.

Later, knowing they were at the end of their purchased transportation, the boys hid in the back of the bus. Hopefully the driver would overlook them, but he did not. So it was they came to be stranded in the middle of the night in Waycross, Georgia. Odus had never been so bone weary and depressed in his fifteen years of mortal existence. At least his unhappy home offered food and a place to sleep. He could not cope any more. He had to rest. Bruce left him sleeping in some bushes and went alone to scout the area.

Sometime later Bruce returned to roust his partner from his troubled sleep. "Come on, man," he said. "I got our transportation." On the street, parked and running, was a 1955 Chevy. Bruce had "borrowed" it from a nearby service station.

Odus did not like the idea. This was a felony. Yet Bruce was insistent, and Odus was desperate. They had been on the highway for just minutes, however, when it became painfully clear why their car had been sitting in a service station parking lot. The transmission was slipping badly.

Ten miles down the highway the criminals were forced to abandon their wheels. They attempted to hide the clunker along a country lane, wiping it hurriedly in an attempt to erase their fingerprints. Then they hustled back to the highway and tried to hitch a ride away from the evidence.

Finally, just as the eastern horizon was painting pink, a brave and kindly soul picked up the two desperados. He was headed for the Sunshine State and would give them a ride as far as he was going, eventually dropping them off in the middle of a city ghetto.

"Now what are we going to do, man?" Odus lamented. His voice sounded as if he were having second thoughts about his decision to leave Ohio. After all, there were some advantages to living at home with an abusive father, as opposed to dying in a Jacksonville, Florida gutter from a slit throat.

Bruce, however, had a brainstorm. The runaways located the local USO and pretended to be new Navy recruits. Fabricating a report for duty date three weeks into the future, they persuaded a staff member to let them stay there. For the next three weeks they barely survived by swiping food from markets.

During that time the price of emancipation became remarkably clear. Disillusioned and ready to face the consequences of their six-week spree, Bruce and Odus called home from the USO and asked for help to get back to Dayton. The two youngsters circled the Western Union office like a pair of vultures scenting carrion, until at last their patience was rewarded. Bruce's folks sent money, but Odus's dad refused. Thankfully, Lynn sent $20, and his mother sneaked in an extra $5.

The featherless friends flew directly from Western Union to McDonald's, where they overdosed on hamburgers and French fries.

With their vacant stomachs finally filled, the humbled buzzards boarded a bus and headed north.

Two days later, back in Dayton, Odus was afraid to go home. He knew too well what awaited him there. Bruce's parents mercifully allowed Odus to stay in their home.

Several nights later Mr. Brown came calling on the Stevenson household. He was drunk, sullen, and demanded to see his boy. Bruce and Odus hid in the next room and listened.

Odus was terrified. This was the brutally abusive man who had done ten years in prison for manslaughter. The stocky man who ruled his home with a merciless iron fist. Surely no one dared stand up to him. Yet the tall and lanky man with graying, bushy hair—Dr. Robert Louis Stevenson Jr.—did just that.

"Your son is here and he is fine," Dr. Stevenson told Mr. Brown, "but he doesn't want to talk to you right now." The gruffness in his voice and the steely set in his pale blue eyes spoke no nonsense. Loud and angry words passed between the two men like grenades, threatening to explode in violence at any moment. At last Dr. Stevenson, full-time veterinarian and part-time president of the Mad River Township Board of Education, ordered Mr. Brown from his property. Amazingly to Odus, his dad complied.

Two weeks later Odus went home and suffered the consequences of his father's wrath.

About the time Bruce and Odus concluded their southern adventure, Bill and three of his buddies—Fultz, Gunter and Turnbaugh—experienced one of their own. This second southern adventure, though, was confined to a single night in southeastern Ohio.

The four young men decided to ride down to Bainbridge in Gunter's 1963 Pontiac convertible and visit their single point of interest in that part of the state. In fact, it was this very point of interest—high school cheerleaders—that provided the gang a valuable lesson: trespassing on a cheerleader camp in southeastern Ohio is ill advised!

Thinking that it might appear suspicious to park the convertible along a country road near a cheerleader camp in the dark, Gunter dropped off his three passengers to secretly explore the camp while he cruised the area. Unfortunately—from the cheerleader camp explorers' point of view—the secret didn't last long.

As Bill, Fultz and Turnbaugh fled from authorities through a dark and unfamiliar forest at breakneck speed, their hearts pounded with fear and exertion. At last, gasping for breath, they crashed out of the rugged timberland onto a dirt lane, thinking they were free. They were not! Instead they were immediately confronted by a group of waiting deputies. Bill and Turnbaugh surrendered immediately. The last they saw of Fultz, however, he was merely a black silhouette disappearing into the blacker summer night. The cops could not catch him.

The two captives were placed under shotgun guard and ordered to sit on the ground in the high beam of a cruiser's headlamps. "If they try to run," the chief lawman ordered, "shoot them."

Bill and Turnbaugh took him at his word. But as if the threat of being blasted in half with a few rounds of 00 buckshot were not enough, the captives were subjected to mortal humiliation as well. "Look!" came a clear articulation from among the gathering voices of amazed young women, "it's Sullivan." Though Bill could not see the crowd for the glaring headlights, he recognized his identifier's voice. It belonged to Stebbins cheerleader, Cathy Link. Being hauled off to jail was a relief.

Throughout their individual interrogation sessions, during which they were badgered for the names of accomplice cheerleaders and the lone escapee, both Bill and Turnbaugh remained as mute as turnips. Gunter, however, who had also been arrested and questioned, squealed like a turnip-fed rabbit.

The following school year, Bruce and Odus continued to struggle against the imposition of school rules and regulations that were the hallmark of an early 1960s education. As they matured physically their inclination toward rebellion became ever more apparent. Nevertheless, they both survived their sophomore year.

Mrs. Bessie Peck had documented Bruce's difficulty with rules, in both spelling and in social activities, on his third-grade report card. Her observations were validated under the signature of Mr. Ewell Singleton, principal of Base Elementary. Summer school was recommended.

Eight more years of education, including two in the fifth grade, did little if anything to improve Bruce's performance in spelling or in the social graces. Despite average scores on standardized tests, his performance was erratic. Finally, and perhaps mercifully, he was expelled from Stebbins early in his junior year for repeatedly smoking on the premises. Officially, on Friday, October 15, 1965, he simply withdrew from school.

Within a few weeks of his expulsion, Bruce and two pals, Clyde Rasnake and Larry Brown, discovered a plan. Uncle Sam called it the buddy plan. So, with the authorizing signature of his father, Bruce enlisted with his buddies in the U.S. Army.

On Monday, January 31, 1966 Bruce officially became a seventeen-year-old, 5' 9", 144-pound soldier. He began basic training on Friday, February 11th as a member of Company B, 19th Battalion, 4th Platoon, 5th Brigade, Fort Knox, Kentucky.

Later in the school year, after repeated skirmishes with school authority, Odus also received a dishonorable discharge from W. E. Stebbins High. His final offense was fighting at a school dance. Shortly thereafter Odus left for California with Dwayne "Cave Man" Helton and eventually joined the army as well.

8

The Flavor of Education

Near the end of his junior year in high school Bill agonized over the registration card he was required to complete. It seemed inhumane to him to require inmates to select their own sentences for their senior year. Though it weighed heavily on his soul, he took the high road and signed up for a heavy college prep curriculum, including classes such as physics and trigonometry.

Two weeks later, though, fate presented an opportunity which Bill's adventurous spirit refused to resist. That opportunity provided him with illicit access to his registration card—*after* it had been reviewed and approved by the proper administrative authority.

His clandestine mission complete, Bill was no longer bound to a senior year of servitude in classes such as physics and trigonometry. Instead he had been emancipated to a life of levity. His new college prep curriculum consisted of such weighty classics as *senior science*, a repeat of freshman general science for low achievers, and *metal shop*, a class in which he was the lone senior among one junior (assistant ringleader, Darrell Norrod) and a bunch of squirrelly sophomores. In short, Bill thought he had died and—by some divine *faux pas*—been admitted into pearly gates of high school sluggard heaven.

Mr. Bennett, who tended the pearly gates of metal shop, was made to order for his class. He possessed precisely the right combination of firmness, patience and humor. Still, his patience was occasionally stretched to the breaking point. There was the time, for instance, when Mr. Bennett discovered that the shop clock mysteriously gained five minutes every day during third period, Bill's period. Since the class was held in the annex, a building apart from the rest of the school and lacking a bell to signal the end of classes, manipulating the clock was a way for students to escape a few minutes early each day.

"I know what you boys have been up to," Mr. Bennett announced in his deep, gruff voice. "You've been moving the clock ahead every day so you can get a smoke in between classes. Well, from now on there isn't going to be any smoking on my time. The next time somebody messes with the clock the whole class gets detention!"

That got the boys' attention! The very next day, at the beginning of third period, assistant ringleader Norrod made a point of engaging Mr. Bennett in conversation. That conversation provided the distraction that Bill needed to move the hands of the clock ahead—*a full hour.*

As soon as the deed was done, Bill interrupted the conversation. "Look Mister Bennett," he said, pointing to the clock. "It's time to clean up already. Time sure flies when you're having fun." The sophomore squirrels roared like lions, and even Mr. Bennett had to chuckle.

In contrast to Mr. Bennett, Mr. Crosswhite, who had the misfortune of substituting in metal shop one day, lacked the skills to manage the class. It pretty much goes without saying that boys who take shop classes are not likely to be thrilled with the idea of sitting in a classroom taking turns reading aloud from a text book. At least it *should* go without saying!

Apparently, though, Mr. Crosswhite either did not know or did not care what should have gone without saying. Or maybe he just did not want to accept liability for a bunch of bushy-tailed sophomores scampering unrestrained around a metal shop with two upperclassmen for instigators. Whatever the case, imposed group reading was a sure recipe for disaster among this menagerie.

Not long after the painfully monotone reading began, Bill saw Norrod's head disappear behind his wide-open book. Suddenly the *needeep* of a frog was heard from his corner of the room. The bushy-tails giggled.

Immediately Kenny Mellon's head went down, and another frog answered the call of the first, *needeep, needeep*. The bushy-tails howled like hyenas.

Soon another head went down, then another. An unseen cow mooed at the frogs. A sick chicken *pluck-pluck-pluuuucked* its way into the chorus. All the while, student after student was called upon to take his turn to stand and read.

By the time Mr. Crosswhite called on Bill to read, the classroom had been transformed into a veritable barnyard. As Bill stood to perform his duty he had no idea what Mr. Crosswhite was about to do. He had no clue that Mr. Crosswhite was about to employ him as a cattle prod in a desperate last resort to redirect his out of control animal farm. Nor could Mr. Crosswhite have foreknown the result of his doing so.

"Class," said Mr. Crosswhite, "Mr. Sullivan is about to read to us and you are acting very rudely. As a fine representative of the senior class, Mr. Sullivan, how do you feel about such infantile behavior?"

Every animal in the zoo fell suddenly mute. Every squirrelly eye focused squarely on Bill's person. For a horrible instant Bill was tortured between embarrassment for himself and commiseration for Mr. Crosswhite. Part of Bill actually felt a twinge of compassion for his beleaguered substitute teacher and wanted to help him. Still, though, Mr. Crosswhite should have known better.

In the end Bill answered the question of how he felt about his classmate's infantile behavior honestly. He simply replied, "Needeep." The squirrels went nuts.

Bill graduated from W. E. Stebbins June 2, 1965. The pleated gray robe he was required to wear made a hot evening hotter. And in spite of the exhilaration pulsing through the veins of more than 500 classmates, Bill perceived the proceeding to be tediously long and boring. When the ceremony was finally over, though, he received a just reward—unsolicited hugs from gorgeous, sniffling females. He also received an unanticipated reward from his parents: a handsome Lord Elgin wrist watch, with a gold wristband, and $150 hard cash!

That night the infamous class of 1965 partied into the wee hours. As those hours wore on, though, the group of revelers slowly dwindled to only a few: Schmidt, Fultz, Chief, Sickman and Bill among them. Those few decided to top the night with breakfast at a 24-hour restaurant.

When the lads emerged from the restaurant, bellies full and eyelids heavy, the eastern horizon was beginning to reflect the colors of their bloodshot eyes. For most of the gang it was "see you at John Bryan Park in a few hours." For Sickman and Bill though, it was a good time to go fishing. As the two of them hopped into Sickman's 1955 Chevy and headed for the Great Miami River, their buddies swore they were crazy.

One thing about John Sickman: he was a sure bet, early on, to become a financial success. His drive to achieve, his capacity to make friends easily, his sagacity (a word he taught Bill in the middle of a hot game of pinochle), his ever present wit, and his competitive nature all combined to virtually guarantee success.

One other thing about Sickman: he enjoyed irritating people. In fact, by the time his family moved from Taiwan to Ohio, just in time for his junior year of high school, he had already developed the art of irritation to surgical precision. It was never enough for Sickman to simply win a few bucks from a buddy in a game of pool or gin rummy, for example. He always had to "rub it in." He always had to use words, inflections and facial expressions to try to trigger a reaction from his opponent.

Bill was also highly skilled with words, inflections and facial expressions. His specialty, however, was using them to burst the bubbles of irritating people. Half the time he did not even try; it just happened. And his competitive nature was no less vigorous than Sickman's.

The joy of going fishing with a good buddy on a beautiful morning, their first morning of liberation following twelve years of captivity, was not enough for Sickman. He had to be irritating. He started badgering Bill to bet a dollar on who would catch the first fish almost before they were out of the restaurant parking lot.

While Bill lacked no confidence in his fishing ability, he had not a dollar to spare. The $150 treasure he had received from his parents was stashed in a dresser drawer at home for an emergency. Sickman had Bill right where he wanted him. "What's the matter, big guy?" he baited in his most taunting voice, while flashing his most irritating grin. "Are you afraid you're going to lose a dollar? Or are you afraid I'll tell everybody over at *Trader's Haven* that I out fished you?"

"Okay, *Sick*-man!" Bill finally agreed. "If you want to donate a dollar, I'll take it. But here's the bet. If I catch the first fish, you pay me a dollar. If you catch it, I'll bite out its backside." Except Bill employed a less polite term than "backside."

Sickman's eyes lit up like sunrise. After rehearsing the terms to make sure there were no tricks, he was thrilled to accept the bet. He knew Bill was good for his debts.

At the river, Bill was thinking *big fish*. He took the time to rig his line with a sturdy Eagle Claw hook and enough weight to cast into the powerful current. Sickman, however, was thinking *anything that bites fast*. He quickly dropped his bait into the still water directly below the elevated bank where they were standing. It barely hit the water when he had a bite and pulled a tiny sunfish out of the water. Bill felt sick to his stomach.

Fortunately for Bill, Sickman was giggling so hard that his fish fell off before he could hoist it up the bank. Seizing the opportunity, Bill dropped his own bait into the exact spot where Sickman lost his fish. Within moments he caught a sunfish of his own and quickly landed it.

Uncharacteristically, Sickman paid the dollar cheerfully. He allowed that it was worth a dollar just to have had the privilege of imagining Bill biting the backside out of a fish.

Two weeks later Bill provided a lasting mental image for two other of his friends, Fultz and Gunter. That image, the friends claimed, was one of Superman—as Bill soared through the air one evening after wiping out on a homemade sidewalk surfboard on Radio Road hill. His crash landing, though, certainly didn't feel like Superman. In addition to multiple bruises, abrasions and lacerations, Bill's guts ached on his right side.

A week later, in the middle of a midnight car wash wrestling match with Schmidt, Bill's aching side began to hurt for real. An hour later his parents took him to the Grandview Hospital emergency room.

Another week later Bill had to be taken to Grandview again. By then his pain was more intense, even with prescription pain medication, than he could endure. Bill's surgeon refused his request to watch his own exploratory surgery, which was possible because of a spinal anesthetic. The surgeon did oblige his patient, though, by holding up the source of his problem, following removal, for Bill to see—a ruptured appendix. Bill was lucky to be alive.

That fall, like many of his friends, Bill found a financially rewarding but mentally boring job with General Motors. He was paid the outrageous sum of $2.64 per hour for sweeping the floors of a GM Inland Manufacturing Division automobile seat pad factory, on McCall Street in West Dayton.

By December Bill had done enough sweeping to put the nightmares he had been having ever since graduation into a new perspective. Those troubling nightmares—always about having a procrastinated school assignment due the next morning—were no longer enough to keep Bill sweeping.

His GM separation report, dated 12-30-65, rated Bill's performance as good in all aspects, including quality of work, attendance, cooperation, and safety habits. That report, signed by supervisor Charles H.

Menker and witnessed by Betty Whitehead, listed the reason for Bill's separation as "returning to school."

Bill was careful not to overload himself with course work for his first trimester of college. Maybe his chosen school, the fledgling Dayton Branch Campus of the Ohio State and Miami Universities, *was* struggling to become a *real* school. And maybe the school it was destined to become—Wright State University—*was* nothing more than a single building, Allyn Hall, in the middle of a cornfield. But Bill had been forewarned by his pals that college was not a joke. Taking his buddies' words to heart, he registered for the bare minimum, twelve credit hours, to qualify as a full-time student. Accordingly, he earned a 3.25 grade point average for that term without exerting himself.

How successful the army was at educating Bruce, at molding him into its system and assuring his conformance to its rules and its regulations, is questionable. It certainly was not successful in correcting his grammar, punctuation, and spelling irregularities and inconsistencies. At least Bruce eventually completed his GED as a serviceman, learned marketable skills, and gained respect for education.

Bruce's basic training experience is recorded in his letters home. A sampling of those letters are reproduced here, with their imperfections, as they fell from Bruce's pen:

From: Fort Knox, Kentucky
Postmark: February 11, 1966

Dear Mom & Dad

The first five days weren't to bad. The first thing we did when we got in was to get our blankets, sheets, and pillos.

We left Cin. Ohio at about 6:00 and arived at about 11:30 at Fort Knox. The next couple of days we had to get three shots. Then we got our I.D. card and later on that day we got our dog tags. On Friday we went a couple of miles down the road to were we would take our basic traning.

We don't have much time to write or do anything. All day long we march and have to have rifle drill. We have to do about four hours of physical fittiness every day so far on Wensday we start in on our marksmanship. I miss being there but it is not all as bad as every body thinks before he does something and your all right tell Eric and Louise that I said high. Larry and Clyde are Ok to and doing all right.

I will tell you what we did going up on the bus. We was messing around. And one of ous decided that we would cutting each others hair. so we was on the bus cutting each others hair. We cut all most all of our hair of on the top and left the sides long it was kind of funny looking but it was fun.

I have made a lot of friends and met some guys that know people that I know well by now I have a lot of work to do we have to shine our boots every day and night to.

Love Bruce

address
Pvt. E1 Bruce M. Stevenson RA15749291
Co. B 19th BN. 5th TNG. BDE U.S.A.T.C.A.
Fort Knox, Ky. 4th PLT.

I would like it very much if you would send me some cookies or candy bars or peanuts or something like that.

From: Fort Knox, Kentucky
Postmark: February 16, 1966

Dear Mom, Dad

Hi I am doing ok. We are under quartine because a lot of people are coming down with cools, flew and a couple cases of Spinal Menengitis. And are not allowed to good to the P.X. to by any thing.

You need not worry about me I am ok. I hardly every see Larry or Clyde any more because we are in different plt. Our plt. has come in first place for the last three days for the cleanest and neatest barrix.

We work almosts every min. of daylight. And only sleep about seven, or eight hours. Tell Eric and the Louise that I said high. The next letter you write me plase send me Bobbys address.

Ho yes thanks for the candy you sent me for Valentines Day. Well got to go now.

Your Son
Bruce
With
Love

From: Fort Knox, Kentucky
Postmark: February 18, 1966

Dear Mom

I would like to know if every body is doing all right. I got a letter the other day from Uncle Bill, Aunt Daphne and Billy. They told me what happened to the store about all the water.

Junior Brown sent me a letter and told me everything that is going on back their and sent me some pictures of some of the guys. I have been getting a lot of mail more that I thought I would.

I want you I you would take some of my money out of the Bank and send it to me. Because I have a lot of stuff to buy that I need. As you can see I brought some stationery. We have a physical traning test friday we have to do 50 push up, craw 40 meters in 30 sec., run a mile in 7 mins. I have to write Junior now so buy.

Love Bruce
TURN OVER

We have had our pictures taken to and so I will be getting them in a couple of weekes.

From: Fort Knox, Kentucky
Postcard Postmarked: February 23, 1966

Hi Eric hope you have been having a lot of fun. And not getting into to much trouble. I have been doing fine it is perty rough but I can do the stuf pert easy well most of it take care of your self.
Bruce

From: Fort Knox, Kentucky
Postcard stamped "Postage due 4 cents"
Date: Winter 1966

Dear Eric

Every thing is all right and I am doing fine. You know Roger Fuller he is getting sent to Vetitnom in about one week. He is just down the street from where I am staying in. We aren't alowed to by any pop or candy. Well by now write you a letter when I get a chance. Bruce

From: Fort Knox, Kentucky
Postmark: March 2, 1966

Dear Dad

I got your letter today. For that last two weeks we have been zeroing our rifles at 25 meaters. But today we went to a different rang were we were shooting at targets that would pop up at 75 meters 175 meters and 300 meters I did perty good I got 34 out of 46 targets. The M14 rifle is a real good rifle for long ranges we were shooting a targets the same size of a man on the 175 meters and 300 meters and the 75 meters were about the size of a man's head.

On Friday we start on hand to hand combat, and next week we start on banet traning. Every where we go we carry a field packs, rifle, pistol belt and canteen.

It has been perty cooled here, but it has not snowed lately. I am perty sure that we will be off quirteen this week end. We probley get post

privelages that means we are able to go where ever we want on the post on off duties.
Your Son
Bruce

From: Fort Knox, Kentucky
Postmark: March 7, 1966

Dear Mother

Well thanks for sending the money, Radio and the candy it was very good. For the last two days I have been laying tile in the day room because I vonlteeryed to do so. Because I didn't feel like have dismanted drill with our rifles.

We get to go to the P.X. about once a week. Grandmother sent me some candy and so did Aunt Daphne did to. We get payed I think Mondy you can't be sure about anything around here.

Me and some of the other guys have a lot of fun when we arn't working around here. Just messing around and telling jokes. I have been getting a lot of mail infact so much I hardly get a chance to answer them except on Sunday. I think that I will probly graduate on April 1 or around then.

Well I got a couple of letters from a couple of girls that I thought I wouldn't they were wondering where I went to. I think that I might get a pass next weeking about 48 hour pass if I do I will come home and see every body but don't count on it a hole lot. Well I got to go now so good by.
Love Your Son
Bruce

From: Fort Knox, Kentucky
Postmark: March 15, 1966

Dear Mother

Haven't had much time to write because we have been studing our rifle marskmanship. On Monday and Tusday we go to qualifie for it. We have to knock down 30 targets out of 84, that is the least.

So earler today we went to the range and we only shoot 56 targets today and I got 34 that was all I needed to qualifie. Tomorrow we shoot 28 targets. If I can't get 11 targets tomorrow I will make sharpshooter but if I can hit 26 targets tomorrow I can get expert but I think I will probly get sharpshooter. We were shooting at targets from 50 meters to 350 meters most of them were 150 and 200 meters.

Didn't get a chance to call Sunday because I was messing around with Larry, Clyde and Junior Brown. We were sitting up at the P.X. and I turned around and Junior was coming in the door. He came up with his Mom and Dad and two sisters. Junior said he was leaving for the Army in eight to ten days. There were up here most of the day, we have been taking some pictures with Larry poloiad camera.

This is the first letter I have had a chance to write all week.

We are or should be getting off this quartine tusday or wensday thats what the Lt. Manning told ous today. We will be taking test for gaurd duty and have to know all of our general orders and chane of comand. Well have to go now so I will try to write Wensday if I get a chance. Well by for now.

P.S.
Here some pictures we took with Larry's camera
Love Bruce
See You Soon
Hope

From: Fort Knox, Kentucky
Postcard Postmarked: Mar 15, 1966

Dear Eric

I hope you have been all right, because I miss seeing you. We have been shooting our M-14 rifles. I like doing it, it is kind of fun the targets pop up and you have so long to shoot at them. Hope to see you soon.
Bruce

From: Fort Knox, Kentucky
Postmark: March 18, 1966

Dear Mom

I told you what I shot 34 targets the first day well I shot 13 more to make a sharpeshooter on the range. Today we started Baynet traning it is not to bad so far. If I could have shot expert on the range I would have got a three day pass but I didn't do it so that shot that pass.

We go on Bivwaky next tusday, thursday and Friday. It will be perty rough, we have to craw about 200 meters with machine guns shooting over the top of ous. Tanks shooting off to the sides of us. I think that we start guard duty next week to.

Junior told me that Jimmy Yancy got put in the hospital for a couple days, because of a fight he was in.

For the last couple of days we were allowed to go to the P.X. and drink beer or what ever we wanted to do. Hope you got the pictures I sent you well I don't have much time have to go now.

Love

Bruce

Bruce graduated from basic training Saturday, April 16, 1966. He did not have to report to his next training station, Fort Gordon, Georgia until April 30th. That left him with a week and a half to swagger through his old haunts on the streets of Dayton, Ohio. Sadly, Bill was too busy with his first trimester of college, not to mention his extracurricular evening activities at Airway Billiards, to pay much attention.

Bruce wrote home much less frequently from Fort Gordon than he had from Fort Knox. Of the two letters that survive from that period, the one reproduced below explains Bruce's attitude toward his new training assignment:

From: Fort Gordon, Georgia
Date: Spring 1966

Dear Mom

Everthing is all right so far, this place is a dump compared to Fort Knox. There is nothing to do at all.

Well I am glad of one thing that I am going to night school I start school at 4:30 in the afternoon and get out at 1:50 in the morning. We will not have to pull KP or gaurd duty.

Larry and Clyde are int the same company but there are about half mile down the road. Robinson and I are in the same barix he is the guy from Richmond Ind. that I was always talking about. So we mess around together.

If you will I want you to send my stationary to me it is in the top dresser draw of mine.

After we get up in the morning we can go into town anytime we want if we are not in class hours. When we came in we stayed over night in Agusta and messed around all that day.

Love Bruce turn over for address.

Bruce Stevenson RA15749291
Tng. Co. Z 5th Bn. USASESCS
Fort Gordon, Ga.
30905

Bruce graduated from the U.S. Army Southeast Signal School at Fort Gordon on June 24, 1966. His mother, Grandmother Garity, and little sister, Louise, proudly attended the event.

Bruce volunteered for Vietnam, but was shipped to Karlsruhe, Germany instead.

9

Karlsruhe Connection

In June of 1966 thousands of American GIs would have welcomed an assignment to Germany. Some may have seen it as an opportunity to tour Europe, savoring the flavor of centuries old cultures. Others would simply have been grateful for being spared firsthand knowledge of another ancient culture in Southeast Asia.

Bruce was among neither group. He found Germany to be a drag. For the time being, however, he had no choice in the matter and simply made the best of it.

On July 5, 1966, Bruce's mother received the following letter from Karlsruhe, Germany:

> Dear Mother
>
> Well this is the first chance I had to write. I had detales all the way over on the boat. We took a train from where we got of the boat to Karlsriulie Germany. Well everthing is all right over here from what I seen hope everthing is ok over there to. We are about 60 miles from Frankfort Germany. I don't even think that I will be working in Siginal from what they say I will be working in the motor pool here.

It took nine days on the boat to come over here. They didn't have to much to do on the ship when we weren't working.

I have talked to a lot of guys of here and they said that I would probly spend two years over here. I was talking to a German girl trying to find out where the train station was she could talk English I didn't under stand to much of what she said but aenough to get where I was going to. I already know how the money system works it is perty easy. Things are a lot cheaper over here than in the States. Have you been getting the allotments and the bonds I took out yet. Well before to much longer I should be making PFC. first class in I guess about a mounth or so. Well I have some work to do so by now.

Love

Bruce

Bill also had some work to do. His work, though, was not on the European continent. His work was at the pool hall in the rear of the Airway Shopping Center. Big Mike Barok, the owner of Airway Billiards, had hired Bill as his Cousin Bob's replacement for the after hours cleaning job when Bob enlisted in the navy. Fifteen bucks a night, for two hours work if he hustled, was good money.

First he would empty all the ashtrays, collect the half-empty bottles and other trash, and put the strewn about cue sticks back in their racks on the walls. Then he would brush down the tables, wheezing from the chalk dust billowing out of the sod green felt. Next he would wipe down the heavy wood card tables with a damp cloth, wipe out the ashtrays, and restore order to the chairs. Finally he would bring out the old Kirby and vacuum the wall-to-wall red carpet.

Most of the time the job was boring. Occasionally, though, adventure burst into Airway Billiards like a late night FBI raid. Bill remembered, for example, a wee hour run-in with old "One Eye," a real-life Barney

Fyfe, and a band of his tin badge flunkies when his cousin was breaking him in on the job.

"Everybody against the wall, hands behind your heads!" the pistol brandishing One Eye commanded, bursting suddenly through the metal door the young men had neglected to lock behind themselves. Everybody—being Bob and Bill—complied.

"Where's the hole? Where's the hole?" One Eye repeatedly demanded. Bill suspected strongly that the hole was in the over zealous deputy sheriff's head.

After being detained for forty-five minutes by a rabid lawman and his boot polishing junior deputies, Bob and Bill finally learned that a burglary had occurred in Airway Fashions. One Eye deduced that entry must have been gained through a hole in the wall or ceiling in Airway Billiards.

When Bill eventually tired of the cleaning job, Big Mike offered him the job of running the pool hall on the nights he did not. The day job was already taken by the old hustler with the thin mustache and thick French Canadian accent, Hank Madon. With his heavily leaded cue stick, Hank specialized in teaching the fine art of nine ball to schoolboys while separating them from their weekly lunch money.

Bill welcomed the opportunity to be paid for spending his evenings where he was already spending them anyway.

Bruce's parents received the following letter from Karlsruhe, postmarked August 22, 1966:

Dear Mom and Dad

Well got your letter yesterday and thought I would write and let you know what I am doing. Well I tryed to call Larry and Clyde but I could get their number because I don't know what company they are in. So of you find out what their address is I will call them.

Do you rember Harold Long you know Sam Long that is his brother, he use to play basketball for Stebbins. Will I called him up today and talked to him for a while.

And he told me what Bobby Fuller address is and I tryed to call him but couldn't get a hold of him.

Well glad you liked the pictures and will take some more when I get a chance to. Hope you took some pictures of the horse show and some of the Mounted Protole if you did send me a couple.

Well Grandmother Stevenson sent me a Dictonary the other day. And I am learning some Germany.

I should start school in about Sept. to get my high School Diapolma. And try to get enough credits to take some night school in college over here.

If you could I would like you to send me some of my clothes, Paints and Shirts and a winter coat. If you would I want you to send me one of Bobbys suit coats if you would.

It is hard to by any american clothes over here, and I don't like the the clothes the Germangs wear. Well tell Louise high fan I am getting so Germany, French and English money for her to have. Well going to the movie so good by and hope to here from you soon.

Love Bruce

Bill had a concern for clothing about the same time as Bruce. Bill's concern, though, was not for what he would be wearing. It was for what he would *not* be wearing.

One night at midnight, after he closed the pool hall, Bill and some of his buddies went to the isolated section of woods at the east end of Eastwood Park and held what Bill called "tactical maneuvers." There the young men divided themselves into two squads: Kenny Earwood, Dick Burton and David Bolser against Bill, Ronnie Taulbee, and Dwayne "Cave Man" Helton. Entering the woods from opposite ends, they intended to ambush and capture one another.

Bill huddled his troops before entering the woods and shared his plan. "The first thing those guys are going to do," he declared, "is take their shirts off for camouflage. We're going to go them one better."

Cave Man chuckled his toothy Neanderthal chuckle. Taulbee, however, objected to running through the woods with no shoes. Bill conceded that they would retain their footwear.

The sight of their white butts bathed in moonlight caused Bill to wonder whether his total camouflage idea was a good one. Still, he could not resist the prospect of seeing the faces of the opposing troops when confronted by a band of naked soldiers.

The nude squad hung their clothes from bushes and tree limbs for decoys and deployed an ambush, using Bill's squirrel hunting strategy of hide and wait. The waiting was not in vain. When their opponents walked straight into the naked jaws of the trap, those opponents were seized upon by simultaneous waves of unclad captors and raucous laughter.

Soon three members of the expedition—Earwood, Taulbee, and Helton—would be playing tactical maneuvers for Uncle Sam. Cave Man would not return, sacrificing his life in Vietnam.

Postmarked September 1, 1966, another letter arrived from Karlsruhe:

Hi Mom & Dad

Well I was laying in bed Sunday night and they woke me up at twelve a clock for a phone call. It was Larry I was so suppised I couldn't believe it. Clyde and him are together in Stuttpgart.

I was also spprised when he told me where his brother Len is because he is right down the road about mile and a half. So I called him up monday and talked to him and went over that night and seen him. He said that he was bring his wife over in about a mounth or so.

Larry and Clyde are coming down this weekend to see us. So I put in and got a three day pass so we will be able to mess around. They are about fourty miles from where I am and will probly have a lot of good time togethe while we are over here seeing how we will probly spend the rest of our time over here.

Well I got your package yesterday and wanted to thank you for sending it to me. Me and some of the other guys sat down and ate it and messed around. And they shure did like that salt water taffe you sent.

Well you will be glad to here haven't been getting into any troble or any thing since I been over her and going to try to keep it that way.

I have been doing fine, but I am gaining a little weight and grew an inch taller so far. Haven't been working hard neigther.

Well though I would write and let you know I am ok and having some fun. Tell Dad to take it easy so he don't hurt his back agin. So by for now.

Love Yall

Bruce

Postmarked October 11, 1966, yet another letter arrived from Karlsruhe:

Dear Mom & Dad

I am fine and having fun. Hope everthing is the same at home.

I been going to school for about a mounth and doing ok. I go the school on Mondays, Tusdays and Thursdays from 6:60 to 8:30

I took a test and the only courses that I am taking is English and Reading.

Tell Louise I will sented some germany money next week when I get a chance.

I finally mad PFC. E-3 Monday and will have a stripe to wear on my arm.

I havent been down to see Larry or Clyde. It seems that I can't get a three day pass or I don't have the money. I went over to Len and his Wife they are dong fine.

Well can't think of much to write now, I liked the pictures that you sent me. I will send some back as soon as I get a chance.

Well I have to go to school now, so I will close for now.

Love Bruce

Bill was also spending time in school—though obviously not enough. At the end of his fourteen credit hour trimester, he received the first failing grade of his college career. Apparently, Bill's rigorous fourth-year regimen of senior science and metal shop had been insufficient to prepare him for the challenge of college trigonometry.

After not even attending his trigonometry class the last six weeks of the trimester, Bill had shown up to take the final exam. Even the professor's open book policy could not help. Bill was unable to intelligently complete a single problem. Instead he wrote a few poems, created a cynical cartoon, and handed them in, hoping he might receive a bit of credit for originality. He did not.

While in Germany Bruce persisted in his desire to get to Vietnam—where the action was—and eventually his wish was granted. He was fortunate enough to make it home for three glorious weeks during November of 1966 before Uncle Sam shipped him to the war zone.

When Bruce awoke on the morning of Thursday, November 24th he could scarcely believe his senses. Was he truly at home in his own bed? Was that exciting aroma really the smell of roasting turkey and baking ham? That afternoon his entire immediate family, except Bobby, who was serving his country in the U.S. Navy, gathered for Thanksgiving dinner. Both Grandmother Stevenson and Grandmother Garity were seated at the table as well.

Bruce savored his mother's home cooked Thanksgiving dinner that year more than he ever had before. In fact, he savored it as if he might never have the opportunity again.

When Bruce's dad learned that his middle son was to be stationed in Saigon instead of a forward battle zone he was relieved. Still, he knew that Saigon was not exempt from violence. He did not expect the army to issue his son a rifle while stationed in the capital city, but when he learned that the army would not provide his son with even a sidearm, he was troubled. Accordingly, the day before Bruce again left home, his dad issued him what the army would not, a semiautomatic Colt 45.

Two years later, Bill would purchase an identical weapon, by special request, and ship it to Vietnam. This one, however, would not be going to Bruce. It would be going to John Sickman.

Bruce heard lots of stories about life in Nam, but like so many other American boys, he really did not know what to expect. He was about to find out.

10

Voice of Vietnam

Bruce wrote home often during his tour in Nam, especially during the first six months. A few of those letters are reproduced here, as accurately as possible, as they fell from Bruce's pen:

From: Saigon, Vietnam
Postmarked: December 13, 1966

Dear Mom & Dad

Well this is the first chance I have had to write. I made it over here ok and with out any trouble. I got in Viet-nam of Dec. 8 and got to my unit where I will be stationed on Dec 10. Were I live it used to be a hotel. There is about one hundred guys that live here. They don't have a mess hall so we draw ratison pay which is $124. a month. There is a restraunt down the street where we eat. It has all government inspected food that is sent from the states. I bought a meal ticket for there for a month which cost only $43. Dollars.

We have our own en club on top of the roof where we live and every night they show free movies. I got another allot that will send about $150. home every mount not counting the other $50. that is coming home.

Well I have to go now back to work We are working 12 hour shifs over here.

You can send me my radio when you get a chance.

Love Bruce

From: Saigon, Vietnam
Postmarked: December 19, 1966

Dear Mom and Dad

Well I got a chance to rite finaly hope I have a chance to send you and the rest of the famialy something for Christmas.

Seeing how I had such a great one before I left. I haven't had a chance to get a camera but I probly will get one before the end of the month more that likely. I have one of the same Sargents that I had a Fort Gordon Ga. When I was there.

I met several guys that live in Cin. Ohio. I know one of them from when Jim Yancy and I used to go up there and mess around with some girls.

You know how I was told that Sigon looks something like Dayton. Well that is not true. The houses and people look worse that the ones that live of the West Side of Dayton a heck of a lot worse.

It isn't nere as bad as what I thought it would be over here. We have Showers Sinks, Rest Rooms they arn't the best they are ok. Better that most G.I. have over here.

I sure would like it if you would send some Cool Aid over to me, the water is perty bad tasting so is the food. We work from 7 in the morning till 7 at night and work an hour and have an half hour off so that isn't so bad. I get a chance to write on breaks.

Tell Eric to keep out of trouble and hope he is doing ok in school. Tell Louise that I will send here some Vietnam money to for her collection. Tell dad that I am doing ok and have had any troble over here so far.

Love Bruce

Write an let me know If every body is ok.

ADDRESS ON BACK

P.F.C. Bruce Stevenson
RA15749291
593rd SiG. Co. (SPT)
APO SAN FRANSiCO 96307

Perhaps he did not want his next of kin to feel badly that he was missing the family festivities. Conversely, maybe he did not want to worry them that he was over indulging in Yuletide revelry of another variety. Whatever his reason, Bruce did not report how he spent Christmas of 1966 in Saigon.

Bill, in contrast, enjoyed a traditional Christmas. He spent Christmas Eve, after helping his parents decorate their tree, at Grandma and Aunt Jane's house visiting with extended family. Aunt Jane's huge, immaculate fir, impeccably accented with perfectly placed icicles, stood in haughty contrast to his family's wildly icicled Scotch pine. Nestled among the exquisitely wrapped and bowed packages beneath Aunt Jane's breathtaking tree, as always, was the ceramic Rudolph with his round nose glowing deep electric-red.

One thing, however, was missing that Christmas. When Bill walked over to Aunt Ginny and Uncle Bob's house on Christmas morning, after opening his gifts at home—neither Bobby nor Bruce were anywhere to be found.

In January Bruce's inclination to write home was rejuvenated.

From: Saigon, Vietnam
Postmarked: January 6, 1967

Dear Mom and Dad,

Well I brought me a camera yesterday it is a 35MM. It is post to be a good camera. I took a hole roll of film with it today. Will send some home when I get them back from the photo shop.

Well their isn't to much to write about over here in Viet-nam. The girls are all skinny and try con you out of you your money. If you go in a bar they come over and talk to you then they ask you to buy them a Sigon Tea witch cost about one dollar and fifty cents.

Hope Eric likes the tape recorder that you and dad brought him. He will have lots of fun with it. I probly will get one before I leave here be cause you can realy get a nice one perty cheep throu the P.X. over here.

Well I am still working twelve hours a day over here get about every fifth day off. Usually sleep most of that. Oh yall the name of the camera I brought is a Petri 75. Well I hope every body is doing ok back home. Tell Eric if he gets a chance to send me Juniors Brown address.

I was wondering if Larry of Clyde have got out of the army yet because they were suppost to get out before long. Well I got to go now so by.

Write soon.

Love Bruce

P.S.

First pictures I have taken
with my camera. Perty good
for first time.

From: Saigon, Vietnam
Postmarked: Jan 21, 1967

Dear Eric

Well I got your letter glad to here that you are doing ok. You take about girls they have some real fine looking ones over here the only thing is that half of them don't believe in taking baths the way the look....

If you see Burton tell him thanks for writing. I sent him two letters and he hasn't wrote one back yet some pal his. Does anybody give you any troble over at the pool hall they better not any way. If they do I'll square them away when I come home....

Big Brother Bruce

Bruce had good cause to be concerned about his little brother's hanging out at the pool hall. Causes such as the night a swarm of heathens overran the place—high on drugs—demanding to know where the "Ants" were. The out-of-control savages were apparently referring to another local gang not known to frequent Airway Billiards.

These barbarians terrorized everyone in the establishment for forty-five minutes, turning over pool tables, threatening and demanding. Their burly warlord even drove a cue stick, with a single powerful stroke, completely through the two-inch thick slate of table number four.

Fortunately for both sides of the altercation, Bill was not on duty that night. Another young man substituted for him. Had Bill been there, he surely would have produced his dad's 44 magnum long barrel from behind the counter and dismissed the unruly hoard from the premises—or from this world.

From: Saigon, Vietnam
Postmarked: January 23, 1967

Dear Mom;

Well I guess that Louise told you that I called home Sunday to 22. She was the only one home it was perty hard to get through but I got through didn't cost any thing either. I called Monday at 4:00 in the afternoon and the phone was bussy so I called the office and no body answred and I could hold the line so I had to hang up the only time that I can call is on Sunday because all the rest of the of the time the line to the States are on higher priority.

Well everything has been going fine over here so far. They are still doing a lot of fighting south of here sometimes at night we can hear the motars going off. The operation is called Ceater Falls it is the biggest operation since the war started. They have killed about 700 V.C. now and have captured about 2 or 3 thousand V.C. and have several suspects that they think are Viet Cong.

We are do to move from where we are because they are trying to move all the troops on the out side area of Saigon.

Louise told me that Aunt Daphne is in the Hospital. She didn't say what was wrong with her. But hope see gets well soon and it isn't anything serious.

Well I hope every body else is ok back home.

Love Bruce

P.S.

Tell Aunt Daphne I said that I hope she get well soon. I write her a letter as soon as I get a chance

From: Saigon, Vietnam
Postmarked: January 26, 1967

Dear Mom & Dad

Everthing thing has been going ok over here. I got of work last night I was driving the truck back to the Motor Pool. We saw three truck loads of Vietneese Solders on the street right next to were we eat. I though that something was wrong. So we went on in and ate breakfest.

Then we left and right in front of were we live there was about 50 more Vietneese Solders so when I got inside the gate. I asked one of the Sargents what was wrong he said nothing. He said it was their Local Draft Board. The just grab people of the street and if they don't show a card that you get when you have a job over here. If they don't have a job or card they put them in a big truck and take them to where they are to be traned.

If they have any money or driving a motor bike they take it and sell it to pay for their uniforms and anything else they give them

I could just see what some of the people would say back in the United States if they did that their.

Will I got my color slide back and they came out real good. Has Bobby heared where he is going to be stationed at over here.

Will hope everybody is ok back home Aunt Daphne to. Bill going back to college this year I got to go to work now so by for now.

Love Bruce

From: Saigon, Vietnam
Postmarked: Jan 27, 1967

Dear Eric;

I want you to send me the address of the pool hall so I can drop Hank a line to let him know that I am doing ok....

I have been working perty hard lately. Hope you aren't getting into any trouble that you can't get out of. Because their isn't to many guys lift back home with any balls that will go out and help you. So you will have to watch out for your self. Take care.
Big Brother Bruce

From: Saigon, Vietnam
Postmarked: February 23, 1967

Hi Mom

Well I have been go along ok over here. Haven't been working to hard lately. But doing a lot of sleeping. I hope that they get Cashos Clay in the service before long.

I should be making SP/4 next mounth or same as copural. How has Bobby been doing. Is he still going to come over here.

Have you heared anything about Odus Brown lately or his brother. I ran into anothe guy that I went to school with he is in Saigon to. Haven't been able to get in touch with that Married Donna. The fighting is getting perty bad up North lately they are really killing the Viet-Cong.

The most stupid thing that they did was when they had the truce for our Christmas and New Years. and the a truce for their Tet. Because you would believe how many more americans will die because of all of the supply that the Viet-Cong moved in. They had trucks on the road twenty min. after the truce started.

Thats the way that just about every body feels over here.

Well I have to go now so by with Love.
Bruce

Bill heard about the controversy over a holiday truce on the news and felt conflicting emotions. On one hand, when he remembered the childhood magic of the Biblical account of the birth of baby Jesus, it seemed that surely there could be a ceasing of hostility for a moment or two. Yet if it were going to cost American lives....

In fact, as were many Americans, Bill was confused about Vietnam in general. Particularly, he did not understand his government's sending troops to fight and die with one hand, as it were, tied behind their backs. If life had taught him anything, it had taught him not to fight halfheartedly. Fighting without total commitment would only get one hurt. If one is truly compelled to fight, he should do so with all the power and intensity he can muster; that was Bill's thinking. Pound one's hostile enemy into submission or oblivion as swiftly as possible! Any other course invites disaster.

Consequently, Bill, unlike some of his patriotic friends: Earwood, McCullough and Sickman for example, felt no compulsion to serve in Vietnam. Then again, when Bill paused one afternoon and listened briefly to a long haired rabble rouser with a New York accent attempting to incite a group of students at Wright State to become active war protesters, he felt sick to his stomach.

From: Saigon, Vietnam
Postmarked: March 15, 1967

Dear Mom;

Well everything has been all right over here been working perty hard lately because on the 14th of March their is some Carnal is coming around to inspect everything. We painted the inside of the switchboard white the out side is a body blue and we even took down the sand bags and built a picket fence.

We also painted the brake room a real light green with a white celling and black wood work. I will send you some picture when we have it all done and you can compare them with the other ones of the switchboard that I sent you.

Thanke you for the money that you gave me for my Birthday I am going to get me a pair of boots with it. I don't mean combat Boots either. The pair that I am getting made is going to be made out of elephant hide. They make real nice boots and shoe over here. When I went down their he measured every inch of my feet and even drew a picture of them.

You tell Eric and Louise I will drop them a letter in a couple of days. Well I am going to go get some sleep because I am so tired I can hardly hod open my eyes to write this letter.

Love Bruce

From: Saigon, Vietnam
Postmarked: Mar 19, 1967

Dear Eric;

Well from what you told me Freddy must be getting perty bad.

I have been working my ass off lately because some colnial is supposed to come down hear and have an inspection where we work. The only fighting I have done over here is with the Vietmeese Cowboys. They usually run in gangs of seven or eight and go around steeling, robbing, and rolling drunk G.I..

I hope you have been doing ok lately and not getting into any trouble. I tell you one thing you better finnish school or I am going to kick you in the ass. And don't think I wont.

If you can get me some salt tablets I sore would like it. At the end of march they are going to cut out our Collon and Rations because they have some mess hall for ous to eat in. So that will be $120. less I will get paided it gave me the ass.

Have you heard anything from Junior Brown or his brothers or Clyde.

I have real great pictures coming back in a couple of days I will send some of them home to you.

I guy that I tould you that I knew from Cinn. O. is driving a jeep for some Captain now. Says he likes it. Well I am fine take care of yourself.
Love Big Brother

Bruce

From: Saigon, Vietnam
Postmarked: April 15, 1967

Well I pulled a real good one the other day. I was backing a truck out of the Villa where we live and backed the truck into a voltswagon bus and some Sargent has his arm hanging out and it got caught inbetween the two trucks. I don't think he hot hurt to bad thought.

I had to go balk to the Old Man (Company Camander). I think I will get out of it clean. They haven't said anything else about it yet. So don't worry about it.

Do you rember the colored guy that I went through basic then to school with named Robbinson. Well I seen him the other day he called me where I work. So I came down and seen him but he couldn't stay long because him and the guys he came down with were on a Convoy to Saigon to pick up some stuff. So he asked to drive down here so they let him. He is stationed about 180 miles from here. Do you rember reading about operation Junction City well he is right in the middle of it.

Haven't been able to locate Junior Brown yet. But if he is around here one of ous will get ahold of the other one.

Well I am working nights again I don't know for how long though Hope everthing has been going along ok back home. Did you get the letter I sent for you to send me $50. Well tell everybody hi for me.

Have to go back to work now.
Love Bruce

Bill "pulled a real good one" about the same time, but it was not a sergeant's arm that was injured; it was his own. Nor was it a truck that delivered the injury; it was a tank by the name of Big Mike Barok—the "big Hunky"—as he referred to himself.

One month shy of his twentieth birthday, Bill was no longer a boy. At 6'2", 225 pounds, with a 33-inch waist—he was a man—*he thought.* "Come on Mike, I want to see just how strong you are," Bill declared, placing his right arm in cocked position on the counter behind which the big man was seated on a tall stool.

"I don't want to arm rassle you, Willy," the gentle giant answered, "you might embarrass me."

"Put that big mitt of yours up here," Bill insisted, "I think I can take you."

Pool hall partisans began to lay down their cue sticks and stare. "I don't feel like straining myself. Rassle one of these young fellas," Big Mike suggested, nodding in the general direction of the gathering gallery.

"Come on you big Hunky," Bill taunted, "let's get this thing over with."

Finally, with a gentle shake of his head and with the hint of an embarrassed smirk on his face, Big Mike conceded. His big arm, sprouting fingers so large that a quarter could easily pass through his ring without touching gold, banged down on the counter next to Bill's. The contestants clasped hands with the firmness of two reunited Vietnam vets. "Show me what you got," Big Mike said softly.

Bill applied pressure, but nothing happened. He threw his shoulder, back and hips into his effort, and nothing happened. He reached down deep inside himself, wrenched his guts and nearly ruptured himself. Still, nothing happened.

Bill forced a glance at his opponent's face. It still wore the embarrassed half-smirk. Then the big man applied pressure of his own. Never before had Bill experienced such raw physical power in a human being. He felt the tendons and ligaments in his elbow begin to snap and pop; the joint itself threatened to explode. It was either release his own pressure and allow his fist to be crashed to the counter in defeat, or his arm was going to be ripped off at the elbow.

It would be weeks before Bill's right arm was back to normal. His psyche would never be the same.

From Saigon: Vietnam
Postmarked: May 8, 1967

Dear Mom & Dad;

I have been doing ok over here and working harder now and don't get so many days off any more. I makes time go faster anyway. I should make E-4 this month for sure if I don't get in anymore truble.

Wether I make E-4 or not I will take over the chief operters job here in about one more month. I will work straight days and only eight hours a day. And about two days a week off. But for now we are working straight twelve hour shifts and one day a week off.

From the picture of Eric you sent he is getting to be a perty big boy for his age. He has a real good looking girl friend to. I hope he is doing better in school and keeping out of truble.

Well I am glad that some one will get some use out of that suit that you brought me when I was over in Germany.

Well I hope that you have a very nice Birthday and a Happy Mother's Day. I have something that I have to mail yet that I brought you for your Birthday that I think you will realy like.

But as the days go by, I know
that I will be home soon.
To the best Mom & Dad that a,
guy could want.
So as I count the day till I come home,
I think every night of the good home
and friends I have to come back to.

Well got to go to work now so good by with a bit of good luck to.

Love Bruce

From: Saigon, Vietnam
Postmarked: May 11, 1967

Dear Mom & Dad;

I have been ok lately. Their hasn't been to much to do lately around here. We probly will be restricted from about the 19th of May till the 26th because it is some Buddist birth day and they usually celebrate for about a week or so. Some guys that was here last year when they celebrated it said that they burn their selves and throw tear gas at people and burns houses and all kinds of stuff. So I will probly take a bounch of pictures of it although we arn't suppost to.

I got a letter from Bobby the other day he said he didn't know for sure when he would be over here if he comes.

I haven't been able to get in touch with Otis yet.

Tell everybody that I said hi and doing fine. Well I can't realy think of to much to write about right now so goodby for now. Take Care
Love Bruce

About half way through his tour in Nam, and about half way around the world, Bruce's high school class graduated. The Walter E. Stebbins High School class of 1967 was honored in a commencement ceremony at the school on Friday, June 2nd, beginning at 8:00 in the evening.

The class of 322 graduating seniors was led by class president, Greg Wylie, and by honor graduate, Joe Goddard. Also marching to the tune of "Pomp and Circumstance" that night was the lovely Miss Donna Marie O'Keefe. The entire affair proceeded under the stern gaze of Principal Orville Edmundson. Bruce and Odus, however, were unavailable.

Later that night—as the graduates danced the jerk, frug, boogaloo and watusi—on the other side of the globe young Americans danced to the beat of mortar shells and automatic weapons fire. Bruce, however, was one of the lucky ones. About the time his classmates began their commencement ceremony, he stripped down to his boxer shorts and removed his Stebbins class ring from his right hand, hiding it in his boot. Then he stretched out on his bunk and dozed. After a twelve-hour shift in a bunkered switchboard shelter, a hot meal purchased on his meal ticket and three hours of "messing around" with his buddies, it was 11:00 A.M. in Saigon, and Bruce was tired.

Time and again Bruce wondered in his letters if and when his older brother would be coming to Vietnam as a guest of the U.S. Navy. In fact, Bob served two six month cruises up and down the Vietnamese coast aboard U.S. Navy destroyers: the U.S.S. *Swenson DD 729* and the U.S.S. *Fletcher DD 425*.

In later years, Bill would remember hearing Aunt Ginny tell, in her best proud-mom voice, how Bobby could have avoided going to the Vietnam theater because his brother was already serving there. "But Bobby wouldn't hear of it," she said. Then she quoted the words of her oldest son: "Where my ship goes, I go too!"

Bruce wondered repeatedly, too, in his letters about the status of his cousin, Bill. Was he in college or not? Was he going to get drafted? In fact, Bill's draft lottery number was eventually drawn, and he reported for a pre-draft physical examination in Cincinnati. By some amazing stroke of fate, though, Bill failed that physical because of a high school football knee injury.

Learning of his failure immediately before the last test on the docket, the hearing test, Bill might have failed that test as well. He might easily have failed to recognize some of the electronic tones sounding in his ear phones because they were obscured by his own euphoric laughter at the capriciousness of life.

Bill did not, however, take the presence of family members and friends in Vietnam lightly. He corresponded occasionally with Bruce as he did with Sickman and others. Yet not nearly so often as he thought he should. Nor did he save the letters that he received in return. Even if he had, they would not have been fit to print.

Fortunately, Bruce's parents saved the letters that arrived at their home from their son:

From: Saigon, Vietnam
Received, June 12, 1967
Hi Mom Dad,

I got the tape that you sent. It sounded real good to hear everybodys voices over it. I will send one back as soon as I get a chance to make one up. It is a real big thing over here because it dosn't cost anything to send them back to the States.

Did you get what I sent your for your Birthday that was the only thing that I could find that you might like. Most of the stuff they sell over here is a bunch of junk.

You can tell Bobby if he gets to a phone over here to call Saigon Port Switchboard and ask for me, if I am not their most likely some one their will know where I am.

I started back to school over here so I can finish my high school. I am taking a four week course then I will be able to take GED test to see if I have an high enough score to get a diopolma.

I realy can't think of to much to write about over here. I do just about the same thing everyday. I went to Long Bien the other day and took some Color Slides and a roll of black and white film to. I will send so home when I get them developed. Did you get the pictures of the swiming pool that I sent home. Well I have to go to work now so good by.

Love Bruce

From: Saigon, Vietnam
Date: Unknown
To: Louise

Hi Sis,

Well I hope that you had a real nice time on your first date. Its sound a though you saw some real good movies to.

I haven't been doing to much because I have been going to school for the last three weeks. So you rember the guy I went to Germany with well he is over here now I haven't been able to talk to him yet but I guess that he put in to come over here to. Because he said he didn't like it over their either.

I see that Eric has a perty good looking girl friend to. I guess that he will be as big as me when I come home. By the way I have only 165 days left over here.

You should see the dresses that the round eyes wear over here. They wear min-skirts about five to six inches above their knees. Ho round eyes are what they call the American girls over here. Bccause all of the Vietneese have slanted eyes.

All the Vietneese people have black hair, black slanted eyes, and most of them are skinny. They are very shy to, most of them don't like G.I. I realy don't blame them one bit because of the way we act over here. Well I have to go to work now so good -by and good-luck

Love

Big Brother Bruce

Odus Brown arrived in Nam on March 6, 1966 and served with the 53rd Signal Battalion in the communication center in Long Bien for a month. Then came a time—a bloody time—Odus will never forget. He was sent into the field as an operator for eight months with a Special Forces unit in the Second Field Force.

It was a wretched time! It was a time wherein the hail of projectiles screeching through the air was propelled by something far more vicious than the puny power of a Red Ryder BB gun, and the resulting slop, splattered on fallen comrades, was something far more profound than the disposable goo of boyhood battles. It was a time so intense as to provide Odus with nightmares for a lifetime. It was a time so brutal as to bring him to recognize that the years of abuse he had suffered at the hands of his father had at least served a purpose. They had prepared Odus for war.

Bruce eventually located his buddy and tracked him down. They hooked up in Bien Hoa and went on a two-day spree. Words fail to express the power of the camaraderie between two boys, forced by circumstance to become men, meeting in a hostile land thousands of miles from home. They tried to cram every bar and back-alley entertainment in Bien Hoa into two action packed days. Together they felt invincible, as Odus put it, "walking their walk and talking their talk."

"Bruce had more balls than anyone I ever knew," Odus would solemnly declare many years later. "He had balls the size of basketballs!"

With their binge complete the two GIs hugged, kissed one another on the cheek, and vowed to stay cool till they met again. The following letter is Bruce's matter-of-fact account of the episode:

From: Saigon, Vietnam
Envelope marked: 150 days left

Dear Mom & Dad & Everybody Else;

Well·I went to BiEN HOA and seen Odus the other day. He hasn't changed a bit except he has got a little taller, not much though. He said that Larry is still in Germany. I could believe that I was setting their talking to him, because it is the first time in a year and a half that I have seen him. He said that his Mom got married again and is still living in Ky.

I have been over here three more months than him. Believe it or not he got over here on my birthday. I stayed up their all night and most of the day. We had so much to talk about an everthing like that.

We are going to take R&R together as soon as we decide when we want to go, and where.

You know the clipping well that is partly true. You can get them sometimes and they are pert crisp. Because they are put in cans. It isn't all that bad over here where I am.

They had the cuttest little girl singer at the, Wolling Hotel where I eat, She could talk real good English to. Let me know if you want anything from

over here because I can get it a lot cheeper over here. Well I can't think of anything else to say. So good-by-
Love Bruce

Following his reunion with Odus, it was back to work for Bruce. Forever true to his impulsive nature, though, Bruce was not destined to remain in one position for long.

From: Saigon, Vietnam
Received, August, 1967

Hi Mom, Dad;

I don't work at a switchboard any more. I quit word their about ten days ago. I drive for a Lt' now so I am perty bussy. But I like it better that working at a switchboard. I drive about seventy or eight miles a day. I drive all over Saigon, Long Bien and all kinds of places.

I get along with the Lt. perty good to. It sure does make you tired driving in all this traffic though. have to keep your eyes open all the time

Has everybody been alright at home and with everybody to.

I went up and see junior again and have been having a good time with him to. Their realy hasn't been to much going on over here though.

You know the doll you sent me I gave it to one of the girls that used to work for me. Because she has a little boy and I though he would like it. Well I can't think of to much to say so I will sign off now.
Love Bruce

From: Saigon, Vietnam
Received, August 10, 1967

Hi Mom & Dad

Well everything has been going fine with me. I am still driving of the Lt's. He had to pay the company the other day and I had to drive him all over with about $96,000. dollar's. It sure would be nice to have it. I carred a weapon but we didn't run into any trouble or anything like that. They are going to split our company in half and start a new one. I think I will probly saty where I am.

If their is anything you want let me know because I can get it perty cheep over here. Like TV, Radios, Record players or just about anything you can think of.

I have been putting in a lot of hours to. It make the time fly by. I have drove close to three thousand miles sine I have been driving the jeep.

I was going down the Bein Wai high to Long Bien and we seen some arvin troops having it out with some V.C.. I sure didn't stick around. Because that was when we were carring about $96,000. Would you stick around I don't think you would.

Have you heard of Billy is going to be drafted or not. Tell him if he has to come in he should go into the MP's because they usualy have it great. Well I have to go now so good by.

Love Bruce

Bill, of course, was not going to be drafted. He did, however, enjoy a memorable experience with the U.S. Army during the summer of 1967. That experience occurred when he flew with John Sickman's mother and sister to Washington D.C. where they visited John in officer candidate school (OCS) at Ft. Belvoir, Virginia.

John was having a difficult time with OCS. In fact, he had been designated "Super Plebe" by an officer who did not like his attitude. The "Kryptonite" buckles on his fellow plebes' belts were determined by the officer to be deadly to Super Plebe. Thus, during various physical exercises, Super Plebe was not allowed within ten feet of any of his comrades.

Apparently, Sickman's surgical skill at getting under the skins of folks had finally caught up with him. Still, Super Plebe was able to obtain a one-night pass and spend it with his buddy. Part of that evening was spent watching the recently released action movie, *The Dirty Dozen*.

Meanwhile, Bruce could have been starring in an action movie of his own.

From: Saigon, Vietnam
Date: Unknown

Hi Mom,

Well I have done it again, I have switched jobs. I quiet driving because I was getting to wreckles.

I am working Installion and repair of telephone. I also climb poles and put up wire. I like it very much as soon as I get some pictures developed I will send you some of them.

We were restricted for three days the only place where we could go was to work. Because of the elections, their was a lot of action all over Saigon because the Viet-Cong had orders to interfere with the voting. They blew up a lot of voting places and killed a lot of people to.

From the way thing look, I might not make it home for Chirstmas because we are going to split our company in half. And half of them are going to Knob Bay to start putting in telephones and switchboards their. I don't know if I will stay here or go to Knob Bay. They haven't said yet. I should take place in about two weeks or so.

I haven't seen Jr. Brown lately because I haven't be able to get off to go see him.

Well I hope everthing has been going ok at home. I hope Eric don't get into any trouble for riding to Motor Cycle with out a lisence.

If their is anything you want let me know and I will send it to you when I get a chance. Well have to go now.
Love Bruce

On November 23, 1967 Bruce left the madness of Vietnam behind. Little could he have imagined the madness that lay ahead. For the moment, however, he was excited—excited to be going home, excited to spend Christmas with his family, excited to see old friends.

He would never again set foot on foreign soil.

11

Welcome to Leonard Wood

Bruce's brief holiday, the time between his arrival home from Nam and his departure for his next assignment, passed more rapidly than enemy fire over a soldier's head. He reported on 12 January to Fort Leonard Wood, Missouri for his last year of army life.

That year, 1968, overflowed with destiny. North Vietnam escalated the war with a Tet offensive that raged across the Mekong Delta to Saigon and north to the highlands. North Korea seized the U.S. Navy ship Pueblo. Back in the states the Green Bay Packers repeated their previous year's performance by winning Super Bowl II. Meanwhile, the Beatles communed on the Ganges with Maharishi Mahesh Yogi. Martin Luther King and Bobby Kennedy were assassinated, martyrs to the cause of civil rights. Helen Keller and John Steinbeck died. Arthur Ashe won the U.S. open. Jacqueline Kennedy married Aristotle Socrates Onassis. Apollo 8 astronauts orbited the moon. Spain rescinded its law—dating back to the same year that Columbus discovered America—banishing Jews. George Foreman won the Olympic heavy weight gold in Mexico City, proudly displaying a miniature American flag. Denny McLain, pitching for the Detroit Tigers, became the first 30 game winner since Dizzy Dean with the 1934 Cards. Richard Milhous

Nixon was elected President of the United States. And a movie about "a man (who) went looking for America and couldn't find it anywhere," was released. That movie was *Easy Rider*.

All the while Bruce's personal destiny continued to press dispassionately toward a looming point—*Eleven Miles South of Half Moon Bay*. A single letter from Bruce to his folks, written during the winter of 1968, survives from the Leonard Wood era:

> Hi Mom & Dad;
>
> Well everthing is ok with me except I sure don't like it here to much. I though that I better send my lisence back to get renewed. I am also sending my Income tax thing back to for last year.
>
> I went up to a buddys place over the weekend and had a real good time. He live in Shipwan Ill. about one hundred and forthy miles from here.
>
> Have you heard anything from Bobby lately. They are sending a lot of guyes out of here to vietnam I don' know if I will go or not. I aint going to let it worry me thought.
>
> I am going up to Springfield Mo. this Weekend to see this girl I met up around their a couple of weeks ago.
>
> She seems like a perty nice girl and everything. She has a car anyways so that makes it nice to. I got the sweeter that grandmother made for me and it is realy nice looking to. Everybody has been asking me where I got it from.
>
> I talked to some of the guys over in my old company in viet-nam and they said their isn't to bad over there not as bad around Saigon as they say. I called them up throught the Switchboard here. Well I hope everybody is doing ok.
>
> Love Bruce

The fact that Bruce did not "like it here to much" was evident in his brushes with authority. He was cited for a series of three conduct violations at Leonard Wood. The first incident was duly recorded 27 June 1968 on a DA Form 2627-1. The form bore the following notification:

> It has been reported that, on or about 25 June 1968, at Fort Leonard Wood, Missouri, you were disrespectful in deportment toward SSG E-6 Anthony W. Valente, your superior non-commissioned officer, who was then in the execution of his office, by bending forward at the waist and saluting in a sloppy manner when told to empty the butt cans on the stairs in front of the Drill Sergeant Classroom, Building 1818, Fort Leonard Wood, Missouri. This is in violation of Article 91.

On a separate section of the same form, dated 1 July, Bruce received this notice:

> The following punishments are hereby imposed: Reduced to the grade of Private First Class E-3 (Suspended for three (3) months). Forfeiture of $35.00 pay per month for one (1) month.

Bruce was handed a second DA Form 2627-1 dated 5 November 1968. This one informed him:

> It has been reported that, on or about 5 November 1968, at Fort Leonard Wood Missouri, you did, without proper authority fail to go at the time prescribed to your appointed place of duty to wit: Headquarters, Building 2362, Headquarters United States Army Reception Station, Fort Leonard Wood, Missouri. This is a violation of Article 86, UCMJ.

The consequence of Bruce's failure to report for duty was recorded on the same date:

> The following punishments are hereby imposed: Forfeiture of $20.00 pay per month for a period of one month. Fourteen (14) days restriction in the company area.

Dated exactly one week later, 12 November, Bruce received his third and final 2627-1 while at Leonard Wood. This one informed him:

1. It has been reported that, on or about 0900 hours 8 November 1968, at Co A, USARECSTA, Bldg 2181 FLW, Mo., you did violate a lawful general regulation, to wit: paragraph 3 and 4, Fort Leonard Wood Regulation 210-24, dated 24 March 1964, by introducing into and having in your possession in Building 2181, alcoholic beverage. 2. It has been reported that, on or about 0900 hours, 8 November 1968, at Company A, USARECSTA, FLW, Mo., Bldg 2181, you did violate a lawful general regulation, to wit: Paragraph 6a, Fort Leonard Wood Regulation 210-25, dated 16 April 1964, by having in your possession in Billets a knife with a blade longer than 2 15/16 inches.

Dated 13 November Bruce received this notice:

The following punishments are hereby imposed: Reduction to the grade of Private First Class E-3 and forfeiture of Ninety-Five dollars ($95.00) for one (1) month.

This was the only one of his punishments that Bruce chose to dispute. His typed appeal, also dated 13 November 1968, was comprised of the following statement:

I Do appeal from this punishment. Because I was never given any rules or regulations on having knives in a locked cadre room or having them in your possession. I know it is against regulations to drink in the billets but I didn't know it was wrong to keep it in your locker with your personal stuff. Also I was wondering what kind of regulations there for having to give a key to the Commanding Officer for your room. Also people can go into it without your permission or you being there.

The appeal was denied.

It was Eric, not yet seventeen years old in the summer of 1968, who suggested to his cousin that they ride out to Missouri on their motorcycles and visit Bruce. Bill thought it was a great idea, and within a few days they were ready to ride. It was early afternoon by the time they left Eric's house on Wednesday, August 21. Clad only in protective helmets, cutoff jeans and low cut tennis shoes, the bikers made their way to I-70 and headed west. The wind of adventure in their faces was magnificent.

If not for the helmet hiding his head from view, Bill could have easily been mistaken for a marine recruit. He had not intended to clip his hair down to its already beginning to gray roots—it just worked out that way. His attempt the previous evening at trimming his own thick head of dark, wavy hair had turned into more of an adventure than he had anticipated.

The electric clippers buzzed like a chain saw in Bill's hand. First he whacked a little off one side, then a little off the other. No, that was not quite even. *Buzz,* a little more here. *Buzz,* a little more there. For a kid who demanded perfection, it was an impossible task. Finally Bill lost his patience and lopped off his entire crop of locks like a logger clear-cutting a section of timber.

When he stepped out of the bathroom, having just completed the defrocking of his pate, Bill's mom and dad were watching television in the living room after a fourteen-hour day of work at Trader's Haven. Daphne Sullivan—the beautiful woman with the graying brown hair flowing to the middle of her back when she unrolled it at night and the peaches and cream complexion undulled by makeup—looked at her son through tired green eyes and said, "Oh my!" Bill Sullivan Sr., a man whose thoughts were most often revealed in the expressions of his broad face and high forehead, simply shook his head with a countenance that demanded more eloquently than words, *what next?*

Bill, however, was not seeking his parents' approval. Though he had not planned his new haircut, he knew his buddies at the pool hall would think it was cool. More important than Bill's haircut—though both would play interesting roles in the young men's adventure—was Eric's transportation. Uncle Bob had warned Eric that his 250cc Harley Sprint, as its name implied, was not made for long distance highway riding. He advised his youngest son to take it slow and easy or he would blow the little Harley's engine.

Bill barely endured the tedium of studying his rearview mirror and glancing over his shoulder frequently to monitor his cousin's progress. His own 450cc, black and chrome stallion surged between his thighs, continually demanding more throttle. By the time the bikers made Richmond, Indiana their plodding progress, combined with the searing August sun on his mostly naked body, had dulled the edge on Bill's zeal.

To make matters worse, by the time they made the 115 miles to Indianapolis they were inescapably trapped in a torrent of rush hour traffic. They stopped to eat, hoping to wait out the jam, but in the end there was nothing to be done but ride through it. In fact, they rode on into the evening, through twilight and into blackness, stopping for fifteen or twenty minutes after every hour of riding for Eric to drink coffee or soda, take a leak, and let his cycle's engine cool.

Bill's back and thighs ached from sunburn, and his leg muscles threatened to spasm into full-blown charley horses from being bent in riding position for so long. His sunglasses became encrusted and his chest embedded with the armored carcasses of thirty-odd species of Kamikaze insects, and his butt grew severely saddle sore. Still, Bill resented stopping so frequently. As usual he wanted what he wanted, and what he wanted just then was to complete the ride to Ft. Leonard Wood before giving up for the night.

As the sun sank in the sea of highway before them, the air immediately above the pavement cooled less rapidly than that surrounding it, attracting swarms of insects. If bugs had been a minor annoyance, now they became a major irritation. Bill's eyes watered at the sting of hundreds of tiny darts smacking into his face, ears, and bare chest in compounding bursts of pain. Breathing without inhaling tiny writhing bodies was at times impossible, and trying to filter the air by sucking it through his teeth only led to unwanted crunchy snacks.

Eventually the highway air became refreshingly, then uncomfortably cool. Pockets of naturally refrigerated air collected in low lying areas near creeks and woods, chilling the riders like cold springs in a gravel quarry swimming hole on an August afternoon. During one of their pit stops Bill pulled a light cloth jacket out of his duffel bag and slipped it over his now prickly skin.

Highway freighters swooshed past the riders and left them bobbing in the turbulence of their wakes like bottles with desperate messages inside floating on the open sea. Bill wondered if he and Eric had been capsized and cracked open upon the concrete sea, their contents exposed for the passing CB captains to view—would those captains laugh? Or would they weep at the messages thus displayed?

Around eleven o'clock that night the western horizon began to glow, as if the earth had reversed its rotation and the sun were resurrecting in the west. Off somewhere in the indistinguishable distance, on the shore of the mighty Mississippi, lay the harbor of St. Louis. The ride from the time the bikers first noticed the western incandescence until they finally reached the big city seemed interminable. Always the source of light seemed just over the next hill or around the next curve in the road, but when the hill was topped or the curve rounded, the anticipated source remained as illusive as a mirage.

The travelers finally made St. Louis shortly after midnight, passing over the inky blackness of the Mississippi that bordered the city like a ribbon of darkness surrounding a galaxy of lights. They glided through the city, two points of light, like comets passing through the Milky Way, and eventually plunged back into the blackness of the Missouri night. Only now they cruised along the historic path of Route 66.

They pressed on through their weariness to within fifty miles of their destination before pitching camp in the tall grass beside a gravel lane that dead-ended at the highway. Sixteen grueling hours on the road made frills unthinkable. Pitching camp amounted to nothing more than spreading their old canvass tent on the grass for a ground cloth and curling up inside their sleeping bags on top of it. Bill deposited his shoes and jacket on a corner of the tent where he could find them in a hurry if required. Despite the improvised accommodations, sleep was instantaneous.

Bill woke in the morning to the sounds of a steady string of traffic grinding its way along Route 66 toward work. He raised his upper body high enough, without getting out of his sleeping bag, to see over the tall grass. He was surprised at how close he and Eric were to the edge of the highway, barely thirty feet off the side of the road. The distance had seemed much further in the dark. He felt as if his privacy had been invaded, as if nosey strangers were peeping casually into his bedroom. "Eric," he called.

The life force within the stuffed fabric cocoon beside Bill did not stir. "Eric!" he called louder. Still there was no response. If not for the muted sounds of respiration, Bill might have feared he had been sleeping next to a corpse. "Eric! Wake up, man!" he implored, reaching out and gently shaking the area of his partner's sleeping bag where he expected to find a shoulder.

"Huh. What's the matter?" Eric responded as if from another dimension.

"Come on and get up, man," Bill encouraged. "It's daylight and we better get out of here before the cops come along and hassle us."

"What time is it?" Eric mumbled without showing his face.

Bill looked at the Lord Elgin with the gold band on his left wrist. "It's almost seven o'clock," he reported.

"In the morning?" Eric moaned. "We just got here. Let's go back to sleep awhile."

Bill sighed. He did not enjoy being on display for passing motorists to gawk at, and he did not want to draw the attention of the law. He dragged himself out of his sleeping bag and put on his shoes. "I'm going back into the woods on the other side of the field behind us to take a dump," he declared. "When I get back here you better be out of the sack Sleeping Beauty, or I'm going to toss you out—into the wet grass!"

Eric's only response was a grunt and a shrug, but Bill was convinced communication had occurred. By the time Bill returned, his feet sloshing in his dew-soaked tennis shoes, Eric was already tying his sleeping bag on the back of his motorcycle. "Let's get out of here," he said anxiously. While you were gone some guy came out this lane and gave me a really hard look. He might call the cops."

"Yeah," Bill agreed, picking up his jacket and laying it over the handlebars of his bike. "I saw a blue pickup come down the lane when I was in the woods. There's a house and a barn and a bunch of junk cars back in there."

The pair worked together hastily folding the tent and strapping it onto the back of the Sprint. Then, with camp broken, the young men kick started their bikes, and Bill slipped on his jacket, anticipating the chill of riding in the cool morning air. The bikers waited on the berm for a break in traffic sufficient to allow them access to the road. They had barely made their entry move when violent, stinging pain stabbed Bill just below the right shoulder blade. He gritted his teeth and twisted back on his cycle's throttle, pulling along side of Eric in a burst of speed.

Zing! The intense pain nailed Bill again, this time between the shoulder blades. He immediately braked and swerved off the road, barely missing the Sprint's back tire. He did not bother propping up his bike on its kick stand but instead killed the ignition and dropped the bike in its tracks. Before he could rip the jacket from his body, the intense pain jolted him again, this time at the base of the neck.

Eric, noting that his cousin had apparently gone crazy—having dropped his bike disrespectfully and flailing wildly at himself as if possessed—whipped his own bike off the road and raced down the berm counter to the flow of traffic. He skidded to a halt at his cousin's side.

"What's the matter?" he asked frantically, the stress of sincere concern engraved on his cherubic face.

Bill sank down on his fallen machine and slumped forward, his head between his knees, his voice a hoarse whisper. "I feel sick," he said faintly. "Some yellow jackets...must have gotten into my coat...and they just stung the daylights out of me...go over there and shake out my coat...would you? Just be careful *you* don't get stung."

Eric walked over and gingerly picked up the jacket by its collar and tossed it away from him into the air. Nothing happened. He repeated the effort, and still nothing happened. He retrieved the jacket a second time, handling it only by the edges of its cotton material, and spread it on the berm. Close examination revealed nothing suspicious on the back of the jacket. He turned it over, again finding nothing amiss. Ever so carefully, appearing as if at any second he expected to be goosed by an ice-cold finger, he lifted the front of the jacket open and looked inside. Again he found nothing. Gaining confidence, Eric turned the sleeves inside out and shook the jacket thoroughly—still nothing. Whatever had made the large, red welts on Bill's back had escaped.

While they waited for Bill to recover sufficiently to travel, Eric removed the rolled up sleeping bag from the back of his bike and used it for a seat. He rested his forehead on his folded arms, in turn supported by his knees. Three quarters of an hour later Bill rose to his feet and, with unusual exertion, lifted his cycle. "We better get rolling," he said, alerting his dozing cousin.

The pair discovered Ft. Leonard Wood, cradled on three sides by sections of the Mark Twain National Forest, an hour-and-a-half later. They rode into the army post town of St. Robert and ate breakfast at a little restaurant, taking their leisure. The way they figured it, they would not be able to see Bruce until after regular duty hours anyway.

It was after eleven before they rode over to the post's main gate and talked to the guard. Bill removed his helmet out of courtesy. "I'll need to see your leave papers before I can let you on the post," the young guard told him.

"Huh?"

"What post are you fellows from?" the guard asked.

"We're not from any post," Bill assured him, his face registering confusion.

"Hey, you guys aren't AWOL are you?" the soldier demanded, peering at one and then the other of the cyclists.

Finally it flashed on Bill what was happening. He reached up and ran his hand across the top of his nearly bald head. "Hey buddy, this isn't a military haircut," he offered. "This is a bad accident. I tried to cut my own hair and screwed it up."

"Me and my cousin here just rode out from Ohio to see my brother," Eric quickly added.

The guard's face still appeared skeptical. "What's your Brother's name?" he asked.

"SPEC 4 Bruce M. Stevenson," Eric replied. "He works in communications."

"He was in the 593rd Signal Company in Nam," Bill added hastily.

"Well..." the guard said hesitantly, "you couldn't see him during duty hours anyway. If you want to come back this evening between five and six you might catch him at the mess hall."

"Couldn't we ride over there now just to see where it is?" Eric pleaded.

The guard's five-second pause was disconcerting. "I guess that wouldn't hurt anything," he finally conceded. "Come in the shack and I'll show you where you need to go. But I want you off this post in one hour! Understand?"

"Don't worry," Bill answered, "we'll see you on our way out of here within an hour."

Inside his shack the guard showed his guests a map of the post and identified the general area where Bruce probably worked. "That building right there," he said, pointing to a particular rectangle with a pencil, "that's where you'll probably find him tonight."

The biker's studied the route that would take them where they wanted to go, then took their leave. "Thanks," Eric offered, as they departed.

"Are you guys sure you're not AWOL?" the guard asked one last time, as if to soothe his conscience for letting them onto the post.

"Positive!" Bill replied, and kick started his Honda.

With some exertion, including stopping to confer and backtracking more than once, the cousins eventually discovered and recognized the area they sought. Finding their way out was only slightly more direct. They waved at the guard as they passed his shack, barely under their one-hour deadline. At least they would be better prepared for their return trip that evening.

The bikers spent the rest of the day exploring the nearby towns of St. Robert, Waynesville and Laquey. They also checked motel rates, finding a room in Waynesville cheap enough to use as a base of operations for the weekend. They did not, however, locate a Harley shop, and Eric wanted to have his Sprint inspected by a good mechanic.

The day passed leisurely and uneventfully, with one minor exception. At the gas station where they filled their tanks they were informed it was against the law to ride shirtless on a motorcycle in Missouri. "That's crazy," Eric argued.

"You boys are lucky you haven't been stopped yet," the attendant countered. "You better get your shirts on and keep them on till you get across the state line. I'm not joking!" The bikers exchanged furtive glances that said *this place is weird*, but took the advice.

Soon it was time to return to the post. The travelers arrived back at the gate, where a new guard was posted, about five-thirty. "We're just here for the evening to visit a relative of ours," Bill told him, making sure not to remove his helmet. "We know where he's at; we were here this morning."

Bill's tactic worked. "Go ahead on," the guard advised, and the bikers did not hesitate.

They found their destination with less trouble this time, and parked their bikes in front of a small frame building. Inside they found a group of five GIs sitting around a table shooting the bull.

"What do you guys want?" one of them asked in a less than friendly tone. "We're looking for SPEC 4 Bruce Stevenson," Bill stated flatly.

"Stevenson! What do you want with Stevenson?" the soldier who had already addressed them asked in a sarcastic tone. "You going to kick his butt?"

"Maybe," Bill replied, looking the two-striper directly in the eye while maintaining his straightest poker face. "Where is he?"

"He's over in the mess hall," one of the other GIs offered. "Come on, I'll take you over there. I want to see this." Apparently the others wanted to see *this* as well. They tagged along behind the two bikers and their guide, making snide comments to one another in muted tones.

After a short walk the lead threesome entered the nearly deserted mess hall, and the guide immediately announced their presence. "Stevenson!" he said, "There's some guys here that say they want to kick your butt."

Bruce, seated at a table with his back to the visitors, spun around in his chair aggressively and greeted the intruders with a mortal scowl. If there was any butt kicking to be performed, Bruce made the distinct impression that *who* would be delivering the performance was debatable.

It was the eyes that registered the first hint of recognition, then disbelief, and finally, unless Bill was mistaken, a hint of misting. "Hey man, what are you guys doing here?" Bruce asked in delayed response, rising from his seat and shaking hands with his cousin and his brother.

"Well, we just rode our motorcycles down here to see if you could get the weekend off and if you need any help kicking some butt," Bill answered, nodding in the direction of the open door full of gaping mouths and bulging eyes behind him.

"Hey man, I was just kidding. I didn't know these guys were your friends," the guide quickly interjected. "See you later," he said, swiftly making his exit and closing the now empty doorway behind himself.

"Where did you leave your bikes?" Bruce asked.

"They're parked out front of the building where we found the jerks who brought us over here," Eric answered, "and all our stuff is on them."

Bruce walked over to the just closed door and reopened it. "Hey Jackson!" he shouted after the last of the retreating soldiers. "You better make sure nothing happens to my family's bikes or any of their stuff." Almost before the words were out of his mouth, he slammed the door shut, cutting off any opportunity for Jackson to respond. Then, turning nonchalantly back to his companions he asked where they were staying.

"We're camping out somewhere tonight, but we don't know where yet. We'll find a roadside park or something," Bill explained.

"Yeah," Eric added, "we brought Daddy's old tent."

"No way," Bruce disagreed, "you guys aren't sleeping in a tent. You can stay with me tonight. I've got a private room in a barracks full of trainees. I just have to stay in the barracks at night to make sure they don't try to pull any crap. I don't have to train the little mommy's boys."

"Yeah, but I don't think we're allowed to stay in your room are we?" Bill objected. "I don't want to get in any trouble down here. The guard didn't even want to let us on the post this morning because he thought I was AWOL from some other outfit because of my haircut."

If Bruce wanted to ask about his cousin's lack of hair, Bill had just provided him with the perfect opportunity, but Bruce ignored it. "You won't get in any trouble," he assured. "No one will even know you're here. Besides, those little snot nose punks wouldn't dare say anything anyways. They know I'd knock the crap out of them. Come on, I'll take you over there right now." Not waiting to entertain further objection, Bruce turned and marched his relatives across the mess hall, out a side door, past several typical frame army post buildings, and finally halted in front of a long, rickety structure.

The threesome entered the barracks through a side door where they were greeted by gazes from several trainees who were quietly mingling in front of a row of bunks. "What are you punks staring at?" SPEC 4 Stevenson demanded. "Hey you, Waverly, you got a problem? How come your eyes are popping out of your head? You need me to kick you in the butt so you can see straight?"

The young soldiers quickly dispersed without a word, their gazes fixed to the wooden floors more securely than if they had been Super Glued.

His mission of intimidation accomplished, Bruce led his companions to the end of the barracks where his quarters were located. His room was nothing fancy but displayed a certain level of having arrived. In addition to his bunk there were a metal wardrobe cabinet, a dresser, a chair, an end table with a lamp, a radio, and a reel-to-reel tape recorder. There was probably even enough room on the floor for two sleeping bags. Bill, however, had already made up his mind he was not going to test the sleeping space.

The young men sat in the privacy of Bruce's compartment and shot the bull. It had been too long since they had seen one another. There was a lot to talk over. Eric, who had outstripped his brother in height, had his high school adventures to relate. Bruce had survived Ft. Leonard Wood for seven full months. Bill had pool hall tales to share. Eventually Bruce inquired how long his relatives could stay in Missouri.

"Just for the weekend," Bill answered. We were hoping you could get a weekend pass."

"Yeah, I can do that okay," Bruce responded. "I can probably get out of here about five o'clock tomorrow afternoon. What are you going to do during the day tomorrow?"

"Is there a Harley shop around here?" Eric asked. "I want to get my cycle checked out."

"You'll have to take it over to Springfield," Bruce informed him. "It's a good ninety mile ride over there."

"That's okay," Bill replied, "we've nursed that bike this far; we can nurse it a little farther. We don't have anything else to do anyway. How about if we meet you outside the main gate tomorrow afternoon about five-thirty? That way I won't have to go through the hassle of getting back on this stinking base again."

"Don't worry about that little gate ape," Bruce snarled. "If he gives you any trouble, stomp the crap out of him. That never bothered you before."

"I told you I don't want to get in any trouble down here. Besides, Eric is a minor. We'll just meet you outside the gate like I said. Okay?"

"Okay, man," Bruce finally agreed. "Let's go over to the rec hall and play some pool."

"That sounds good to me," Eric agreed.

"Yeah, me too. This place makes me antsy," Bill added. "But let's go over and get our bikes first. I don't like leaving our stuff out for temptation." His companions concurred.

12

Weird Missouri

The ride to the rec hall, with Bruce on the back of Bill's Honda, was short. Inside, a few soldiers watched TV in a darkened room. In the larger, lighted room, two others played Ping-Pong. The single pool table was in use by a no-striper, looking barely old enough to shave. "You want to play some nine ball for a dollar a game," Bruce snarled in the kid's direction.

"No thanks," the youngster whispered, his gaze focused on his superior's boots.

"Then give me that cue stick and get your butt out of here," Bruce commanded.

"I don't have to get out yet," the youngster answered almost inaudibly. "My sergeant told me I could come over here for an hour. I still have twenty minutes before I have to leave."

"And I'm telling you to get out now before I kick you out!" Bruce growled into the soldier's beginning-to-tremble face. "Me and my family want to play pool."

The youngster flinched heavily at Bruce's sudden snatch of the cue stick from his hand.

"What's going on in there?" another voice demanded from the TV room. This new voice projected the qualities of habitual whiskey and tobacco abuse and many years of barking orders. The short, stocky owner of the voice appeared at the edge of the light. "Stevenson, you got a problem?"

"No First Sergeant," Bruce answered the bulldog of a man with short cropped, graying hair. "I don't have a problem. I'm just trying to teach this thick-headed recruit the rules around here."

"Do *you* have a problem, son?" the first sergeant asked the wide-eyed lad. The youngster's only reply was to hang his head even lower.

"I ain't in the habit of repeating myself," the bulldog growled. "Now what's your problem?"

"I…I was trying to finish a practice rack, First Sergeant, when Corporal Stevenson told me I had to quit," the no-striper reported, never looking up.

"Is that right Stevenson?" the bulldog barked.

"Yeah, that's right," Bruce conceded, glaring at the feet shuffling youngster.

"Go ahead and finish your rack, son," the first sergeant declared. "Stevenson, leave him alone! Understand?"

"Yes First Sergeant," Bruce replied, still glaring at the lad. Then, as soon as the older soldier disappeared back into the TV room, Bruce whispered a message to his about to cry adversary: "Around here they call me the rash, and from now on I'm in your arm pits, punk."

Eric and Bill stood aside, silently watching the episode. Eric's dark brown eyes were wide as a starry night, while Bill's face flushed crimson. The trembling soldier took two more shots, neither of which he came close to sinking, then left the rec hall without a word. The door had not closed behind him before Bruce was racking the balls. "Want to play screw your neighbor?" he asked cheerfully.

For the next two hours the trio shot pool and trash-talked each other. With a dime a game at stake the competition was fierce and the talking fiercer. Yet the three pool players had not an ounce of ill will between them. At last, with fatigue rapidly overcoming the thrill of competition, Bill announced that he and Eric needed to go find a place to sleep for the night.

"Hey man," Bruce suggested, "if you guys don't want to stay with me, there's plenty of places you can camp on the post."

"You mean campgrounds?" Bill asked.

"No," Bruce answered, "just good places to camp where nobody will bother you. Let me go get my cycle and I'll ride out there with you."

Bill was not comfortable with the idea, but he lacked the heart to further refuse his cousin's genuine attempts at hospitality. By the time the threesome rode away from the occupied portion of the post to find a camping spot, it was dark, very dark. The beams from their headlamps slashed through the night to reveal not much of anything.

On and on they rode, looking. The night air became chilly. Bill tried to convince himself that they would find the perfect overnight hideout any moment. They did not. Finally, with a burst of speed, Bill pushed past Bruce's 350cc Honda Scrambler, slowed, and pulled to the side of the road. His cousins followed his lead. "Man, thanks for trying to help us out," Bill began, "but I haven't seen anyplace that I want to camp. I guess I just don't feel good about camping on post. How about just getting us out of here, and we'll meet you tomorrow evening."

Wearing only a T-shirt on his upper body, Bruce was shivering. "Okay, man," he agreed, "follow me."

It was no small disappointment for Eric and Bill to discover that their long delay in getting off base had caused them to barely miss last call at the local fast food restaurants. They were all closed. The duo settled for a midnight supper of Baby Ruth candy bars from a vending machine. Bill washed his down with water from his old boy scout canteen. Eric guzzled Dr. Pepper. With their hunger temporarily appeased, the cousins bedded down for the night at the hidden, grassy base of a highway embankment. Sleep was sweet.

Bill did not stir until nine the next morning, and then only at the insistence of an over extended bladder. As he stretched his arms and yawned, he had a curious thought. Accordingly, before he crawled out of his sleeping bag, he carefully checked his jacket and shoes for stinging insects.

The bikers took their ease preparing for the new day. They ate brunch at a fast food restaurant, then checked their map for the best route to Springfield. The course was not complicated.

The ride was pleasant if uneventful. Bill was no longer in a hurry to get anywhere. In Springfield, it was no problem finding the Harley shop, and the proprietor was friendly. His mechanic inspected Eric's Sprint and took it for a quick spin. The diagnosis was exactly what the cousins already knew; the engine had a lot of miles on it and needed a complete overhaul. In the short term, there was nothing to do but continue to pamper the cycle. The bikers dared not exceed forty-five miles per hour, and needed to stop every hour on long rides and let the engine cool.

It was time for one of those stops during the ride back to Leonard Wood, via the scenic route, when Eric spied a roadside store and rolled into its gravel driveway. It appeared to be a family operation: a country store and living quarters under one roof. The lads parked their bikes on opposite sides of the driveway, in the shade of friendly oak trees, and strolled toward the store, thinking to quench their hot afternoon thirst.

"Hey man," Eric reported, "the door is locked."

"Are you sure it isn't just stuck?" Bill asked.

"See for yourself," Eric replied, stepping aside.

Bill twisted the doorknob back and forth. It appeared to be locked. He put his shoulder against the door and applied moderate force. It was solid. He pressed his face against the door's window, peered inside past the hanging cardboard "OPEN" sign. The lights were on but no one was in sight. "That's strange," he muttered, pounding on the door. There was no response.

The young men retired to the shade and stretched out on the ground beside their cycles to rest. Bill dozed to the strident singing of a chorus of lonely cicadas. Sometime later, he had no idea how much later, he was ripped back toward awareness by an even harsher cacophony. Screeching and shouting reverberated across the chasm between sleeping and waking as if a wrongfully condemned soul were being hauled down to Hades. There was a confused, semi-cognition of chaotic motion. Then, as the focusing of a lens, the action congealed into consciousness. Bill recognized a voice.

"What's the matter with you, are you nuts?" Eric was shouting, while frantically trying to kick-start his Harley.

"You better get out of here and never come back!" shrieked his unlikely assailant, wearing a granny dress and wielding a broom.

The moment his cycle started, Eric fishtailed in the gravel driveway, creating a miniature dust storm, and making his escape. But even as the Harley sprang into motion, the ranting Harpy took one last wicked swing with her broom. "You crazy old witch!" Eric shouted back at her.

Bill was totally baffled but did not wait for explanations or invitations. Neither did he take the time to kick-start his engine, his usual practice, but instead employed the electric starter. He held his breath as he passed through Eric's dust devil: half because he did not want to suck the debris into his lungs, and half because he was afraid the female devil's disciple might take a swipe at *him* as well. Succeeding in his escape, Bill chased Eric's backside. He had not seen the Sprint move so fast since they left Dayton.

A safe distance down the road, the bikers pulled to the berm. "What happened back there?" Bill asked, thinking his cousin must have somehow provoked the old crone.

"Don't ask me!" Eric shouted, his eyes wide and wild. "One minute I was asleep and the next minute this crazy woman is beating on me with a broom and yelling all kinds of stuff that doesn't make any sense."

"Did she act like she was drunk?" Bill asked, still thoroughly puzzled.

"I didn't smell any booze on her," Eric answered.

"That doesn't make any sense," Bill concluded. "She must have been in there all along but didn't want to wait on us. Maybe she thought we were going to rob her or something. Who knows? Maybe she never saw a motorcycle before. This place is weird!"

The rest of the ride back to Leonard Wood allowed seething emotions to settle. The site of Bruce waiting for his kin at the gate, astride his orange and white Scrambler, was an invitation to catharsis. The biker's anger and bewilderment were transformed and vented as stark raving hilarity. The three young men laughed so long and hard, as Eric and Bill recounted the story sparing no detail, that Bill had a fleeting thought that his side might split open along the seam where his appendix had been removed three years previous.

When the trio regained sufficient composure, they rode to their previously selected motel to rent a room for two nights. "What in the world did you guys pick this place for?" Bruce wanted to know.

"Why? What's the matter with this place?" Eric thought out loud. Bill was wondering the same thing. Bruce, however, offered no explanation except to snicker his *I know something you don't* snicker.

After checking in and stowing their gear, Bruce led his companions out of town for an evening spin along country roads. At times, Bruce left the road, playing follow-the-leader across a field or through a wooded lot. The terrain was no problem for him on his Scrambler, nor for Eric on his Sprint. Bill, however, was at a serious disadvantage: his street bike was heavier and rode lower, and his tires lacked the traction of his cousins' machines.

Attempting to follow his companions down a steep, sandy wash on the side of a wooded hill, Bill laid his bike down before he even got a good start. Bruce was at the bottom of the slope before he recognized his cousin's predicament. Bill had righted his cycle but was in a quandary as to his next move.

"Are you okay?" Bruce hollered.

"Yeah!" Bill hollered back. "I just bruised my leg a little bit when I laid this thing down!"

"Stay right there," Bruce instructed. Without hesitation he zoomed back up the steep slope past Bill and parked his bike on relatively level ground at the top of the hill. Then, shuffling on foot back down the slope to his cousin's rescue, he said, "Let me show you how to ride that thing out of here!"

Though embarrassed, Bill did not object. In fact, he watched gratefully as his cousin restarted the Honda and rode it skillfully to the bottom of the hill. Then, after positioning the cycle for a running start at the slope, he revved the engine and popped the clutch. The Seventh Cavalry would have been proud of his charge up the hill—a soldier on a spoke-wheeled stallion—shouting *EEEHAAA!*"

"Thanks, man," Bill said sheepishly, after the dust had settled.

"No problem. I ride in motocross races out here almost every Sunday," Bruce replied, as if to excuse his cousin's lack of off-road experience. "I'd like to ride this thing out on the blacktop. Do you want to trade for awhile?" That was fine with Bill.

Back on the road, Bruce leaned forward and flattened his body on his cousin's 450. He twisted back on the accelerator with his right hand, reached down and grasped the shift lever—intended to be manipulated by foot—in his left hand. Then, without benefit of the clutch, he popped the screaming machine into gear and exploded into motion. The big bike's back end fishtailed, then grabbed the pavement, leaving a long narrow patch of black rubber. Simultaneously, the front end raised two feet off of the ground.

As if he were the master of some mysterious governing force, Bruce kept his raging steed under control, and, with a mighty "*EEEHAAA!*" literally rode into the sunset. A lingering glance between Eric and Bill revealed their mutual admiration for Bruce. Then they laughed and followed his path toward the golden glowing horizon.

Back at the motel room, Bruce broke out a deck of cards. "Are you guys ready to loose your money?" he taunted.

None of them had any money they could afford to lose and knew it. Yet that would not stop them from jiving each other. "When is your next pay day?" Bill wanted to know.

"First of the month," Bruce answered, feigning a snarl.

"Okay," Bill announced with a grin, "I'll take your I.O.U. till then."

"When do *you* get paid?" Eric echoed.

"At least I got a job to *get paid*, you little peach-fuzz schoolboy," Bill slammed him.

"Poker *is* my job, you whisker-faced pool hall flunky!" Eric slammed back.

"Okay, if you guys are so hot, let's play dealer's choice, hundred dollar ante, pot limit!" Bill declared.

The three card sharks did not have a hundred dollars between them, but since they were playing "owesies" that did not matter. Moreover, the absurd stakes was a signal to both his cousins that the only real stake was bragging rights. Still, since this latter agreement was unspoken, one could enjoy the thrilling fantasy that the big loser might actually pay him a huge sum of money. The horrible thought of having someone actually expect to be paid a huge sum was equally thrilling. Bill's contingency plan—just in case, by some fluke, he were the big loser—was to pay off in *Monopoly* money.

The poker war raged into the wee hours. The combatants played five card stud, five card draw, seven card stud, baseball (both daytime and nighttime), Indian poker and more. In short, they played every variety of poker known to Hoyle, and many that were not. At various times they played deuces wild, treys wild, one-eyed jacks and the king with the axe wild, treys and nines wild, fours draw an extra card, and a dozen other combinations.

When the shuffling and the betting were finally finished, Bill was the undisputed lucky, no-good, bottom-dealer of the night, with total winnings in excess of three million dollars. Just as he reached to switch off the light, Bill had a flash. "Don't you guys try to pay me off with *Monopoly* money!" he warned.

The card sharks slept late, not venturing out of their casino until ten-thirty in the morning. They ate brunch at a fast food restaurant and made plans for a glorious afternoon at the Lake of the Ozarks. The day was warm, and they traveled light, wearing only T-shirts and cutoffs. As the young men rode their motorcycles out of Waynesville, chasing the serpentine coils of State Route 7 through the fields and woods of a Missouri summer; though their metal thunder was less than heavy—these Nature's children were living true to Steppenwolf's "Born To Be Wild" lyrics: "looking for adventure and whatever comes our way."

They found the Lake of the Ozarks, a beautiful body of water, winding through a valley surrounded by wooded hills. It sported a resort area complete with the usual tourist attractions: boat rides, amusements, souvenir shops and restaurants. The main strip through the resort area was bumper to bumper traffic.

The bikers were singularly astonished by one particular exhibit, the "Sky Faucet." A large spigot hung in mid air, unsupported, and spewed forth a smooth unending torrent of sparkling water into a fountain eight feet below. It was as if Eden's fountain, ordained to water the whole earth, were alive and active in Missouri.

The threesome sought shelter from the sun under a large canopy, pondered the mystery of the Sky Faucet, and ate sandwiches of sizzling meat, hot off an outdoor grill. Eventually they figured out the fountain's secret. Still, they all had to insert their fingers into the six-inch-diameter, flowing stream just to be certain. After satisfying their curiosity and their hunger, they moseyed on down the strip, soon discovering another site of mutual interest.

Inside an open building, a group of young people was demonstrating various arts and crafts. A pleasant young lady, Susan, showed the bikers how to create personalized medallions from copper blanks and powdered paint. The blanks were flat and oval, about the diameter of an over-sized chicken egg, with a hole drilled in one end allowing access for a cord or fastener.

Bill was excruciatingly careful in designing his pattern and applying his paint. His background was a symmetrical lavender center, darkening in concentric rings into purple then blue-black. Emblazoned in the foreground in bright yellow was a one-word message: "LOVE." Bruce, in stark contrast, was utterly nonchalant in his approach. He sprinkled on some of this color and some of that, a few flecks here and a few there, with the same reckless abandon he brought to life in general. His creation was finished baking before Bill's had even entered the kiln. Yet the finished product was certainly no less striking than was his cousin's. It was the epitome of chaotic beauty in a random universe. Eric's approach fell somewhere in between those of his brother and his cousin.

Looking back, years later, Bill would realize how powerfully those medallions, purchased for a buck fifty apiece, had defined their makers' paths through mortality.

When Bill's medallion was finally finished baking and cooling, the bikers were ready to ride. "We're having a folk/gospel sing here tonight at eight o'clock," their hostess said gently. "It's free. Would you like to come?"

Bill did not want to hurt the sweet young lady's feelings, and for the moment it was the only invitation he had. "I don't know if we can make it or not, but if we're still down here tonight we'll try," he hedged. "Thanks for the help, Susan."

"Yeah, thanks for the help," Bruce and Eric echoed.

"You're welcome," Susan assured, "I hope you can come back tonight."

Bill led the way back to their bikes, forging into the street through a narrow seam in the slowly moving traffic. He barely made it to the other side when he heard the unmistakable thump of something—a fist or a foot—slamming into the fender of a car, followed by loud cursing. He spun in his tracks to see Bruce standing on the centerline of the road gesturing wildly, still yelling at the driver of a car whose taillights showed no sign of braking. Eric stood by, puppy-eyed and mute.

"Hey man, calm down!" Bill warned, "we don't want any trouble."

"That punk almost ran over my brother!" Bruce shouted back. "Come on Eric," he said, wrapping his arm around his sibling's shoulders like a hen protecting a chick under its wing. Then he swiftly ushered his little brother across the opposite lanes of traffic.

As the bikers rode away from the bustle of the strip into the unknown, searching for their next adventure, their new medallions were proudly displayed on their chests, suspended from their necks by cords. It took some exploration, but they eventually located the object of their search: a secluded area accessible to motorcycles. Bill laid his bike down again getting to it, but this time he handled the difficulty on his own. The effort to get there was worth it.

Cropping out from the side of a steep slope was a huge boulder, overlooking a large expanse of lake. It was easily large enough for all three young men to lounge on at once, basking in the sun and absorbing the panoramic view. For a time they sat in reverent silence, each appreciating nature's beauty in his private way.

It was Bruce who broke the mood by suggesting they dive into the lake, twenty feet below. Bill peered over the foreboding edge of his stony perch and examined the wet blackness beneath him. "We better go down there and check it out first," he advised. "It looks pretty deep, but there might be a rock or stump not far under the surface."

Bruce stood on the edge of the precipice, silently surveying the shimmering surface. Then suddenly, with a mighty "*EEEHAAA!*" he sprang into the expanse and crashed, cannon ball style, into the waiting caress of the Lake of the Ozarks. Eric and Bill stood and witnessed the exploding fountain of Bruce's entry. When their comrade popped to the surface, blowing water from his nose, they exchanged glances filled with abhorrent admiration and shook their heads.

"The water is warm as whiz," Bruce called up to them. "I'll swim around down here and check for rocks and stuff."

Bill was the next to take the plunge. He stood on the brink of decision, contemplating whether to be persuaded by his cautious side or by his impetuous side. In the end, caution won out, and he jumped instead of dove. Nevertheless, the moment of departure was exhilarating. A rush of adrenaline hit Bill's heart, lungs, stomach, brain and gonads all at once. For a time-suspended moment he was full of rushing air and anticipation. Then—suddenly—he crashed feet first into the awful reality of shocking coolness. Bruce had lied.

Down into the silent immersing depths Bill descended, greenness above and abysmal blackness below. In an instant he felt an incredible loneliness and a longing to be reunited with the warm and lighted, breathing world above. Kicking and stroking powerfully, he rose, and bursting gloriously through the water's surface he emerged reborn among the living. "Come on in man," he called up to his remaining dry cousin, "the water's great."

With an impish grin, a loud "*YAHOO!*" and total confidence in his older relatives, Eric leapt from the ledge. Upon resurfacing, however, he gasped through bluish-tinted lips, "I thought you guys said this w-w-water was w-w-warm."

Bruce laughed his *Har! Har! Har! I got you guys a good one*, laugh. Bill just plain laughed.

The climb back up the steep slope to their staging platform was a chore, but to the young adventurers it was an enjoyable one. When they completed it, there was unspoken recognition they had just passed through a rite of initiation, and they could not wait to leap again. Thus they spent an invigorating hour, taking turns jumping and diving, then climbing to renew the cycle.

When at last they paused upon their prominent rock to catch their breath and soak in the warming rays of the sun, which now hung low in the western sky, a speeding boat approached. Riding in the back of that boat, and gazing intently at the three lean, perfectly formed bodies posing on the boulder above her, was a lovely, tanned young lady wearing sunglasses and a bikini. She smiled and waved, and the threesome returned her gesture. Then she waved again, but this time with a beckoning motion, inviting them to display their diving ardor for her delight. The young men obliged, one by one, soaring from their lofty perch to the lake below.

When they climbed once more to their exalted rock, the boat made a second pass. This time the lovely young lady and her companions applauded. Standing there in their near nakedness, the slanted rays of the sinking sun engulfing them in a golden glow, and pierced by the adoration of passing strangers, the initiates felt much as the gods must have felt when they first ascended Olympus.

The power of the setting sun was too weak to completely dry the adventurers before it slipped below the trees. They shared Bill's beach towel to dry themselves as best they could and returned to their cycles. Still, the ride back to the strip was chilly. After eating and discussing their options, they decided to check out the folk/gospel sing, whatever that might be. At least they might meet some friendly young ladies.

Susan greeted the bikers pleasantly. She was obviously pleased with their attendance, and she introduced them to other young people, who, like Susan, were part of a religious organization that sponsored summer activities in an effort to share their brand of gospel with young strangers.

Eventually a sort of entertainment with a message began in the form of guitar playing and singing, punctuated with gospel testimonial stories and remarks. Though the bikers were not particularly participative in the sing-along moments, they enjoyed the laid back evening. While they were not seeking the message, neither were they offended by it.

The ministry activities concluded at ten o'clock, and light refreshments were served. Bill was amazed at how quickly the time had passed. He was actually feeling a portion of serenity and brotherly love.

Furthermore, judging from his cousins' peaceful countenances and gentle speaking, it seemed they shared his sentiment.

Bill finally got up the nerve to ask Susan if it was possible for him and his cousins to spend the night at the facility where she and the other youth ministers had their quarters. "We're not allowed to have visitors," she explained, "but there is a motel about two blocks down on the other side of the street."

Mildly dejected, the biker's said their good-byes and walked outside. The temperature had dropped dramatically during the two hours they had been inside. "Are you guys sure you want to ride back to Waynesville?" Bill asked.

"I didn't bring any clothes besides what I'm wearing," Bruce answered. "Riding back tonight would be awful cold. What do you think little brother?"

"I think we would freeze our butts off!" Eric answered without hesitation. "Let's see if we can afford a room."

"Sounds good to me," Bill agreed, "if we can find one cheap enough. I don't have any clothes with me either, except for my raincoat. Let's just walk down to the motel."

Unfortunately the motel was full. To make matters worse, the tidily dressed young attendant was obnoxious. "You can try the motel on the other side of the street about two blocks down," he whined, barely glancing in their direction. His nasal tone oozed sentiment that seemed to say, *Kindly remove your unkempt persons from the premises. Are you so dull as not to notice that I am busy?*

"Thanks," Bill said curtly.

"Yeah! Thanks for nothing, you ugly little lobby-monkey," Bruce snarled on the way out the door. In an instant, any warm and neighborly inclination that lingered from the gospel activity flew like a flock of bats into the night.

Minutes later the trio's apprehension was confirmed. The second motel was full as well. "Now what?" Bill asked. "It's a long cold ride back to Waynesville."

"Let's go get our bikes and see what we can find," Bruce offered, with no apparent concern. Forty-five chilly minutes of riding up and down the strip later, however, even Bruce was ready to concede defeat.

At last the bikers settled for picnic table bunks in a roadside park. Bruce and Bill shared a tabletop, huddled under Bill's raincoat. Eric was banished to a private planked-berth and left to fend for himself with only Bill's still damp beach towel for a blanket. A slab in the morgue could not have been less comfortable. To speak of sleeping in such conditions would be an exaggeration, but fatigue was heavy, and after a time of tossing, turning, raincoat stretching and snickering at Eric's muttering and cursing, Bruce and Bill dozed.

Vroomm! Vroomm! The delicate partition that barely separated frenzied dreaming from frosty consciousness was shattered in an instant. Bruce sat up and looked toward his brother, allowing a rush of icy air to invade the sanctity of the raincoat bubble. "What's going on now?" Bill growled.

"Eric's over there revving up the Sprint," Bruce explained.... "Now he's firing up my Scrambler.... Now he's spreading your towel on the ground. He's making a bed between the cycles to try to stay warm off their motors."

The bunkmates laughed and began again—but with less vigor than before—the tossing, turning, butt knocking, raincoat stretching exercise. Snoozing was close behind but short-lived. Headlight beams pierced the darkness like swords, startling Bill awake in a flash. "Oh no!" he whispered, "it's the cops." Neither he nor Bruce so much as twitched, but watched pensively.

"Maybe they'll just leave us alone," Bruce whispered. No sooner had he spoken, however, than Eric rose from his soggy bed and approached the cruiser.

"What is that fool doing?" Bill asked incredulously.

The police officers were apparently wondering the same thing. "What are you boys doing down here?" one of them asked in an authoritative tone.

Eric walked right up to the side of the cruiser and answered in a non-stop, shivering voice: "M-m-me and my b-b-brother and cousin didn't have anyplace to s-s-sleep tonight because the motels are full and it was t-t-too far to ride back to Waynesville without any clothes s-s-so we decided to try to sleep here but it's impossible because it's so c-c-cold we're about to f-f-freeze to death. Do you guys have any b-b-blankets we could use?"

Bruce and Bill nearly wet their picnic table trying to keep from laughing out loud. The officers did not even attempt to hide their amusement. "We don't have any blankets," one of them said when he was able to stop laughing, "but you can sit in here with us for awhile and get warm if you want to." Eric did not have to be invited twice.

Then one of the officers called to the other two makeshift campers and invited them to come and sit in the cruiser. "No thanks," Bruce answered, "we're fine." There was no way he or Bill was going to sit in a police car voluntarily.

Half an hour later, Eric got out of the cruiser and thanked the officers. "You boys be careful down here now," one of them warned, and at last they drove away. Bruce and Bill laughed, then dozed again—until the next *Vroomm! Vroomm!*

Mercifully, the first light of dawn bloomed early in the morning. The pilgrims rose and built a small campfire, warming their souls as much as their bodies. "We about freaked out when you went walking up to those cops last night," Bill told Eric. "We were afraid they would lock us up for vagrancy."

"I could care less what they did with *me*," Eric reported, "I was about to freeze to death. What could be worse then that?"

Bruce and Bill laughed hysterically.

"You guys had a raincoat to share," Eric continued, seemingly unamused, "all I had was a wet towel."

Thus they spent the early morning hours, sharing idle chatter around a campfire and enjoying the camaraderie known only to those who have shared sincere adventure and affliction.

13

Hobbling Home

The ride back to Waynesville, in contrast to the harshness of the previous night, was wonderfully gentle. The adventurers rode lazily, more because it felt right than because of any desire to spare Eric's engine. They made the motel about one in the afternoon.

Bruce and Eric entered the room, while Bill checked in at the office. A voluptuous older lady—Bill judged her to be in her late twenties or even early thirties—was on duty. Her tinted red hair and heavy makeup struck him as garish for a motel attendant.

Bill, who hated asking favors, turned on the charm: "Ma'am, my cousins and I rented room 112 for Friday and Saturday night, and we didn't even stay there last night. Our stuff is still in there, and we were wondering if it would be okay if we went ahead and took showers and rested up a little while before we check out. I know it's past check out time, but we would really appreciate it."

"Well, how come you boys rented the room for two nights," she snapped, "but only used it Friday night? What did you do, spend last night with *friends*?"

Bill blushed. He could not tell from her demeanor whether the insinuation in his inquisitor's voice was teasing or serious. "Oh no ma'am," he quickly explained. "We rode down to the Lake of the Ozarks yesterday without any warm clothes. Then last night it got too cold to ride all the way back up here. Then we couldn't get a motel room down there; so we had to sleep in a park. We all need showers in the worst way."

"So I noticed," she quipped, completing the disarming of Bill's fancied charm. "Now what can *I* do for you?"

Again the voice of innuendo: Bill blushed, gazed at his feet and stammered, but never quite said anything intelligible. The lady let him flounder for a protracted moment of silent harassment, then laughed out loud. "Well," she said after her guffaw, "we're almost empty anyway, so I guess you boys can shower and rest for a bit. But if you decide to throw a party, you better invite *me*."

Bill's eyes snapped up from the floor and performed a reflexive double take on his grinning antagonist. He still did not know how to take her. "Oh we're not going to throw a party!" he insisted, "but if we do, you're invited."

She laughed again, then told him to be sure and drop-off the key on the way out. Bill assured her that he would, and gratefully made his exit.

"What took you so long?" Bruce quipped when Bill walked in their room. "Were you trying to make a pass at that motel woman?"

Bill shook his head. "You wouldn't believe," he replied.

Bruce laughed his "Hee! Hee! Hee!" *Bill loves a wanton woman* laugh. "You still haven't figured it out, have you?" he asked seriously. Bill and Eric looked at one another. No, they had not figured it out. "Half the men on the post come over here on the weekend," Bruce continued. "What do you think they come for?"

Bill's ruddy blush indicated that he finally "figured it out," and they all had a hearty laugh.

By the time Bill walked out of the bathroom, he being the last to shower, his cousins were both fast asleep. Unfortunately for Bill, both beds were taken. It occurred to him, for a fleeting moment, that he was the beneficiary of the perfect opportunity to prank his partners. He quickly decided, however, that it was not worth the effort. Instead, he sank down in one of the room's two stuffed chairs and slept.

Bruce had to be back on post by six o'clock Sunday evening, and it was nearly five before the bikers were fully recovered from their afternoon siestas. A nearly tangible tone of solemnity hung over them like a Missouri morning fog. They sat mute around their room, gazing at the floor. It was as if they each knew, without speaking it, that something special—something near sacred in the Flow of Life toward a point *Eleven Miles South of Half Moon Bay*—was about to end.

"Eric, we better ride," Bill announced, shattering the awkward silence. "I want to make a pit stop at that souvenir shop on 66 east of Leonard Wood before we hit the road." He could not bring himself to address Bruce, somehow feeling guilty for leaving his cousin behind.

"If you guys are going to stop at the souvenir shop," Bruce offered, I'll ride out that far with you."

Bill took his cousin's gesture to be his way of saying thanks for coming, his way of trying to make their parting easier on his companions. Bruce turned in the room key, sparing Bill the embarrassment, while Eric and Bill loaded their bikes. Moments later the trio were creeping slowly east on Route 66.

They reached the souvenir shop all too soon. There could be no more prolonging of their parting. The adventurers grasped hands, arm wrestling style, signifying their unspoken love and appreciation for one another. It was plain that Bruce had been deeply touched by the visit of his brother and cousin. "You guys be careful riding home," he advised. Then he was gone.

Eric and Bill stood as helpless as statues among the shop's gaudy lawn ornaments and watched their loved one ride away. Bruce looked back over his shoulder once and waved.

Inside the barn full of curios, Bill moved quickly to fill his emptiness with shopping. None but the perfect souvenir would do. It took him more than an hour of deliberate searching, but at last he found it, the pure-white fleece of a lamb.

Their shopping done and dusk descending, two-thirds of a mighty trio rode out, looking for a place to eat. Finding it in a little roadside diner, indistinguishable from ten thousand other diners strung across the highways of the land, they ate a quiet meal and reflected inwardly, bracing themselves for the return ride home. That ride would prove to be drastically different than anything they might have anticipated.

By the time the duo left the restaurant, however, dusk's gray curtain dictated the use of their headlamps. Unfortunately, Eric's was not working properly, occasionally flickering off and on like a lovesick firefly. Soon the night was darker than dark. Near Rolla, even the road added to the blackness, having just been resurfaced with several inches of fresh blacktop. There was not a painted line to be found upon it.

Bill rode far to the right, contrary to conventional wisdom, just inside the edge of the road. This technique allowed him to keep an eye on his cousin's progress in his rearview mirror. Once, when he was unable to locate Eric's headlight in his mirror, he looked back over his left shoulder to get a better view. Eric was there all right, the intensity of his headlight beam waxing and waning.

Bill's gaze returned forward barely in time to see his front tire drop over the edge of an eight inch ledge of freshly rolled blacktop. The time for thinking was past. Bill reacted. His unusually quick reflexes, however, instead of working to his advantage as they had many times in the past, this time sealed his downfall. Instead of riding his cycle off the road and taking his chances, even laying it down if need be, he instantly twisted his handlebar in an effort to whip the front wheel back onto the road.

The wall of asphalt was unyielding. The cycle went into a violent wobble. In a sudden instant Bill felt a sickening rush of adrenaline. This is it! he thought, resigning himself to his fate. It was precisely this instant—the infinite instant between recognition and consummation—

when he came to know that time is truly relative. In the same millisecond he went airborne.

For a time, time was suspended. Mental activity was accelerated exponentially, creating the effect of viewing physical activity in slow motion. Furthermore, though Bill did not realize it at the time, there were gaps in his perception. Afterward he did not remember, for example, the non-time during which he flew over the handlebar, somersaulted in the air and crashed to the pavement. Eric would provide these details later.

What Bill did remember was finding himself sliding east on Route 66, his whole body rotating counterclockwise in the road as he slid. When his head rotated to the west, he spotted his capsized motorcycle pursuing him, also sliding and rapidly closing the gap. He tightened his muscles anticipating the steely embrace. Then, in a single bone crushing moment, his Honda took its revenge on his person.

Again there was a gap in Bill's perception. Eric swore that when Bill and his vindictive steed had finally skidded to a halt, Bill leapt immediately to his feet, kicked his motorcycle and shouted, "You dirty son of a two-bit tin can!" before collapsing back to the pavement.

Bill's next recollection, though, was of two good Samaritans from a gas station on the other side of the road pummeling him for a response. "Hey buddy, are you okay? Are you okay?" they demanded. Could they not see that he was already adequately pummeled?

Bill was trying to answer, but it is difficult to speak when every last wisp of wind has been bashed out of one's body by unyielding asphalt and unforgiving steel. Finally, he wheezed out a hint of a whisper, "I'm okay…just don't touch me."

"Huh? What did he say? Hey buddy, are you okay?"

These fellows, as dazed as Bill was, made him nervous. "I'm okay. Just don't touch me," he whispered again. He knew he was hurt, knew he had sustained some specific injury beyond the obvious pounding, bruising and scraping. He was struggling, however, to isolate it. He wobbled slowly to his feet and removed his helmet. He noticed deep grooves ground into its surface, which otherwise would have been ground into his head. He was glad he had followed Uncle Bob's advice and worn it.

The next thing Bill noticed was his left arm dangling uselessly from its shoulder. He began to inspect the limp limb for breaks with his right hand, working his way from the wrist up to the shoulder but finding nothing out of order. Next Bill placed his hand gently onto his left trapezius muscle and slid it forward. There he discovered the major damage to his body—the protruding splinters of a shattered collarbone threatening to pierce the skin.

"Is there anything we can do for you buddy?" one of the good Samaritans asked.

Bill looked down and noticed his shoes were missing. "Yeah," he replied, "would you find my shoes for me?"

"Find your what?" the Samaritan asked.

"My shoes," Bill repeated.

The assembled members of the "Rolla Branch of the Missouri Good (but very weird) Samaritans Club" looked at one another blankly. "We can't understand what you're saying," one of them needlessly explained.

"Maybe his buddy knows what he's talking about," another one suggested.

Eric was approaching the group after having had sense enough to dash across the highway and phone for an ambulance. "Your buddy here keeps asking for his *shoes*," the Samaritan told him. "Do you know what he's talking about?"

Eric looked down at his cousin's feet. "He got knocked out of his shoes," he answered, "he wants his stinking *shoes*!" Then he went and searched until he found them.

"I'll get your bike taken care of, then I'll ride over to the hospital," Eric offered, when the ambulance arrived.

"Later," Bill answered, then added, "Be careful."

The ambulance ride to the Rolla's little hospital did not take long. Neither did Bill's examination once he arrived. He overheard the on-duty intern's careless comment to a nurse, "*There's nothing we can do for him here.* We'll have to send him to Jefferson City."

Not only were they unable to do anything for Bill, but neither could they spare an ambulance for the ride to Jefferson City. Instead he was hauled in a patrol car driven by a sheriff's deputy. The ride was made barely tolerable by the kindly deputy's professional concern, but as the patient's body revived from numbness and pain staked her claim, Bill's mind began to ramble.

His thoughts wandered off into the darkness away from Jefferson City, across the back roads toward Springfield, toward the country store where he and Eric had met the charter member of the "Missouri Wicked (and extremely weird) Samaritans Club" just two days before. Bill wondered what the old hag was using her broom for at the moment—transportation? He was glad she could not swat him with it just then.

There was not much to be done for Bill in Jefferson City either. He was examined and admitted, then spent a miserable night in a sleepless hospital bed. To his great surprise and relief, however, he was discharged the next morning into the care of his visitor. That visitor, his father, had driven the Trader's Haven bait van all the way from Ohio during the night to take his injured son home.

Bill Sr. called his sweet wife, Daphne, back in Mad River Township to let her know that her "little boy" was okay. This was neither the first nor the last time Bill Jr. would be sustained by his father's steadfastness and his mother's prayers.

After making sure Bill thought he could travel, his dad wanted to know where Eric was. Bill had no idea. "He was supposed to meet me at the hospital in Rolla," he answered. "But I haven't heard from him. I told the people at that hospital to tell him where they were sending me."

"Well then, I guess we'll just have to backtrack till we find him," Bill's dad declared.

Bill struggled to climb into Trader's Haven's white Ford van with his left arm in a sling to keep the weight off his fragmented clavicle. The truck had only two seats, but Bill's dad had come prepared. He strapped his son into a reclining chair, previously lashed down to keep it from sliding, and wrapped him in a blanket.

"Are you going to be able to ride like that," his dad asked.

"I can ride just fine," Bill replied. He hurt so badly from the exertion of climbing into the truck that he felt sick to his stomach, but there was no way he would admit it. Nothing was going to stop him from riding home with his dad.

As they sped down the road toward Rolla, they passed a pitiful site: a young man in a roadside rest area. He was straddling a motorcycle, vainly trying to kick-start it. Even from the fast moving van, his exhaustion and utter exasperation were plainly visible. Bill's dad shouted something out the window to the youngster who looked up from his labor with a bewildered expression. His countenance seemed to wail, *Oh no, this is the last straw! Everything possible has gone wrong! Now I'm stranded in the middle of nowhere and some weird Missouri punk is giving me a hard time.*

In fact, the young man was feeling much as a stray puppy, cruelly cast into an unknown and friendless countryside with no way home. Whatever the depth of desperation the young man was feeling, it was dwarfed by the height of his appreciation when he saw the white Ford van backing up and recognized his Uncle Bill behind the steering wheel.

Eric had been on his way to Jefferson City the night before when he halted at the rest stop to cool his engine and look at his map. Then his cycle refused to restart. He had spent the night wishing to sleep, then spent the entire morning trying to start his motorcycle. In fact, Eric had given up hope an hour before his relatives arrived, but had continued kicking mindlessly through his exhaustion for lack of any alternative. (Examination of Eric's bike back in Dayton would reveal the cause of both his starting and headlight problems: completely worn brushes in the generator.)

Eric and his Uncle Bill loaded the Sprint into the back of the van and lashed it to one side. Next they completed the drive to Rolla, where they retrieved Bill's bike and lashed it to the other side of the van. Then, though he had driven all through the previous night, Bill's dad drove the bruised and weary bikers home.

Later, when he examined the personal belongings that had been held for him in the hospital, Bill noticed that the crystal cover on his Lord Elgin had been marred by the hard Missouri asphalt as severely as himself. Somehow he was vaguely aware that although time had not ended for him and his cousins, it had been permanently altered. Somehow he knew, down deep in the crease between conscious and unconscious knowing, that the three of them would never share such an adventure together again.

Unlike another trio of "Easy Riders" that year, more chromed and famous, who "went looking for America and couldn't find it anywhere," Bill and his cousins found America in abundance—but could never drink their fill.

Bill did not feel inclined to have his hair cut for a long time after the Missouri adventure. And all the while his hair was growing, he often remembered the Missouri adventure, visualizing himself and his cousins gliding along country roads on their motorcycles, cruising through wooded hills and grassy fields.

During those moments he would hear the haunting strains of G. Goffin and C. King's "Wasn't Born To Follow" as performed by the Byrds:

Well I'd rather go and journey
Where the diamond crest is flowing;
And run across the valley
Beneath the sacred mountain,
And wander through the forest,
Where the trees have leaves of prisms,
And break the light in colors
That no one knows the names of.

14

Hello and Goodbye

Bruce was honorably discharged from the army January 30, 1969 and came home to Ohio to let his hair grow. He found a job as a construction laborer, worked long hours and moved into a fifteen foot by twenty foot shed with Jack "Snack" Barber as his roommate. That shed was all that remained of the original Stevenson's Animal Hospital. Most of the old office—the part which had been Bill's home for two years, and beside which childhood wars of marbles, apples and turtle eggs had been waged—had been torn down while Bruce was in the army. It did not take Bruce and Snack long to try to demolish what little remained.

The antique cannon stored in a corner of the shed by Bruce's dad, with its supply of black powder and rags, proved too tempting. The explosion knocked the two jokers on their butts inside the shed and rocked the entire neighborhood. Neighbors and family members came running, fearing the worst. What they found, though, instead of the feared carnage, were billows of white smoke pouring out of a blasted open door, and two temporarily deaf pranksters lying on their backs laughing. Bruce's mother simply shook her head and walked away.

Not satisfied with terrorizing a single Mad River Township neighborhood, that night the daredevils loaded the cannon into the trunk of a car and hauled it to a party at a house on Harshman Road. There they hid in the weeds and fired another blast. Fortunately, the partying parties neither suffered a heart attack following the explosion, nor sustained a broken a leg during their hurried evacuation.

Because Bruce's 1969 home season was destined to be a short one, there was only limited time for him and Bill to enjoy each other's company. Yet they managed a few memorable occasions. It would have to be enough.

One such occasion began with a Saturday night out with the guys. Bruce and Bill walked into the Showbar in Fairborn along with five other young men. Gloom hung in the air as thick as cigarette smoke over three-quarters of the establishment. Pretty girls clustered in small groups and glanced furtively over their shoulders. Male patrons sat silently or spoke in low tones.

The remaining quarter of the club, however, the northeast quarter, reeked of baboon urine and raucous surliness. It was staked and claimed by the denim colors of the Dayton Satans. The weather was still too cold for even the Satans to be riding their Harleys, but the bikers themselves were there in force.

The seven intruders walked straight to the rear of the club and staked out their own corner. They arranged their tables and chairs, ensuring none of their number was left with his back unprotected. "We can take these guys," Jimmy Yancey declared." It was clear that Jimmy was eager to backup his words with action.

"I get the big, fat, ugly one," Buddy Yancey called, as if the situation were no more serious than a schoolyard game of marbles. "Don't anybody else take him. I want him." Buddy spoke in his whinny younger brother voice: the one he used whenever he claimed dibs on something he thought Jimmy would want. It was well known that Jimmy Yancey liked to fight, and he was good at it. He enjoyed fighting so much, in fact, that when he could find no stranger with whom to start a fight, it was not unusual for him to engage one of his brothers in fisticuffs.

"Forget those guys," Bruce snarled, "I'm going to go dance with that blonde over at the bar," and skulked off in her direction. Soon every member of the back-of-the-bar gang, except one, was dancing. Bill was too shy. Instead he sat and kept a watchful eye on the Satans who grew ever more surly, a pack of baboons whose territory was under invasion.

Eventually it happened. Someone took offense to a remark and the skirmish line formed. All seven of the newcomers stood on one side of the line, Jimmy Yancey in the forefront jawing the apparent leader the Satans antagonistically. A dozen Satans stood on the other side, watching their hero do verbal battle with Jimmy.

The two contestants stood nose to nose and toe to toe. Jimmy—with his narrow, protruding chest and his longish, light brown hair flared on the back of his head like hackles—was a 6'1", 170-pound gamecock watching for an opening to spur his opponent. The Satan's mouthpiece was shorter and stockier than his cocky adversary. His blue-black hair hung straight on the sides of his head, and his eyes were intense. One tiny spark of action would ignite the scene into an explosion of pounding, kicking, biting and gouging violence. This would be a barroom brawl of classic proportion.

At the very moment when war seemed inevitable, one of the Satans in the background spoke. "Hey Jimmy, Jimmy Yancey, I know you." The voice was mellow, even congenial. It was the voice of former Stebbins schoolmate, Larry Duncan.

Duncan's simple act of confessed recognition defused the tension, preventing an ugly explosion. The Satans and the intruders began to observe an unspoken truce, even began to slowly intermingle. Two hours later, when most of the intruders left for a new adventure at another club, in Xenia, the leader of the Satans declared, "If you guys run into any trouble you can't handle over at the Cast Aways, call us and we'll give you a hand." Only two of the intruders, Larry Stamps and Bruce, remained behind, saying they would catch up with the rest of their buddies later.

There had been a brawl the previous night at the Cast Aways, and Jimmy wanted to be there in case the action resumed anew. He did not have to wait to arrive in Xenia, however, to find action. Bill "Mooch" Marsh, distracted by the arguing between Jimmy and Buddy over which radio station they would listen to, lost control of his 1966 Chevy on a curve on Beaver Valley Road. The car ended up in a field of corn stubble.

"Now look what you did!" Jimmy shouted at his brother.

"It wasn't my fault!" his lanky, 6'3" sibling whined back. "You're the one that grabbed my arm."

"It was too your fault!" Jimmy countered. "You shouldn't have tried to change the radio."

"I had too," Buddy whined. "Your hillbilly crap was driving me crazy. I just wanted to listen to some rock and roll for awhile."

"Would you two idiots knock it off?" Mooch finally intervened. "We're knee deep in mud, and it's going to take all of us just to get Bessie back on the road." Even when he was angry, though, Mooch's face was fixed in his perpetual, impish grin.

Eventually the group arrived at the Cast Aways and entered trailing mud. Their greeting was less than cordial. There were more bouncers than usual, and they did not pretend to be friendly. Bill felt like a side of beef under the scrutiny of a platoon of USDA inspectors, as the bouncers eyed the newcomers up and down.

Roger Fuller and Richard Wamboldt saw their former schoolmates enter and immediately walked over to warn them. "Be cool you guys," Wamboldt advised. "Don't start any trouble. These guys want to hurt somebody tonight because of what happened in here last night."

"Yeah," Roger added, "they have a shotgun behind the check-in counter. They can't wait to get their hands on the guys who tore this place up last night." That remark unnerved Bill. Bruce had been involved in the brawl the previous night. Would the bouncers remember his face? Bill went to the phone and called the Showbar, but he was too late. Bruce and Stamps had already left.

Bill and his buddies were sitting at a table near the entrance when Bruce and Stamps arrived. "That's one of them right there!" one of the bouncers roared with the enthusiasm of a hungry lion spotting an untended goat. A second lion seized his intended prey by the shoulder.

Bruce's eyes flashed wide. He did not wait to be asked to dance. In the same instant that Bill and the Yanceys jumped to their feet, Bruce jerked himself free from his assailant, kicked him in the groin, and dashed back out the door with two bouncers in hot pursuit.

Before Bill and the Yanceys could take two steps toward the door, they were looking straight down the ugly end of a sawed-off twelve-gauge. The shotgun was leveled at their guts. "You boys sit back down now and stay cool and nobody will get hurt," the large and grotesquely bald shotgun wielder ordered.

Bill felt a rush of nausea churn in his stomach. He had blasted the bowels out of more than enough rabbits to know what a twelve-gauge can do at close range. Yet there was more. There was the old intense emotion of guilt. Bill felt as if his failure to act were an act of extreme disloyalty.

Judging from Jimmy's angry fuming and Buddy's facial contortions, the Yanceys were feeling it too. Their comrade needed their assistance; they knew he needed it; but they could not—did not—deliver it. What greater punishment could be inflicted on true warriors? Buddy literally burst into tears.

Later, Jimmy would try to round up a gang to completely destroy the Cast Aways and burn it to the ground. As it turned out, however, Bruce did not need his companions' help. Exiting the building, he ran through the parking lot into a vacant field. There he quickly found an old wooden fence post, and in an instant the roles reversed. Now it was the bouncers, two cowardly whelps, who fled, and Bruce, a goat with a club, who eagerly pursued.

In May, when warm weather finally emerged from her winter's hibernation, Bruce and Bill shared another adventure. The cousins teamed with Snack, Fat Jack Zindorf, and Crazy Mike for a Sunday of gentle river rafting.

The crewmen constructed their own raft of thin plywood sheets lashed atop automotive inner tubes and launched it in the Mad River below the Harshman Road bridge. Clad only in cutoffs and tennis shoes, the crew climbed aboard. Applying their two homemade push poles to propel themselves away from the bank, a sense of giddy exhilaration overpowered them as the current pulled them into motion. It was as if all limitations had been lifted from their joint existence. With the river as their highway and each other as companions, all things were possible: The Mad River dumps into the Great Miami; the Great Miami empties into the Ohio; the Ohio pumps its power into the mighty Mississippi; and the Mississippi flows all the way to the sea!

"Hubba, hubba," declared Fat Jack, rubbing the black hair on his distended belly, "we could float all the way to New Orleans if we wanted to." He spoke with such characteristic nonchalance it actually seemed plausible. Their overblown expectations, however, were soon deflated. As they tried to ride out the first rocky riffle, they punctured two inner tubes. From then on, whenever they came into a rocky riffle they dismounted and walked their raft through to the safety of deeper water.

Nor were rocks the only hazards to be avoided along the Mad. "Hey! What do you boys think you're doing?" The fisherman's voice startled the self-absorbed crew of the passing raft.

"Hallelujah! We've been saved!" the impetuous Snack shouted. "Hey mister, where are we? We've been floating on this river for a week."

"Yeah, we're from New York," Crazy Mike added in his elfin voice, matching his diminutive stature.

"This river doesn't go anywhere near New York," the grizzled old fisherman growled.

"Oh yeah," Crazy Mike added hastily, "I meant…uhh…"

"Canada," Snack whispered.

"Canada!" shouted Crazy Mike.

"Mister, do you have any food you could spare?" Fat Jack asked, patting his oversized belly. "We haven't eaten for three days."

"Yeah mister," Bruce joined in, "we would even settle for a few of your night crawlers."

"You boys are crazy!" the fisherman snapped. "I have half a notion to turn you in."

"Forget you old man!" Bruce snarled back. "You're having a hallucination."

"Yeah," Fat Jack agreed, "you've been eating too many Trader's Haven dough balls."

The old angler was livid. His face flushed blood poisoning red. He grabbed a hand full of small stones and stood up as if to throw them at his disrespectful tormentors who were drifting quickly out of range.

"Be careful old man," Fat Jack taunted, "you might rupture yourself."

"Lighten up you animals," Bill implored in a brief, self-imposed respite between laughing convulsions, "you're going to give the old man a heart attack."

"Aw, he deserves it," Bruce countered. "We weren't bothering him none. Anyway, he started it."

"Yeah, but I like to fish over here myself," Bill argued. "And if the old geezer dies he'll just stink up the river for everybody."

Soon the voyagers were well out of the crusty old carp catcher's territory and peace resumed. The journey to the mouth of the Mad, the area's swiftest river, took only an hour in spite of a near shipwreck on a logjam against a concrete abutment beneath the old railroad trestle adjacent to Eastwood Park. Once the young men made the slowly rolling Great Miami, however, their progress slowed to a dog paddle.

"I'm thirsty," Fat Jack declared, straining to hoist the burlap bag tied to the side of the raft out of the water. "Anybody want a cold one?" Everyone did.

Snack dove nimbly into the river, his bulky, rubbery body barely making a ripple. Surfacing, he clung to a corner of the raft. His longish hair glistened black, flat against his skull where the river had washed it. Rivulets of water streamed down his olive complexioned face. With his free hand he grasped an open bottle of fluid refreshment and hoisted it into the air a foot above his head, resembling one of his Cherokee ancestors raising a tomahawk as if to strike. Tilting back his head, Snack poured a stream of amber liquid into the reservoir of his mouth, swallowing repeatedly as he continued to pour, while the sunlight made golden magic as it danced in the cascade of sparkling fluid.

By the time they made downtown Dayton, the crew was bored. It was already past noon. They poled to shore beside the old YMCA building on Monument Avenue and discussed their options. Ironically, though Bill had swum naked in the same YMCA only a few years previous, he was now too shy to run around town dressed only in wet cutoffs. His companions, however, were not. Bill was left alone to guard the raft and worry.

An hour later the crew returned—a scrambling horde of pirates. "Let's get our tails out of here fast," Crazy Mike shouted animatedly.

"Yeah," gasped Fat Jack between heaving breaths, "this town doesn't appreciate class."

"Well if Bruce hadn't kicked that guy in the privates…" Snack began to respond.

"It was his own fault," Bruce interrupted. "He shouldn't have tried to grab me. I was going to pay him for his stinking hot dog."

Bill wasted no time to debate the relative merits of his cousin's behavior. He was already busy launching the escape craft as his crewmates clamored and splashed aboard. Bruce and Snack grabbed the push poles and shoved vigorously until they were once again freely drifting upon the wide and lazy Great Miami.

The afternoon was warm, and after the fluid refreshment was depleted there was nothing to do but loaf. One by one the crewmen dozed, stretching out to sun themselves as turtles on a floating log.

It was late afternoon when Bill awoke. He knew about where they were because he could see Deed's Carillon behind them on the east side of the river and the heavy abutments supporting I-75 dead ahead. Only partially raising his upper body from its prone position, he surveyed the raft. His companions were all asleep. Though the river was still mildly swollen from spring rains, its downstream progress was so slow as to pose no serious threat, in Bill's estimation, even if the raft made a direct hit on one of the concrete abutments. Silently the craft glided into the shadow of I-75 and was swallowed by its coolness without even coming close to an abutment.

When they emerged, Bill gazed downstream. Something did not look quite right. The river seemed to break plane slightly at some point in the distance. It was as if the low angle of the sun were refracting light on the water's surface, creating an optical illusion. Bill stared and puzzled over the phenomenon momentarily, then went back to sleep.

"Wake up you guys! Wake up!" a pixie voice screamed. Though he was frantic, it was difficult to hear Crazy Mike over the roaring in the background. The rest of the voyagers struggled to consciousness only to discover themselves within thirty feet of sudden death. The breaking point Bill had detected earlier was no illusion: it was a low-head dam completely transecting the river.

Thousands of gallons of water were driving over the dam every second, creating a mighty waterfall. The deafening roar that nearly drowned Mike's alarm was the roar of a monstrous river anticipating Sunday dinner. The voyagers had reached Dayton Power and Light's Tait Station.

The white frothing turbulence below the crashing waterfall was chilling. Bill was distinctly aware of the river's musky scent, as if it sought to attract him to its wicked embrace. His stomach growled, but not from hunger. Although the sudden drop in the river's level was only eight feet, surely no one could hope to survive a rendezvous with such a raging torrent.

During the brief seconds Bill gazed into that churning, watery grave he was transfixed by echoes from the past. There was an echo from the day when he had nearly drowned in Crystal Lake, and another from a day in December 1963 when he had nearly drowned at a low-head dam on the Mad River. In those same seconds, had he been as sensitive to whispers from the future as he was to reverberations from the past, he might have seen a glimpse of another roaring torrent, somewhere downstream in the flow of life, sucking in people like debris. That other torrent was the unforgiving undertow of surging surf—*Eleven Miles South of Half Moon Bay*.

Snapping out of his nightmarish reverie, Bill noticed something more sickening than the swirling liquid death. He saw a small crowd of citizens, gathered on the riverbank below, gawking as spectators at a Sunday sporting event.

"What are we going to do?" Crazy Mike shouted.

Bruce and Snack were already doing it. Each of them had one of the push poles in his hands and was trying to use it to anchor their craft by probing the river bottom. As the raft approached the dam, the water became more shallow, and the push poles grabbed hold of the bottom. "Help us hold this thing!" Snack shouted. Fat Jack jumped to his assistance, and Bill aided Bruce.

"Now what do we do? Now what do we do?" Crazy Mike chanted like a moon-maddened pixie. Though he was displaying no overt signs of rationality, Crazy Mike's question was a reasonable one. They certainly could not impede the raft's destiny indefinitely.

"Come here and help Fat Jack hold this pole," Snack directed. "I'm going to see if I can stand up in this current." Crazy Mike obeyed.

Snack eased over the end of the raft nearest the dam while maintaining a death grip on one of the inner tubes. To everyone's relief, the rushing water was only waist deep, and Snack was actually standing against the current. Demonstrating profound courage, utter ignorance, or just plain desperation, Snack released his grip on the inner tube and shuffled cautiously toward the dam. The water grew even shallower, thigh deep immediately behind the dam.

Still, the current was powerful, and the footing was slick with slimy moss. One slip and Snack would be flushed, with no more respect than a huge lump of fecal matter, down the apron of the dam to sure destruction. He inched his way laterally across the dam wall a few of the fifty yards which separated him from the west shore opposite the power station, demonstrating the possibility of literally walking away from danger.

"Bruce, can you hold this side?" Bill asked.

"Yeah, I got it," Bruce assured.

"Okay, I'm going to take over the other side so Fat Jack can get off; then he can help Mike."

The plan worked. Soon Fat Jack and Crazy Mike had edged their way several yards clear of the raft. "We're going to have to let go and jump off at the same time," Bruce advised his cousin.

"Okay," Bill agreed, "on three—ready? One...two...three!" Both cousins jumped as far away from the raft as they could and struggled to establish footing against the current. Fortunately, both succeeded. Meanwhile, the unpiloted raft slipped toward the dam, teetered momentarily on its brink as if contemplating suicide, then plunged. The crushing, ripping results were sobering to its shipwrecked crew.

The voyagers edged their way tediously across the dam, struggling to maintain their precarious balance against the current, until at last they all made it safely to solid ground. Then, disregarding the Great Miami's full-bodied aroma, which suggested finny creatures and silted river muck, they knelt down and kissed the riverbank's crusted rocks.

One evening shortly after the river adventure, on a whim, Bruce, Bill and Eric rode their motorcycles to Rona Hills Estates in Fairborn. There they visited the Stevensons' former next door neighbors. When the young men left the Martineau home, Bruce asked Fred and Mary to "tell

Ronny hi." That night Ronny was given the message. It was the last he would ever receive from his childhood nemesis.

Bill wondered why his cousin was leading their motorcycle procession over a less desirable route back to Mad River Township. Then, without warning, Bill's question was answered. Bruce hopped his Scrambler from the pavement onto a railroad track—between the rails. Eric followed, and reluctantly, so did Bill. His street bike, however, was not designed to take the pounding of railroad ties at forty miles per hour. Or maybe it was Bill who was not designed to take it. The vision of a capsized motorcycle, pursuing him down Route 66 in Missouri the previous summer was still fresh in his psyche. Whatever the excuse, he was soon trailing far behind his cousins.

Trailing behind his cousins, however, was far from Bill's major concern. His major concern—the one that caused him clammy arm pits despite the cool, dry licking of the wind—was the speeding locomotive gaining on him in the distance. Once, twice, three times Bill tried unsuccessfully to jump his cycle out of the deadly valley surrounded by steel cliffs. He simply could not get the angle he needed.

By now his cousins, far ahead, had noticed the charging iron beast. They easily rode their lighter and better hoofed steeds out of the path of danger. They stopped, looked back in Bill's direction and waved their arms in frantic motions that screamed *get your crazy butt off the tracks!*

Wild thoughts rushed through Bill's brain. Maybe he would have to sacrifice his bike, just drop it and leave it. But what damage might be done to the freight train and its crew? Could there be a derailment? Even if there was no danger to the train and its crew, the demolition of a motorcycle by a locomotive was sure to make the news. Bill would not only have to endure the loss of his bike, he would have to endure the well deserved heckling of his buddies for a long time:

"Hey Wild Man, I heard you got lost the other night and decided to hop a freight train home. I heard it was a real drag.

"Hey Wild Man, you didn't have to dump your bike for the insurance money. I would have spotted you a couple of bills to pay off your poker debts."

Hornnnk! Hornnnk! Shock shot up Bill's spine as mercury shoots up a thermometer suddenly plunged into super heated steam. He felt the raw power of the mighty engine's horn as the impact of its sound waves, compressed by speed, slammed into his auditory canals and threatened to burst two tiny drums. It was truly the time to do or die. Fortunately for Bill, some railroad employee had chosen the section of track dead ahead to leave his work undone. For there, between the rails which imprisoned Bill as securely as bars in a jail cell, was a long pile of crushed limestone forming a ramp for his escape. Some laborer had quit before his job of spreading the white rock around newly replaced ties was complete. Bill shot up the ramp to safety, and the train jockey shook his fist angrily as he sped past.

When Bill caught up to his cousins, Eric was still staring in wide-eyed disbelief. Bruce, in contrast, wore a gentle smirk on his face. "What were you waiting on, man?" he asked. "Were you just showing off?" The irony of Bill's having been saved through the indolence or incompetence of some invisible comrade was lost on Bruce. For in the self-assured ignorance of youth, he knew they were immortal.

Despite his occasional adventures, life in general had become tedious to Bruce. Work, eat, sleep—get up and start all over again. The long hours and lack of liberty were cramping his style. Bruce was growing restless, and Bill could feel it. As the season wore on, a vague apprehension invaded the borders of Bill's consciousness. He became anxious whenever he talked to Bruce: anxious that after Bruce's three years of military separation, they should so soon be parted. One day in late May Bill's apprehension bore fruit. "I'm leaving for California next week," Bruce said simply. "Do you want to come with me?"

"How long are you planning on being out there?" Bill asked. He had always wanted to visit California. In those days it was common for boys in the Midwest to dream of traveling to golden California.

"I'm heading out to Kansas first," Bruce answered, "to hook up with Odus. As soon as he gets discharged from the army we're moving to California."

"You're moving to California?"

"Yep."

"Oh wow, man, I can't move to California right now," Bill said defensively. The terrible truth, though, was that he could have. Bill was not attending the spring quarter at Wright State; his part time job at the pool hall would be no loss; and his girl friend would get over it. "Let me know where you're living and I'll come out and visit you later on," Bill added with real intent.

Bruce accepted Bill's answer without argument. "Okay, he said simply, "I'll write and let you know where I'm at."

For the next week Bill reflected again and again on his decision not to accompany his cousin to California. He was sorely tempted to trade the security and connection he felt at home for the thrill of the road and the unfamiliarity of a strange land, but in the end, his conservative side held fast.

On the appointed day Bruce packed his few necessities onto his Scrambler. Straddling his loaded motorcycle in the gravel driveway outside his vacated shack, he visited with his cousin one last time. His light brown eyes were uncharacteristically soft and glistening. "I wish you could come with me, man," he pleaded.

Even though it was warm, Bill felt the cold rush of winter in his face—as if he and Bruce were walking and talking along some dark and frigid city sidewalk on their way home from some downtown coffeehouse. He felt disloyal to the depths of his soul. He knew Bruce would not have permitted him to ride off by himself because of a girl, a job or college.

"I can't leave right now, man," Bill insisted, "but I'll come out to see you." (If only he had known then the circumstances under which his promise would be kept!)

Bruce reached inside his striped, Mexican-style poncho and pulled a package of Lucky Strikes out of his shirt pocket. "Here, man," he offered, "take these. I have more."

Bill was touched by the simple parting gift that bound him to his promise. He wished he had something in his pocket to give to Bruce, something of great value. He wished he could give him back the fistful of marbles he had extracted by force so many years before only a few feet from where they now stood.

The cousins shook hands and Bruce rode into destiny, never to pass that way again.

15

Exodus

Bruce reached Manhattan, home of Kansas State University, without mishap. There he stayed with Odus in a rented house shared with friends. Those friends included Jeff Patterson, who, like Odus, was an indentured servant abiding his final days of indebtedness to Uncle Sam at Fort Riley. Jeff was from Pennsylvania. An adopted son, he received a monthly allotment of $1300—a fortune for a young man with few obligations—from a trust fund. He demonstrated little responsibility, however, in the management of his resources.

Odus became a free man on the second Friday in June, forever dispelling any superstition in his mind regarding bad luck on Friday the thirteenth. The next day he bought a 1949 Mercury for the trek to California. Soon thereafter he climbed behind the wheel with four pilgrim passengers, including Bruce and Jeff, and headed west.

It did not take long for the combined weight of five bodies, their accumulated belongings, and a trailer loaded with two motorcycles to prove too strenuous a load for the old Mercury. In the middle of the afternoon—and in the middle of nowhere—the Merc overheated. Bruce was quick to volunteer. "You guys wait here while I ride ahead and get some water," he offered.

Within minutes Bruce had his Honda unloaded and rode into the wavering horizon. It took more than an hour, though, for him to return and water the hot and thirsty flock. For the rest of the migration, Bruce rode in front of the procession across the barren west—a modern Moses—leading his people out of bondage to the Promised Land.

The group settled for a short time in Santa Anna, California, where they lived in a remodeled garage. Here Jeff enjoyed racing around the area on the 305cc Honda motorcycle owned by Odus. He was no more responsible with the cycle, though, than he was with his inheritance. He wrecked the little Honda on two occasions, and once nearly killed himself in the process. Then Jeff bought a motorcycle of his own, a magnificent 650cc Triumph.

New faces came and went continuously at the garage home. Two of the people who joined the congregation in Santa Anna were Larry Brown and Snack Barber. Bruce and Snack survived any way they could, including begging for food on local beaches. One weekend, when Odus traveled to Oakland to visit his girlfriend, Karen, the gang traveled with him.

In Oakland, Karen introduced Bruce to her friend, Jan. He was instantly attracted to Jan's long blonde hair and pretty smile. Jan liked Bruce's lengthening locks, hanging in brown waves down the back of his neck. She also liked his unpretentiousness.

Soon Bruce, along with Jeff and Snack, moved to Oakland. Bruce and Snack both found jobs pumping gas, and the trio rented a house at 2514 38th Ave. Odus remained in the LA area where he studied music at the Orange Coast College in Costa Mesa. When Jeff's Triumph stopped running, just before the move to Oakland, he quickly tired of trying to figure out why. "Hey Odus," he asked, "do you want this pile of junk?"

Odus hesitated. His Native American ancestors seemed to whisper, *beware of white man bearing gift*. It took a moment for him to overcome his shock and regain control of his deep, resonant voice. Maybe this was

Jeff's way of making up for crash testing the Honda a couple of times. "Yeah, sure man," Odus finally agreed, "I'll take it off your hands."

After his former housemates relocated to Oakland, Odus discovered his new cycle had a bad magneto and replaced it. Late that summer he rode the Triumph triumphantly up to Oakland. There, with Karen riding on the back, he promptly crashed it into a car.

"Hey Junior," Bruce taunted one day as Odus lay convalescing from his injuries, "you need me to give you some riding lessons?" It hurt to laugh.

Odus remained under his buddies' care in Oakland until October. During that time he was impressed with a significant change in his best friend's attitude. Bruce no longer went to bars and got into fights as he and Odus had done so many times in the past. He was no longer into alcohol and aggression. He was into love and peace. Bruce adopted a new philosophy of goodwill toward his fellow man. Even Odus—who never related personally to the West Coast peace movement, who saw it as phony and hypocritical—knew Bruce was absolutely sincere.

In September, Robert Louis Stevenson III was honorably discharged from the navy aboard the U.S.S. Isle Royale at Long Beach. Shortly after his discharge, Bob caught a bus to Oakland and spent two weeks at the Oakland house. Regrettably, he did not spend much time with his brother while there. The morning Bob left from Oakland for his Ohio home, Bruce drove him to the airport. They shook hands just before Bob stepped on the boarding ramp.

"Take care of yourself *big* brother," Bruce told him. This was Bruce's way of saying to his brother, *You may be older, but I am tougher*. It was also his attempt to express affection.

"Try to keep your nose clean," Bob replied. This was his way of saying, *You may be tougher, but I am wiser*. It was also *his* attempt to express affection.

Bob boarded his plane, and soon his homebound flight disappeared into the morning sun. He watched out the window until earth and ocean evaporated in a sea of mist. It occurred to him that rabbit and quail hunting season would be opening in Ohio in November. Perhaps he would have the opportunity to spend Thanksgiving morning hunting with his cousin, Bill, for the first time in several years. Bob picked up a *Scientific American* and began to read about glacial movement. A shiver slipped down his spine as it occurred to him that destiny was inching toward him as surely and irrevocably as a huge cake of ice grinding across a continent. Yet there was no way for him to know that he would never again sit down to Thanksgiving dinner with all the members of his immediate family present.

Early October was a kaleidoscope of change in Oakland. Odus was awarded $2000 in insurance money and bought himself a sporty, red 1961 MGA. Soon thereafter—as if summoned by the ritual of changing seasons, like salmon on a spawning run, or by the Midwestern festival of fall colors, like Sunday afternoon sightseers—the Oakland band dispersed. First Bob, then Jeff (with Snack riding on the back of his reclaimed Triumph), and finally Odus began their pilgrimages east.

Bruce, alone, remained in Oakland. Postmarked October 12, 1969, he sent the following letter to his little brother in Dayton:

> Hi Eric
>
> Well I hope you don't get into to much troubl with that I.D. card that you got busted with. So be cool about it and you will probly slip throught the hole thing.
>
> Snack and Jeff should be in Dayton by now so say hi to them. Also Odus is leaving to day for Dayton so I will be the only one left in Oakland of the guys that I have been traveling with the last five months.
>
> But I think I can make it on my own because I have been lately. Tell Bill I said hi and to drop me a line some day and let me know how he is doing.
>
> I have been saving my money so I can buy a truck a van to fix up to live in, for when I start traveling again.
>
> I will probly move to Los Angloes in Feb. or March….

Also tell mom and Dad that I am all right and still working and keeping out of trouble to. So hope you keep out of trouble to and be cool and tell Linda to stick it in her ear.

Later Bruce
best brother
a guy could have

Left to fend for himself without the moral support of his rambling companions, Bruce moved to a cottage in the secluded yard behind 3227 38th Ave. He rented the cottage, equipped as an efficiency apartment, from old Bessie Mikulos for $40 a month. It was not easy supporting himself on his meager wages, but he liked his job at Roble's Chevron station at 3587 Redwood Road. What is more, his boss allowed him to adjust his work schedule to accommodate his new pursuit: attending classes at Laney Junior College. Between work, school and his blossoming relationship with Jan, Bruce had little time to miss his buddies.

At the end of the year, Eric received a cash Christmas gift from his brother in a card the size and shape generally used for that purpose. It was postmarked December 22, 1969 from Oakland. The commercially printed message was short and to the point: "MERRY CHRISTMAS and a VERY HAPPY NEW YEAR." Bruce's handwritten message was equally succinct. It would be the last he would ever pen to his younger brother in this life: "To the Best Brother a guy could have."

Bruce did not move to Los Angeles in February or March as he had suggested in his October letter to Eric. His growing romance with education was part of the reason. A bigger part of the reason, however, was his flourishing romance with Jan. Although Bruce was well experienced with girl friends, this young woman was different. She stimulated an emotion in Bruce with which he was only vaguely familiar. That emotion was genuine affection. Remarkably, Bruce began to show signs of settling down.

While living alone in Oakland for the next six months, Bruce compiled a group of handwritten poems in a notebook under the misspelled heading, "Poes of Life." Most were assigned numbers instead of titles. It is not clear whether Bruce composed all of them or only part of them, but either way they capture the essence of the person he was becoming. Read in the light of events that were shortly to transpire, they seem prophetic. Following are most of Bruce's "Poes of Life":

1st

Travel is my name
…is my game

I came and ventured into
the land of never land

Wondering what it was all about
then it came to me one day
from the moon lighter…

A man said to me live life and
love it; but don't try to figure it out.

Because when you do there is nothing
really there in which I found out

Traveling from one land to another

So get loose; and dig a while

2nd

I came to say a word
and I shall say it now.
But if death prevents me,
it will be said by tomorrow
For tomorrow never leaves a
secret in the book of eternity.

3rd

I came to live in the glory of love
And the light of beauty
Which are the reflections of GOD I am here
Living and I can't be reexiled from
the DEMRIN of life
For through my living word
I will live until death

5th

A time ago
Or else a life
Walking in the dark
I met Christ

Jesus my heart flopped
Over and lay while
He passed

As close as I'm to you
Yes closer
Made of nothing
Except loneliness

6th

Ballad of a way Faring-Stranger

I am just a poor, lonely, way faring stranger.
Traveling this land of ours yours and mine just the same
I've traveled from East to West and North to South
Looking for what I know not.

But I think what I want is just to be free
And people leave me do my thing.

Because I am just a poor lonely Way-faring-stranger

Not making any laws, but trying not to break any

For I don't understand some of them but they tell
me they must be.

So that's why I am the way I am and you the way you are.
So that's why I'm just a way-faring stranger

7th

The only religon one really needs, is peace
and love of his fellow man.
The one who finds both, has truly
found a treasure

Life is what you make of it.
So make the best of it.

8th

Moss Landing
Sittin by the docks
Playing with rocks
People passing bye
Always wondering Why

Love

Yea though I walk through the Valley of Death

I shall not fear death for I am love of Gods love

And love shall live long after death in each and every man

More in some than others

"Be fruitful and multiply"

We Came From Two

I have love to give in handfulls
Love of what I am and nothing more.

I have a heart; and cries which are not mine alone.
I come from a country which does not yet exist.

Oh, I love in plenty to give of what I am.

I, a man among many citizens of a Nation
which has yet to exist.

Traveling

Traveling is to be
But not for all

But surely for me
But not for you

Thought

I thought there was
But there wasn't
Thought there should be
But who could say there is
So if there isn't it's to you
To decide if it's to be for you

The winter of 1969-70 fled swiftly in Oakland, more swiftly even than a human soul passing through the portals of birth and death. Bruce and Jan looked forward to spending a beautiful spring day together the first Sunday in April. The two lovers climbed into Bruce's black 1957 Chevy, made their way to Highway 1, and drove south along the coast. Jan did not know exactly where they were going, nor did she ask. She preferred leaving such details to Bruce. She felt secure when she was with him. She knew he would protect her.

All too soon, they reached their destination: North Pescadero Beach—*Eleven Miles South of Half Moon Bay*. As they arrived, a rescue effort was in progress. Someone was in trouble in the notoriously dangerous undertow. Bruce did not wait to be asked, or even to strip off his clothes. He merely placed his car keys in his pants pocket and handed his billfold to Jan. Then, without so much as a goodbye, he dashed into the angry water to assist with the rescue. He moved so quickly that Jan had no opportunity to protest.

That same afternoon, April 5, 1970, Eric stretched out on the living room couch in his Ohio home and snatched a late afternoon nap. Sometime between five and six in the evening he awoke from a dreadful nightmare. In his own words, Eric "...experienced a tossing, tumbling uncontrollable moving sensation, as though I was experiencing millions and millions of somersaults. The colors of frothy Blue-White mixed with a color of sand, my body scraping along what felt like sandpaper.

"I woke up sweating and full of fear, of what I didn't know. My body hurt and I could not get my breath. At the time I didn't know what it was all about. Later...I understood."

That night, in little Otway, Ohio, Snack Barber also had a troubling experience, the profound influence of which remains with him to this day. Awaking suddenly, he sat straight up in bed. He knew he was not dreaming; yet the vision before his eyes could only be rationalized as a dream. Bruce was there with him in his room: smiling, waving his arm as if beckoning, but speaking not a word—until he gently faded from Snack's view.

Snack puzzled over the source and meaning of the disturbing visit until daylight. He finally decided that Bruce was calling him, by some mystical means, to come back to California. So sure was Snack of the reality of what he had seen that the next day he began to prepare to return to Oakland.

A week later, Snack drove to Airway Billiards in Dayton and told Kenny Earwood he was going back to Oakland to rejoin Bruce. The troubled look on Earwood's face startled Snack. Nor was he prepared for what Kenny had to tell him.

16

ALPHA: The Beginning of the End

It was Sunday night, early but darkening. The April air poured over Bill's bare arms, causing a shiver. His upper body seemed to writhe against the restriction of his striped T-shirt. To a casual onlooker, his dense, dark hair, with a few scattered flecks of accenting white, must have seemed to spring from his head like an untended shrub. Add to that the natural intensity in his steel-blue eyes, and it was easy to understand the nickname, Wild Man. He was the essence of virility, wild and undocked. It would be two years after the events of this night before he would allow his hair to be trimmed.

Bill drove the peace-mobile, his black 1957 Ford, down the half-block of North Garden Avenue from his home to its three-way intersection with Northcliff Drive and Springfield Pike. Looking to his left, he gazed for a fond moment at Trader's Haven, the stone and aluminum-sided log cabin at 4726 Springfield. He wondered how many millions of night crawlers his parents had sold there over the years, eking out a meager day-to-day living.

Bill turned left and drove west toward no particular destination. As he passed Stevenson's Animal Hospital at 4720 Springfield, he had a fleeting recollection of rubbing newborn puppies in paper towels until they whimpered and took their first breaths. As he drove, the Sunday Evening Phantom was his invisible companion. He knew the phantom was there because of the way he felt, the way he always felt on Sunday nights—hollow—as though his vitals were missing, like a just gutted fish. The Sunday Evening Phantom seemed to whisper, *the dance is over; the lights are low; only you are here alone. You and the shadows, listening to the silent echoes of some Electric Guitar Band.*

Absent mindedly, Bill rubbed the fingertips of his right hand gently back and forth over the surface of the peace-mobile's clear plastic seat cover. Had he pressed more firmly he might have discerned the outline of the decorations he had placed beneath the plastic. These decorations were in the shapes of stars and peace signs, cut from red, gold, and blue pieces of felt and sewn to a background of burlap.

He passed the frame house at 4712 Springfield where, with Bobby and Bruce, he had played during years past with neighborhood boys. He wondered what had become of the Owens and Schulke families, who had both rented the house at one time or another. It was impossible for Bill to know then that just two years later he and his bride would rent the house themselves. Nor could he have foreseen, or even imagined, what treasure he would discover there. That treasure hangs to this day, on a beaded chain, suspended from the lance of a brass Don Quixote in Bill's home office. It is the last communication he would ever receive in this life from his cousin, Bruce.

The peace-mobile's headlights momentarily illuminated an object that caught Bill's attention. The slowly moving dark form beside the road, lean and six-feet-tall, was instantly familiar and instantly warned of disaster. The peace-mobile braked and halted as if by its own volition. Its tangible occupant rolled down the passenger side window and addressed the form. "Eric, what's the matter, man?" Bill asked with genuine concern.

His puppy-eyed cousin stopped his forward progress in a rapid series of sputtering heaves, like a faltering engine or a young man suppressing sobs. Moments passed like painful boils aching to be popped. At last he spoke. "I just found out," each word was a tortured tangle of emotion, "Bruce died today."

Bill felt a lurching thump deep in his chest. It was the lump in his throat colliding with the knot in his stomach in the immediate vicinity of his dead-stalled heart. His brain and his car simultaneously switched to automatic pilot. "Come on and get in, man," Bill heard himself implore.

Silently, Eric complied like a cringing puppy, expecting a blow for an offense it does not understand. The peace-mobile resumed its course toward nowhere and everywhere. A new phantom—stark, black and previously unknown to Bill—ripped the fabric of his consciousness and demanded his soul. This was not the familiar Sunday-Night-The-Thrill-Is-Gone-There-Must-Be-Something-More-Phantom, but perhaps a distant relative, some hostile ancient ancestor. Bill's emptiness was deeper, blacker, and more ancient than his limited experience could comprehend. It was as deep and black and ancient as time and space. This phantom was Death.

"What do you mean?" Bill asked desperately, unwilling to believe. How could he believe? He was an only child, and Bruce was the closest thing to a brother he had. There must be some horrible mistake. Vigorous, twenty-two-year-old fellows do not just up and die. "What are you talking about, Eric. What happened?"

Stifled-sobbing pause, then, "Mother and Daddy got a call from California." Emotion choked, throat-aching struggle to vocalize, and finally, "He went to the beach with his girlfriend. Some kid was drowning in the surf and Bruce went in to help him, but he drowned instead. They saved the kid but Bruce died."

Eric's dark, puppy-dog eyes refused to make contact with Bill's, whose in turn radiated intense, pale-blue nonacceptance. Shock! Denial! Neural overload! Thank you God for the numb-unfeeling of shock.

"No, man," it was Bill's voice again, "are you sure?"

This could not be happening; it made no sense. A kid does not survive the trauma of birth, the vulnerability of childhood, the reckless rebellion of adolescence, the brainwashing of basic training and the insanity of Vietnam just to die one afternoon at the beach. Absurd! Where is the purpose in that? This could not be happening.

Yet it was.

Bill's virility curled up in his gut like an abruptly docked puppy. Someone had just ripped his crystal universe from the life-giving rays of the sun. All was cataclysm.

Bill does not remember anything else for sure that night. He does not remember letting Eric out of the peace-mobile or how long he was in it. He does not remember where he went or how he got home. Maybe he went to Uncle Bob and Aunt Ginny's house in the vain hope this nightmare was a morbid mistake. He seems to have a shadow of a memory about something of the sort. Everything is foggy and garbled. Thank you God for the numb-unknowing of shock.

Tears came later. Maybe it was the same night, maybe the next. It was, however, late at night, and it was intense. Thank you God for the purging gift of bittersweet tears.

It was Jan's parents who called Dr. Stevenson and told him of the tragedy, but there was not much they could say. Jan was incapable of conversing; she was in shock.

Eventually, Bruce's sister, Louise, would request and receive a copy of the police report filed in the California San Mateo County Sheriff's Office describing the scene at North Pescadero Beach the day Bruce drowned. In a synopsis to that report, under the signature of H.E. Elvander, Captain, Investigation Division, would be provided the following explanation:

> ...Teresa Jan...accompanied Bruce Stevenson to the beach. None of the other people present were acquainted with either Miss...or Mr.

Stevenson....Miss...and Mr Stevenson arrived at the area known as North Pescadero Beach around 2pm on April 5th, 1970, and immediately observed that someone was in trouble in the surf, and that a rescue was in progress. Mr. Stevenson entered the water to assist, still wearing his clothing, and was subsequently swept away and drowned. The man mentioned in the report in the first paragraph on the last page as being the original victim and leaving the water unidentified, did so before Mr. Stevenson entered the water.

There is no question in our mind that Bruce Michael Stevenson entered the ocean at North Pescadero Beach around 2pm on April 5th, 1970, in the County of San Mateo, and drowned. His body was never recovered, which is not unusual along this coast. Only about 70% of the drowning victims are recovered from the ocean in this area.

According to the report, Bruce entered the water around 2 p.m., or around 5 p.m. Dayton time—coinciding with Eric's horrifying nightmare. The report only confirmed what Eric already knew—he had been a participant in his brother's experience of drowning. The same bond that united them in life, though they were oceans and continents apart, likewise bound them together in Bruce's final struggle against death. The connection Eric felt with his brother is expressed in his poems:

The Adventurer

For I once had a brother, or
should it be said he had me,
bound in his ways, and desires
My world was the same as his
for we were always together in mind
Until one day he ventured across the sea
To see fields of Green grass,
and, of rolling hills, to be
covered with blood of unknown
friends for no cause
After his war was fought he
had returned home but not to stay
The home that he had once
lived, was not his way, for
he had found another way of life
So off he was again to venture,
and to see the world of which
he lived, fought and did not die for
But now he shall see no more
For he was swallowed up by
the sea, for another unknown
I believe now that I am of the
age, to venture and see as he
and, to be swallowed by the sea as he
Me and he will venture further
to what no one knows
A peaceful sleep me and he will Pray

Lost and Found

For I am the brother of a way faring
stranger, lost in a cloudy sea
He is me and I am he
Me, and he will rest in peace
we believed in peace
When he is where he is to be, free
Found and Unlost

There Were Two

There were two of the same
Now there is one
For one has met deathe
face to face
We pray he shall sleep in
a peaceful eternal sleep to
be undisturbed
There were Two now there is one
Who knows how long he will be
Sleep my brother in Heavenly
peace, for I will join you
God is looking over
There were two
Then there was one
Now there is none

The last of Eric's poems was written in memory of the great Missouri adventure:

The Trip

Two tripped to see another
Two then became Three
They never more were to part
They tripped together to have
a never ending peaceful journey
One from Three leaves Two
Two remain to protect
and love each all the
more on this Earth
The two that were left
behind, remain to Pray
that the Third will sleep
in a eternal and peaceful sleep.
Guide the Two that remain my brother
We Three shall meet again.
May the Gods look over.

Bruce's dad also expressed his feelings at the time of his second son's death through a poem:

My Rebel Son

A Rebel died this day in a sea
of Sand—Tide—and Sun
A Rebel he was born
unwanted by some
In violent times reared
and his own song he sung
His own thing he did, right or
wrong; it was done
In "Nam" he fought his war;
no glory won
He did, what need be done;
and a little more; than some
In the cold and roughened sea
his Life he gave for an unnamed one
And his soul the sea did keep!
"To each his own they say;" and I
ask only; in peace, he sleep.
For he was my Rebel Son

Days after Bruce's death, his mother drove to Oakland and closed out his affairs. Two of his three siblings, Bob and Louise, went along to share the driving and support their mother. Louise, a junior at Stebbins, had only recently acquired her driver's license. Unlike Eric, she was a good enough student to afford to miss the time away from school.

They found Bruce's cottage apartment in Oakland just as he left it. In the windowsill above the kitchen sink, Louise discovered Bruce's class ring. Though he had not even come close to graduating with his class, he wore his Walter E. Stebbins class of 1967 ring with pride. For some reason, as if he had a pressing date with destiny, he had not slipped it on his finger the morning of April 5th.

The discovery of the ring creased the curtains of defense behind which Louise concealed her heart. Her business length hair, dishwater-blonde, hung limp, and her blue eyes moistened. Old memories of her lost brother flooded her thoughts involuntarily....

Suddenly Louise was reliving a terrifying moment wherein she had nearly drowned. She was playing, with the joy only a young child can muster, in the shallow end of a motel swimming pool. It was the motel where she was spending the night with her mother, her Grandmother Garity and her siblings on the return drive from a visit with Aunt Jo and Aunt Jean in New Jersey.

Louise ventured out to the rope marking the division between the deep and shallow ends of the pool, hung on it and bounced up and down. Not knowing about the steep ledge just beyond the rope, in a careless instant her hands slipped off the rope and she slid down the ledge into water over her head. Panic gripped Louise as nothing in her young life had previously done. She flailed wildly with her arms and legs, but her uncoordinated motion was useless as if she were nothing more than a crocheted doll.

Suddenly, someone grabbed her by the arm and pulled her, coughing and sputtering, to the surface. It was Bruce. With a quizzical look on his face, he asked simply, "What's the matter with you?"

How could it be that the brother who had saved her young life from drowning had so soon lost his own life to the same fate? Louise's thoughts, however, did not linger on the tragic. She could not allow it. Instead, a new scene impressed itself upon her mind's eye. This new image of her brother, though she did not understand it, was the way she wanted to remember him.

Again Louise was a young child, just seven or eight years old. She and Bruce, he being four years her senior, were left in the car while their mother ran into a store at the Page Manor Shopping Center. While Ginny was in the store, however, there was a minor traffic accident at the intersection of Airway and Spinning. When she came out, she noticed the flashing lights of two police cruisers. "What in the world happened out here?" she asked.

Louise, even in her tender years, was bewildered at her brother's unhesitating reply. "They just had a bank holdup!" Bruce exclaimed. "You should have been out here. The cops was chasing the crooks down the street, and one of them stuck their head out of the window to look at the cops just as they passed another car, and he got his head knocked off, and it went rolling down the street."

For a shocked moment, Virginia Stevenson was aghast. Then she saw the hint of a smirk curve the corners of her son's mouth. "Oh, Bruce!" she exclaimed, expelling air through her nostrils in her characteristic snorting fashion. "I don't know where in the world you come up with these things."

Neither did anyone else….

The title to Bruce's Chevy was discovered among his belongings. His mother took it to the vehicle registrar and had the car transferred to her name. Bob made arrangements for the car to be towed to a junkyard from the fire station where it had previously been towed. Before turning the title over to the junkyard manager, however, Bob removed a necklace made of seeds from its hanging place around the rearview mirror.

He also removed a physician's report from the glove compartment. That paper reported the results of a recent pregnancy test. It was positive.

When the task of cleaning out Bruce's apartment was complete, the family stood and silently surveyed the cottage, etching the image in their minds. That image was as empty as the void in their hearts. Before leaving, they stopped at the main house to say goodbye and thanks to old Bessie Mikulos. Bessie must have felt powerless to console her former tenant's family, but made the attempt nonetheless. She told Ginny "what a good young man" her son had been, and she gave Louise a memento, a crocheted doll.

On their way out of Oakland, the family stopped at the home of Jan and her parents. Bob went to the door, but Jan's parents did not want her to talk to Bruce's family. She was having trouble coping.

How much trouble Bruce's mother had coping no one knows save she and God. Whatever her suffering, six aching years passed before she was able to have her son declared legally dead. She then applied for and obtained a bronze plaque, memorializing her son, from the Veteran's Administration.

Bruce's body was never found. Emotionally, that is not an easy thing with which to come to terms. For years after Bruce left his living loved ones, Bill dreamed about his cousin. The essence of those dreams was always the same. One fine day Bruce would show up at home, unannounced, but alive and well. Bill's joy would be overflowing. Then he would recognize something had changed between them. They were not close anymore; they could not communicate. Always Bruce would depart again without word, leaving Bill to grieve anew.

Yet the details of the dreams were always different. It was as if an unconscious shred of Bill's psyche were playing a cruel hoax on his conscious self—forever holding out a glimmer of hope of Bruce's survival. It was always the same false hope, but always slightly disguised—so Bill could believe—so he could be conned into thinking he was not dreaming.

Maybe Bill still has those dreams once in a great while. He thinks he does. If so, his conscious self has become an expert at repressing them.

17

Rendezvous at Virginia Beach

In the minds of two young men, the four months following Bruce's death were blurs: two rolls of film overexposed to the light of day. Still, two years had passed since the great Missouri adventure, and Eric and Bill were restless. They needed a new quest, but there was not much incentive to ride out to Fort Leonard Wood. Bruce would not be there to meet them.

Early August found the young men loading their gear into Eric's old green GMC and heading southeast. They had decided to seek the next chapter in their ongoing saga on the sands of Virginia Beach. If someone had asked, "Why Virginia Beach?" however, the cousins could not have provided a satisfactory answer. It just felt right. It was as if a gentle, almost imperceptible, magnetic force were pulling them in that direction. Yet, from time to time throughout their adventure, the magnetic poles of that force seemed to reverse, as if an opposing force sought to repel them from their mission.

The cousins drove straight through from Dayton, except for short intermissions, taking turns behind the wheel. Nevertheless, it took them much longer to drive than they expected. Instead of the five hundred miles they had anticipated, they drove closer to six hundred and fifty.

Their intent was to spend their first night in Virginia Beach with Bill and Nora Schieman, former residents of Mad River Township. Then they planned to find a place to camp for the rest of the week. The Schiemans, however, insisted the young men stay the week with them in their middle class, ranch style home. Their hospitality was superb.

Bill Schieman was an avid and accomplished fisherman. The ten pound two ounce largemouth bass hanging on the wall of his den attested to that. The following spring, he sent a clipping out of the local newspaper to Bill Sullivan Sr., detailing his latest catch: a whopping eleven pound six ounce largemouth.

Although August was the slow season for fishing in Virginia Beach, Bill Schieman insisted that his guests take his bass boat, trolling motor and fishing tackle for a day of fishing on the local reservoir. He did not have to twist their casting arms. The young men spent the morning pulling large plastic worms, rigged weedless, through thick brush sure to hold lunker bass. The fishing was great. The catching was lousy.

The early afternoon sun was hot as dragon's breath. The fishermen decided to beach their craft on a grassy bank with a little shade to eat their lunch. Before half finished, though, they were assaulted by the roar of the dragon itself passing overhead. The huge firebird seemed to hover momentarily above them, threatening to burst their eardrums with its raging, singe their hair with its fiery exhalation, and devour them like two roasted hot dogs. Then it passed, dipped beneath the trees, and skidded its rubber-clad claws on the tarmac surface of the nearby commercial landing strip.

This was neither the first nor the last such monster that day to cause earth, sky and water to quake, as if by the portentous and cataclysmic voice of God, proclaiming some miraculous event about to occur. Still, as with most miraculous annunciations, it was soon forgotten.

After lunch the lads basked in the sun and dozed. Later they refreshed themselves in the reservoir's cooling waters. "Watch out for cotton mouths," Bill warned. He did not want to have to use the snake bite kit, complete with razor blade and rubber suction cups, his dad had given him for just such occasions.

"Don't worry," Eric assured, "if I spot any kind of a snake I'll be out of this water before you can flip your Bic."

That evening after work, the bass master himself joined his guests in the boat. But even Bill Schieman could not coax a bass to strike before the reservoir's curfew of dusk.

The fishing trip excluded, the young men spent their days at the beach playing in the water and relaxing in the sand. They enjoyed themselves, but the anxiety of unfulfilled expectancy was growing in the middle layers of their psyches between conscious and unconscious knowing.

One afternoon, Bill met an attractive and pleasant young lady who shared her phone number. When he called the next day, however, she was not home. Neither did her father provide encouragement. Bill never called back. No fulfillment there!

The cousin's evenings were active, always flirting with but never obtaining whatever was lurking just beyond the touch of the five human senses. Once they visited the Edgar Cayce Foundation, which Bill found disappointing. In his own way, since his cousin's death, he had begun searching for "Truth," but he did not find it in Edgar Cayce, the so-called "sleeping prophet." Eric, however, when considering the Cayce visit in retrospect, felt it had prepared him, had opened the door, for the later culmination of his own quest.

Another evening was spent at a drive-in theater with the Schiemans. They were so hospitable it was impossible not to enjoy the experience, but it was weird for the young men to watch the movie *Woodstock* with a couple who were old enough to be their parents.

The foursome agreed that the music—the hard driving soul sound of Richie Havens, the wildly rocking havoc of *The Who*, the psychedelic strains of *Jefferson Airplane*—was fantastic. But the film also powerfully documented a rising generation with values vastly different from those of the Schiemans' generation. Those values included drugs, rejection of moral restraint and total disrespect for the established culture. That disrespect was epitomized by the haunting glare of the "Star Spangled Banner" as rendered by the ultimate electric guitar of Jimi Hendrix.

Yet another evening, Eric and Bill escorted the Schiemans' daughter, Pauletta, and her girlfriend to a local nightclub. It was not really a date, though. Pauletta, who was midway between Eric's almost nineteen years and Bill's twenty-three years of age, already had a steady boy friend. She was just being gracious. The quartet danced and made mostly trivial conversation. The main event of the evening was a vicious fight between two sailors. The thought occurred to Bill that had Bruce been with them *in the flesh*, they would likely have been involved in a brawl. He had not yet learned about Bruce's conversion, during the last year of his life, from barroom brawler to peace freak.

Pauletta needed to be home early, but Eric and Bill did not. The two comrades spent the wee hours at the beach waiting for sunrise. Bill was repulsed by the chilling discovery of a pentagram, with apparently Satanic inscriptions, exquisitely drawn in the sand. He wondered who had drawn it and why. Was it meant for him? Surely whoever had drawn it knew it would be destroyed by the tide before morning light.

Equally distracting to Bill was the unending assault of ruthless marauding mosquitoes. It was as if a horde of tiny scientists had selected him as the donor of vital fluids for a Frankensteinian experiment to resurrect the dead. Eric, however, was impressed only by the sunrise. For him, the blazing orb rising from the sea spoke deeply and symbolically to his soul. That enlightening experience further prepared him for what was still to come.

Another night found Eric and Bill at a house party with an assembly of young people who were strangers to them. One giant fellow, known as Tiny, had a form of epilepsy and was not supposed to imbibe alcoholic beverages. "Tiny is a real nice guy," someone warned the cousins, "until he starts drinking. Then he goes crazy. Don't let him get close to you when he's drinking." Tiny happened to be drinking heavily.

Shortly after Tiny went berserk, requiring half a dozen friends to subdue him, the cousins decided it might not be such a bad idea to accept an invitation from a strange young lady to go meet her pet boa constrictor. Though her Gypsy-like clothing seemed out of place, and her choice of fragrances failed to conceal the combination of serpent scent and BO that clung to her obese body, hers seemed a better alternative than anything Tiny and the gang had to offer.

Even at night the snake lady's apartment building appeared dilapidated on the outside. Inside, the miniature dwelling was no better—dark and creepy with an eight foot rat disposal coiled in a corner. The rapid-fire, rambling conversation of the hostess, mostly about her problems with her hot tempered, live-in boyfriend, made Bill even more uncomfortable.

Though the snake lady spoke rapidly, her bursts of speech were interrupted by silent pauses. Bill thought that maybe her irregular speech was due to her self proclaimed ability to think in several channels at once. Whatever the reason, she often failed to complete her thoughts. Instead, her sentences seemed to flake off and fall away like scales sloughing off a sick snake.

Eric and Bill exchanged furtive glances with raised eyebrows. There was no doubt this woman was big-time weird. "Where at in Ohio?" she asked. Her question seemed disconnected to anything they had been talking about.

"Huh?" Eric and Bill echoed.

"Your license plates," she snapped indignantly. "You must be, you know, Cincinnati? Columbus? Cleveland?"

Bill was bold in answering. After all, they were hundreds of miles away from home. Not much likelihood they would ever run into this strange lady again. "We're from Dayton," he admitted nonchalantly. "Well, actually we live in Mad River Township, just east of Dayton.

"You…are?" she said, as if gazing into the distance at some pleasant vision. The way her witch-black eyes suddenly lit up the features of her corpulent face made Bill cringe.

"Springfield!" she said, as if it were some divine revelation.

"What about Springfield?" Bill asked apprehensively.

"My home…family…parents and sisters still there," she beamed. "Take me with you…when you…. When are you…?"

Bill got the message, and it gave him goose bumps. He could not endure a twelve hour drive with her: not if she showered for an hour and succeeded in lowering her BO level below her pet's putrid pungency, and not if she were completely fabricating the graphic descriptions of her boy friend's jealous rages.

"We're not sure when we're leaving, but when we do we know where to find you," he said. "Listen, we have to go now because we promised the people we're staying with that we'd be in early tonight," he lied, "and we're late already. Don't get up; we can find our own way out. Thanks for having us over."

"Yeah, thanks for having us over," Eric added, as the two young men let themselves quickly out the door.

"Don't forget…Springfield," their hostess implored pathetically, as Eric closed the door.

The two young men walked swiftly to the GMC. "Let's get our buns out of here!" Eric exclaimed. Bill couldn't have agreed more. Still, he wondered what Bruce would have done in the same situation. Would he have hauled this strange lady back to Ohio? Yes, Bruce probably would have—but not Bill.

Their last night in Virginia Beach, Eric and Bill went nowhere. Instead they remained at "home," sitting in the darkness on the Schiemans' back patio, sipping lemonade. Something was missing; they both felt it. Though neither of them knew consciously what the object of their quest was, they would be leaving in the morning, and they were both vaguely aware they had yet to obtain it.

The young men reflected on their current adventure and reminisced about previous ones. The silver thread binding the volume of those adventures together was the memory of their escapades with Bruce. "I remember one day," Bill offered, "when your brothers and me were riding home from downtown on a bus. Bruce never said anything about feeling sick, but when we got off the bus he threw up right beside the driver. I can still see the look on that driver's face when he grabbed some paper to clean up the mess. He looked like he was about ready to lose it himself. But when he reached for the puke, Bruce grabbed it real quick and jumped off the bus. It was rubber!"

"Oh, man, I remember hearing about that," Eric laughed. "I must have been eight or nine years old." Then, after regaining his composure, he asked, "Do you remember the time we were all snowballing cars from underneath the house the Millers moved onto the field next to our house?"

Bill remembered all right.

"When the cops came," Eric continued, "everybody went running out the back of the hole."

"Yeah," Bill offered, "that was old Red Williams, the Riverside constable. We thought we were safe because there was eight inches of snow on the ground, but he cut right down through the field after us. Bobby was half way back to Motcos' cornfield when Red cut me and Bruce off in our tracks. When Bobby saw we were caught he came on back and surrendered. He probably figured we would rat on him anyway."

"Yeah," Eric laughed, "and me and Danny Miller were the only ones who didn't get caught because we were too little to climb out of the hole."

Bill laughed too. Suddenly, he was reliving the experience in his mind's eye. He saw anew the expression of abandonment in his little cousin's eyes as he struggled futilely to climb out of the ground. Seeing the police cruiser cut off his flight, Bill had abandoned all hope of escape. He turned and faced his captor just in time to witness the precise instant Eric's eyes registered the realization that he had better hide than run. Those big brown eyes and the wispy body dressed in a ragged jacket had reminded Bill of Pinocchio. Then, as if he were a puppet with its strings suddenly cut, Eric had collapsed and disappeared within the hole.

Reminiscing about the snowballing incident reminded Bill of another Northcliff Drive episode. "Do you remember the time Phil Conway gave us a piece of telephone cable, and we used it to make a trapeze in one of the big sycamore trees across the street from Martineaus' house?" he asked.

"Just vaguely," Eric admitted. "I think I was pretty young at the time. I just remember being over at the office one day when you guys come running in with Bruce bleeding all over the place, and Mother rushed him off to the hospital."

"What happened was," Bill explained, "we used a piece of galvanized steel pipe for the trapeze bar. We ran the cable clear through it and tied the loose end back to the main cable, then tied the other end up in the tree. That cable was real strong, but we didn't realize that the pipe had a sharp edge inside, and after awhile it cut right through the cable.

"We would climb up on the first limb of the tree and swing off it. Bruce happened to be the unlucky one who was swinging when it broke. I was standing right there beside him when he got up and showed us the inside of his elbow. A big triangular flap of skin and meat was peeled away like an orange. When he first jumped up I could see his muscles and tendons and everything. Then all of a sudden little red beads of blood started popping up everywhere, and then blood just started gushing out."

Recalling the incident so graphically seemed to fix Bruce's image in Bill's mind almost as if he were actually there with them, tangible flesh and blood, perhaps sitting inside the house on the living room sofa.

The cousins turned in shortly after eleven, wanting to get a good night's sleep before the long drive home. Bill awoke in the wee hours of the morning, though, curiously perplexed. He fumbled his way into the dark living room and was startled to find Eric sitting in a stuffed chair. "What are you doing up?" Bill whispered.

The quaver in Eric's voice alerted his cousin that he was, or had been, or was about to cry. "I just saw Bruce," he replied.

A million minuscule electrochemical impulses flashed through Bill's brain at once, overloading his synapses in their search for sense in what he thought he had just heard. They were not successful. "What do you mean?" he demanded.

"I couldn't sleep," Eric explained, "so I went outside for a smoke. When I came back in, Bruce was sitting right there on the couch." Eric's voice still quavered.

Bill's eyes had adjusted to the dark, and he stared at the couch just across the room. There was no one on or near it. He wondered if maybe Eric had mistaken one of the Schieman family members for his deceased brother. "Are you sure it was *Bruce*?" he asked.

This time there was no hint of wavering in Eric's declaration: "I'm positive! It was my brother!"

A thought sprang from the deep abyss of mystery and terror that surrounded Bruce's death in Bill's psyche. Half hope and half horror, Bill had entertained the thought before but had suppressed it. What if Bruce had not really died last March? After all, his body had never been found. What if his death had been staged? What if he were still alive but could not or would not make that fact known? "Did you talk to him?" Bill asked.

"I asked him if he was okay," Eric answered, "but he didn't say anything. He just smiled at me and gave me the peace sign." The quaver in Eric's voice gave way to quiet sobbing.

Bill did not ask again if Eric was sure of what he saw. He knew Eric believed, and he wanted to believe as well. "Where did he go?" he asked gently.

"I started to cry…then closed my eyes for a second…while I wiped them," Eric explained, trying to suppress his tears. "When I looked back at the couch…he was gone. I don't know where he went. I looked around the house, inside and out. He was just gone. But it was him, man. I swear it."

Bill felt like crying, but did not. He wished he could have seen his beloved Bruce as Eric had. He wished he could have seen him smile and flash the peace sign. Why had Bruce not appeared to him as well? Why had Eric's quest been fulfilled, but not his own?

Maybe in Bruce's judgment Eric was more needful, or more deserving. Or maybe Bruce had tried to communicate with Bill but had been unable to get through his tough, skeptical exterior. Maybe he had been unable to pierce the veil between Bill's temporal and spiritual eyes.

Eric was privileged with a second visitation from his deceased brother at another time and place. This time he was more prepared. After this second incident, he could not say whether they had actually spoken to one another or not. He knew, however, they had communicated. In Eric's words, Bruce conveyed this message: "…all things are ok, for me (Eric) to complete my destiny of all good, to help and heal others, to continue with life and growth, to learn and to be educated, to know there is no reward in violence but only in good. He wanted me to continue where he left off with education; to him that was the most important thing I could do for him and his spirit."

It would be another two years before Bill would receive personal confirmation that Bruce was truly okay. It would not come, however, in the form of a dramatic spiritual manifestation. It would come in the form of a simple youthful token.

18

Pilgrim's Trek

October 1970 brought with her the restless stirring of autumn. Eric, Bill and John McCullough celebrated the fall festival at "Wrightstock," an outdoor rock concert at Wright State University. There, on a "megadecibel" Friday night, Eric introduced Bill to the beautiful Miss Donna Marie O'Keefe. She was an older sister of Eric's girlfriend, Suzanne. Bill was smitten with Donna's sparkling green eyes and bubbly personality. She was equally smitten with his penetrating blue eyes and long, wavy hair. They soon became sweethearts.

In the chill of December, Bill confided to his new girlfriend that he was troubled. Bruce's body had not been found; neither had there been a funeral for him. That did not feel right. Bill planned to drive to California after the holidays and perform a memorial service. Not that he possessed any ministerial credentials: unless that possession came by birthright from the ancients, passed down through the lineage of some unknown priestly ancestor. It was simply something he *had* to do. It was as if he were a celestial body placed in purposeful motion by some unseen, omnipotent hand. Though he gently resisted his accelerating inertia, Bill knew intuitively that he was ordained to press forward through time and space, a shooting star, until mission complete, he would descend to earth in a fiery display—forever changed.

Bill began to grow a beard in preparation for his errand. It's reddish-blonde tint contrasted with the bushy, dark hair of his head, which now approached his shoulders. Then, on the night of Monday, January 4, 1971, Bill trekked alone into the clear and frigid western blackness. He had planned to drive his own car, but his dad changed his mind. Maintaining that the peace-mobile was not safe for such a long drive, Bill Sr. had insisted his son borrow his big, black 1968 Ford LTD. Bill Jr. was grateful.

As he drove, Bill rehearsed the arrangements in his mind. He had shared his intent with his two closest remaining male relatives, his dad and his cousin, Eric. He was to notify them of the appointed time for his lonely service. They would participate, though far removed by physical standards, in the experience. Bill's dad was to observe a silent vigil of solemn contemplation. Eric would provide music for the memorial, playing their chosen album, *Easy Rider*. Thus Bill sought to share with those he loved and trusted two powerful gifts: his grief at his cousin's passing, and his compulsive mission to commemorate Bruce's mortal walk.

Bill thought of the carefully chosen articles packed securely in the trunk of his car. These were the items he had resolved to cast into the ocean in token of the bond between Bruce and himself. In his own misguided thinking, these objects would become sacraments signifying his undying love for his cousin.

In later years Bill would look back on this time and hope that God would look gently upon his ignorance, and smile upon the intent of his heart. He hoped that God would forgive him for employing base objects as symbols of his relationship with his cousin, which employment could be misconstrued to be in mock of the sacred sacrament symbols representing the relationship between mankind and the Son of God.

Bill felt a tingling blend of exhilaration and anticipation, akin to Huckleberry Finn adrift on the mighty Mississippi. Like Huck Finn, he knew he was impotent against the powerful current now sweeping him along its course. He acknowledged the destiny awaiting him across the continent to the west. Yet that destiny seemed faraway. He was in no hurry; he would ride with the flow.

In fact, Bill was not far into Indiana when he pulled his car into a roadside rest and slept. The winter chill, however, soon penetrated his lodge, and he was back on the road within the hour. Thus he proceeded, alternately driving and catnapping, along the way.

Somewhere in Illinois Bill picked up Larry, a short and pudgy young man near his own age. "Where are you headed?" Bill asked the scraggly looking hitchhiker before unlocking the passenger side door.

"I'm on my way to see my Brother in Wichita," Larry replied. "How far are you going?"

"I'm going all the way to California," Bill answered. "I'm not sure how close I'll be getting to Wichita, but I can get you closer than you are now if you want to ride along."

The newly formed traveling troop arrived at Bill's planned overnight resting point Tuesday afternoon, the home of his old buddy, John Sickman. That home just happened to be located at Fort Leonard Wood, Missouri. Captain Sickman and his wife, Jeanne, welcomed Bill and his charge graciously. That night after dinner John and Bill played gin rummy and swapped tales till midnight. Larry made himself scarce.

Bill had forgotten how infuriating it could be to play cards with John, whose whiny voiced taunts were annoying; whose ostentatious, fat fingered dexterity at shuffling and dealing was irksome; and whose excessive amusement each time he ginned was insufferable.

John's time at Leonard Wood had briefly overlapped with Bruce's. Captain Sickman had not appreciated SPEC 4 Stevenson's familiarity toward him. Nor had he appreciated Bruce's helping himself to his liquor without invitation. "I used to warn Ellen about boys like him when she was in high school," John said with chubby cheeked animation. "No little sister of mine better ever bring home a Bruce Stevenson or a Junior Brown I used to tell her."

Bill laughed aloud. It amused him to think of Bruce's casual fraternization with Captain Sickman. It also amused him to think of Super Plebe's protectiveness of his sister. Ellen had a mind of her own.

Bill slept late the next morning. When he finally rolled out of the sack around noon, the Sickmans' had additional company, John's brother, George, and his companion. The twosome was touring the country in a VW hippie van. Bill did not want to impose, and planned to leave that afternoon, but John and Jeanne insisted he stay the night. Thus, Bill rose early Thursday morning, thanked his accommodating hosts and departed with his apprentice.

The two young men ate dinner that evening at a drive-in diner in Oklahoma City. The weather was surprisingly mild, and the carhops were kept busy delivering orders to young customers. Soon Bill was engaged in a pleasant conversation with a carload of local ladies. It seemed to him that Oklahoma girls tended toward friendly and pretty, not an altogether unpleasant combination. Then he thought of his sweetheart at home and knew it was time to leave.

Bill had discerned his passenger's passion for Wichita cooling over the past two days. When the time came to nudge Larry from the nest, he was ready. "Where do you want me to drop you off, Larry?" he asked, suggesting either the bus station or an on-ramp to Interstate 35 North to be the logical spots.

"I've been thinking," Larry began, "there really isn't anything for me in Wichita. My brother isn't expecting me or anything. And I've always wanted to see Los Angeles. I think I'll just ride along out there with you."

Bill did not mind helping somebody out, but he was not about to take a stranger on to raise. He did not particularly care for Larry's company anyway. He impressed Bill as being half wimp and half sticky booger. "I'm not going straight to LA," Bill explained. "I'm stopping to see a friend down in Odessa, Texas."

"That's okay with me," Larry countered. "I'm not in any hurry." Of course he was in no hurry. Why should he be? He was traveling across the country in the luxury of big Ford; he was not spending a nickel for gas; and Bill's friends were providing half his meals.

"I think you better stick with your plan to go to your brother's," Bill insisted. "At least you have a place to stay there until you can find a job. What would you do when you got to LA? You don't know anyone out there. You don't have a place to stay. You're better off to go to Wichita until you get on your feet. Save yourself some money; then check out LA if you want." He was trying to be polite, but he had made up his mind that Larry was not going to sponge off him or his friends any longer. Larry elected to be dropped off near I-35.

Bill had been driving all day long and part of the night by the time he made Amarillo, Texas. He was tired and debated within himself whether or not to drive out of his way, as he had planned, to visit Richard Wamboldt in Odessa. The distance did not look too terribly far on the map. He decided to go for it. Thus began Bill's education regarding distances in Texas.

On and on he trekked into the desolate night. He drove until weariness weighted his eyelids like highway sandbags, and fatigue pounded at his temples like a jackhammer. Never had he driven so far and seen so little. Two hundred and fifty five miles later he made Odessa just as dawn was beginning her assault on the eastern horizon.

Bill drove around the area until he located Wamboldt's home, a tattered little house in a neighborhood where luxury was an unknown companion. There he parked along the street, locked the doors, and crashed. He awoke around noon and knocked on Wamboldt's door. To his surprise, he was greeted pleasantly by a fair and slender young lady. Richard was at work out in the oil field. Bill would go exploring and return in the evening.

Wamboldt's dark eyes sparkled when Bill reappeared at his door around dinnertime. He was obviously elated to see his high school chum so far from Dayton. In fact, Bill had never seen his typically shy friend so demonstrative. Wamboldt insisted that his guest stay for dinner and spend the night as well. "I'm sorry we don't have anything but coffee to offer you to drink with supper," he apologized.

Bill remembered an unopened bottle of newly popular wine in the trunk of his car. Yet he hesitated. *That* wine was reserved for a special purpose. He was hauling *that* wine most of the way across North America in memory of his cousin, for his *cousin*. Then he remembered the night at the Cast Aways back in Ohio when Wamboldt had warned him to be cool. He remembered, too, what had happened when Bruce had tried to enter the Cast Aways later the same night. What would Bruce want him to do with the bottle of wine in the trunk of his car? "I just happened to think," Bill offered, "I have a bottle of Boone's Farm out in the car. I need to save some of it for California, but we can drink some with supper."

During dinner the two friends caught up on what had happened to each other since Wamboldt had been discharged from the army and moved to Texas. "I just got promoted from roughneck to roustabout," Wamboldt announced proudly.

"From what to what?"

Wamboldt chuckled. "Out on the oil rigs we have roughnecks and roustabouts. My foreman just made me a roustabout, that's a step up from a roughneck. It's all dangerous work though. People get hurt all the time, and some get killed." Wamboldt was short, but strong and tough.

After supper the two friends got out their guitars and demonstrated their respective skills. Wamboldt was far more accomplished, and attempted to teach Bill's inarticulate fingers new techniques, but with limited success. By ten o'clock both young men, despite the pleasant company, were yawning. By eleven they were ready for bed.

They slept late Saturday morning and toured the town during the afternoon. From Bill's perspective, however, there was not much to see. Tragically, the young man they visited in the hospital that evening would have probably agreed with Bill, had he been able to respond. A friend of Wamboldt's young girlfriend, the patient did not even acknowledge his visitors' presence. Instead he laid silently in a self-induced coma. The drug culture had taken root in Odessa and was grabbing hold like a strangler vine.

That night the fellows again played their guitars and talked. "So you're going out to Oakland to hold a service for Bruce Stevenson," Wamboldt said gently.

Bill recognized Wamboldt's open-ended statement as an invitation to express the "E" word. "Yeah, he hasn't had one yet because they never found his body," Bill confirmed. "But first I'm going to look up your old buddy, Denny Robeson, in Los Angeles," he continued, quickly changing the subject.

Had their roles been reversed, Wamboldt would not have exposed his emotions either. Bill knew he would not. The memory of the drowning of another hero, just a few years previous, was still too fresh. It had not been terribly traumatic for Bill, just upsetting. He had not known Jim Myers well. He had, however, witnessed the stark impact of Jim's loss on an entire neighborhood of young men: Jack and Tom "Trash" Myers, Ron and Steve "Fat Boy" Piatt, and Richard Wamboldt. No, Wamboldt would not have shared his hurt either.

For a moment Bill was lost in his own thoughts. He was back at the low-head dam on the Mad River. The one which splits the river into two channels forming Rohrer's Island just a mile below Huffman Dam. The one where Jim Myers drowned after rescuing two people and trying to save a third, after a long line of hand grasping youths had been washed off the apron into the turbulence below. The one where Harold Long described how pleasant it was to be dead after being pulled from the river by Bill Hoskins and revived. The one where Bill Sullivan himself had nearly drowned when he slid off its slimy-slick surface while snagging carp during the Christmas break of 1963.

Wamboldt snapped Bill's reverie. "I just saw Denny a few months ago," he said, respecting Bill's privacy. "He's living in a house on Kingsley with Bill Hoskins and Bill Myers."

"Yeah, I have the address, and I knew that Hoskins was living there. But I didn't know about Bill Myers. You mean Bill Myers from Dayton, Jim and Jack and Trash's older brother?"

"Yep, that's the one alright."

"I've never met him. Is he pretty much like his brothers?"

Richard paused before answering, as if his brain were processing the question. "No, Bill is different from his brothers. But he's okay; you won't have any trouble getting along with him."

"What do you mean *different*?" Bill asked.

"Oh nothing, he's just different. You'll see what I mean," Wamboldt hedged. Bill's curiosity was piqued, but he dropped the subject. The two friends went to bed early again that night. Bill was beginning to think that going to bed early was pretty much a way of life in Odessa.

Bill rose early the next morning, Sunday morning, with the intent of getting in a full day's driving. Richard wanted him to stay another day, but he was already feeling the irresistible pull toward a plot of sand—*Eleven Miles South of Half Moon Bay*. It was as if he were the tide and California were the moon. Unfortunately, the gravitational pull of the moon and California combined were not enough to start the big Ford's engine. The battery was dead.

"Don't worry about it; my next door neighbor is a backyard mechanic," Wamboldt offered. Two hours older and twenty dollars poorer, Bill was traveling gratefully west on Interstate 20 with a rebuilt alternator under his car's hood.

He did not drive long, however, before hunger was gnawing at his gut like it was homemade jerky. He stopped in a little dive in Pecos, ate barbecued chicken and was back on the road by noon, licking the remnants of the savory sauce from the corners of his mouth. Forty miles west of Pecos, Bill connected with Interstate 10, not stopping again until he made El Paso. Then he only stopped on a whim, wanting to see the Rio Grande.

What a disappointment! The Rio *Grande* was hardly grand. In fact, it was just a trickle of water that could not pass for a respectable Ohio creek. It seemed in jeopardy of being swallowed entirely at any moment by the arid country surrounding it. Bill picked up a stone and hurled it across the Rio dribble onto foreign terrain. Mexico did not seem to notice.

Bill found his escape from El Paso to be a magician's stunt worthy of Harry Houdini. After his third loop through the same run down section of town, he was convinced someone had intentionally misplaced the signs that were supposed to point the way back to the interstate. Perhaps forcing traffic repeatedly through its dismal streets would result in some percentage of motorists stopping and spending.

The solemn dark faces with the straight black hair and the shining black eyes that watched his passing made Bill curiously uncomfortable. There was no way he was stopping. When he finally discovered a ramp leading back to I-10 West, there were two hitchhikers standing along side it. They were not scruffy looking, but like him, they had long hair for this part of the country. He picked them up.

Bill's new companions, two new stars in a growing constellation, were traveling to Oregon. They had spent their Saturday night in a little West Texas town jail for vagrancy. It was not that they were destitute, but they lacked transportation. Furthermore, they did not appear as if they belonged in Texas. They figured the vagrancy charge was just an excuse to get them out of town.

Around six-thirty, the group stopped for gas in a little town in New Mexico. One of Bill's guests struck up a conversation with a young man who appeared to be stranded there, discovering that the fellow was a penniless, nineteen-year-old GI traveling to San Francisco. Furthermore, he was AWOL.

The three older fellows attempted to persuade the youngster to turn himself into army authorities and get his affairs straight. They did not want to see the kid mess up his life. The young soldier agreed think about it while he traveled to San Francisco. Now Bill had three traveling companions.

After gassing the car, the unlikely quartet stopped at a cowboy restaurant just down the road. Before they left the car, though, one of the vagrants shared some advice: "If any trouble starts in here, guess who's going to jail?" he asked, pausing to let his words sink into his listeners' brains. "We need to mind our own business and try to avoid trouble. But if a fight does start, we need to stick together."

"I have a knife," his partner added.

All agreed to be on their best manners and to fight together if fighting was necessary. In Bill's mind, that was good operating procedure no matter where one was, but he thought his outspoken rider was exaggerating a bit. He was not.

The young men walked down the sidewalk, behind a husky cowboy, to the restaurant. The cowboy stopped in front of the door, swung it open wide, and grinned broadly. With a sweeping gesture of his free hand, he beckoned the out-of-towners inside like honored guests.

"Thanks," Bill said, smiling as he passed the cordial cowboy.

"You're the grimiest lookin' bunch of lizard lickers I ever seen," the doorman responded, eyeballing Bill's shoulder length hair, while never breaking his grin.

Bill was close enough he could have leaned over and taken a bite out of the brim of the cowboy's black Stetson hat. He feared the worst.

The lizard lickers found a table as far away from the cowboy and his posse of eight or ten assembled deputies as they could. They spoke softly to one another, making emergency plans. They would tolerate all the verbal abuse a crowd of rowdy New Mexican cowboys—who, judging from the fact that there were no obvious horse droppings clinging to the soles of their fancy leather boots, had apparently prettied up for

Sunday night dinner—could dish out. That, however, would be it. The moment one of the big, bad bovine-busters got physical, all hell was going to break loose.

Verbal abuse was plentiful. Rowdy ridicule and cowboy guffaws rolled across the room and rattled the walls like thunder. Especially nasty or perverse insults were reserved for frequent hikes to the jukebox, which trail led conveniently close to the lizard lover convention.

The "grimy lookin' bunch of lizard lickers" ordered short orders and devoured them as quickly as possible. After paying for their meals, they walked as inconspicuously as possible—which was about as inconspicuous as four bloated horse droppings floating in a punch bowl at a wedding reception—past the obnoxious horse-hoppers and out the door. After his first encounter with New Mexican rednecks, Bill felt as if he were an escapee from an Arlo Gutherie tune. He was anxious to put as many miles between himself and New Mexico as possible.

Around midnight, a Ford LTD, a black speck of antimatter in a material world, glided past Phoenix. Only its pilot was awake to see the city lights sprawled, saucer-like, across the flat desert floor, resembling a huge UFO. The city appeared as if it might rise anew at any moment from the desert ashes. As if it might soar through the midnight heavens to a new world, as did the ancient City of Enoch.

Bill did not know then that he would be returning eastward through Arizona and New Mexico via a different route before the month was out. Nor did he anticipate the awesome spectacle of the Grand Canyon, which would exceed his expectations in even greater proportion than the Rio Grande had disappointed them. Nor did he know he would spend a frosty night sleeping in the front seat of his car on the rim of that canyon with yet another hitchhiker sleeping in the back. The only thing he did know about the Grand Canyon was that if he ever got the chance, he would spit into it.

Nor could Bill have known that he would drive out of his way to deliver the same hitchhiker to his destination in Albuquerque. Or how outraged he would feel with his first experience of southwestern bigotry to American Indians. He could not have known how the young stranger he would befriend would become indignant with a drunken old Indian staggering across an Albuquerque street in front of them. How that befriended stranger would show his gratitude to Bill by declaring, "Run that raunchy old reservation rat over! Who does he think he is walking in front of a white man?" As if the white man's fragile short-term lease on this vast western land were absolute. As if the ancient culture of the red race were not as deeply embedded in the land as are the Rocky Mountains, the Colorado River and the Mojave Desert.

Bill could not have predicted any of these experiences. Yet they would flow naturally from the course of events already set in motion and from the spirit of the land, so intermingled as it was with the spirits of its ancient inhabitants, which spirit was already whispering to Bill's own, preparing him for his mission.

About two hours out of Phoenix Bill's companions were forced into semiconsciousness at the California border town of Blythe. Bill was required to get out of the car and open the trunk for a fruit inspection, but it was just as well. He had been only semiconscious himself, and the activity was invigorating. Soon enough he was pressing on into the wee hour darkness, struggling again to stay awake.

Nothing in his experience had remotely prepared Bill for the predawn rush hour traffic on a densely fogged LA freeway. He was panic stricken. He literally could not see ten feet in front of his car. He could not see road signs. He did not dare change lanes or slow down for fear of being smashed from the rear. All the while traffic ripped past him unmercifully.

The only viable option Bill's drained brain could muster was riding the tailgate of a big Peterbilt, focusing on its red running lights. Mile after torturous mile he plunged into terror, praying constantly that the trucker would not slam on his brakes. The strain of the situation on top of twenty hours of driving was desperately close to unbearable. How long could any human maintain absolute concentration under such harrowing circumstances? It was all Bill could do to remain sane.

An hour later—or an eternity—the sun rose and the fog began to lift. At last Bill found his weary way to Highway 1 and freed his fellow pilgrims to hitchhike up the California coast. Relieved they were gone, yet feeling suddenly alone, he drove back the way he had come.

Bill found the Kingsley house in a quiet neighborhood of tired but stately old homes. "Denny won't be home until two-thirty this afternoon," Hoskins informed him after they exchanged greetings and brief small talk. "You can hang around here until then if you want."

"Thanks, man," Sullivan answered, "but I think I'll drive down to the beach and rest for awhile. I'll be back this afternoon to see Denny."

"The beach around here isn't much to look at," Hoskins warned.

"Yeah, but it beats anything in Dayton," Sullivan grinned. When he arrived at the beach, however, he saw immediately that Hoskins was right. The nearly deserted stretch of coarse sand was dismal in comparison to the beautiful Florida beaches he knew, and even the ocean chopping at the shabby shore appeared dingy. Though the scene was hardly romantic, Bill knelt and drew a figure in the sand, a heart pierced with an arrow. Inside the figure he wrote "Bill loves Donna."

Before returning to his car to rest, he observed four outlandishly dressed young people, three females, cavorting on the sand fifty yards distant. Pausing to see what they were doing, he realized they had a tripod and what appeared to be a movie camera. They seemed totally self-absorbed. Probably college students, Bill thought, *bent on producing a new film classic in Cinematography 101. Then again, maybe…*

Bill was disappointed that the only other members of his species on the beach did not invite him to participate in their party, nor even notice him at all—as if nothing in his paltry existence were worthy of recording. Or, as if he were already nothing more than a recorded celluloid image, watching reality proceed without him. Or, as if he were a shaman—*in the world, but not of it.*

19

Farewell

Boarding at the Kingsley house was an adventure. It was as if the structure, whose architecture exhibited the artistry and craftsmanship of a slower paced era, were a portal placed at the seam between two dimensions of time. If so, Denny was a lens, focusing light through that portal from one dimension into the other, imparting to it golden and rosy hues reflected from his own soul.

Denny was delighted to loan his extra mattress, the one on his bedroom floor along the opposite wall from his own, to Bill. It would have been difficult, for the sparkling moment, to find two more compatible roommates. Denny was a wizard of California culture, Bill his eager apprentice.

The friends enjoyed browsing together for hours in New Age bookstores and grazing at vegetarian restaurants. Both of these experiences were new opportunities for Bill, and he partook abundantly. He found the California scene exhilarating, much as his cousin had before him. He felt as if he were in a theater where ten classic movies were being projected on the screen at the same time. His mind raced to keep up with it, to absorb and make sense of it. When he returned to Ohio he would be taking back a hundred pounds of books and a commitment to vegetarianism that would last for the next eight months.

Denny thrived in his role as mentor. His charming smile, long pony tail, intellectual inclination and charismatic spirit (too large to be contained by his smallish physique) all conspired to make it so. All he had heretofore lacked was a suitable student. Sometimes they read; sometimes they listened to Denny's fantastic collection of what would come to be known as the classic rock sound of the Doors, Joplin, Hendrix, Harrison and Lennon; sometimes they made the nightclub scene; sometimes they just kicked back and philosophized on the nature of the universe.

Bill also enjoyed chatting with Denny's housemates, Hoskins and Myers. Hoskins had added some pounds to his well proportioned, six-foot frame since Bill had last seen him. His straight black hair had grown longer, while his hairline had receded. More noticeable, however, than these physical characteristics was the mellowing of his attitude. Bill had known Hoskins to be a fighter to the core: one who not only refused to run from a fight, but often sought one out. Now, however, the aggressive edge was gone. In its place was a quiet, albeit misguided (from Bill's perspective) serenity.

As for Bill Myers, Wamboldt was right; he was *different*. At 6'3", he was easily the tallest of the Myers brothers, and he was a dedicated college student. He was also an amiable conversationalist, bright, soft spoken and intriguing. Those mundane details, however, did not begin to explain how he was different. When he invited Bill to join him for a Saturday afternoon in San Diego, Bill readily accepted.

As the two new friends walked barefoot along the beach, chatting about the universe, Bill began to pick up pretty pebbles which caught his eye. This had been his custom ever since Aunt Ginny introduced her cub scouts to rock collecting fifteen years before. Myers followed Bill's lead, and soon they were sharing each newly discovered treasure with the glee of two born again children.

"Oh wow, look at this one," said Bill. "See the fine, dark lines? They make it look like a three-dimensional jig saw puzzle don't they? But it isn't a puzzle, it's a miniature world. Those lines are the borders of all the countries in that world. And see how those flecks sparkle in the sun. Those are the gold and jewels that kingdoms rise and fall to possess."

"Oh yeah, I see it, man!" Myers declared. For a long moment the two of them were lost in a shared fantastic vision. Then Myers broke the reverie. "Look at this one I just found!" he said, extending his hand with a small smooth object nestled in its palm.

Bill looked. There was a stone of exquisite contrast, two opposing elements perfectly fused at a curving seam—half anthracite-black and half Antarctic-white. Myers explained its significance. "This is night and day, good and evil, life and death, yin and yang."

"I see it. I see it," Bill admitted. "Lighten up, you're blowing me away!"

"You know," Myers suggested, "everybody should take the time to pick up a few rocks every week and mellow out. They could carry a little sack of their best ones wherever they went. And whenever anybody asked how they're doing, they would just pull out their sack of rocks and say, 'This is where I'm at.'"

At the moment the thought made perfect sense. Even now, in comparison to the material possessions so sought and flaunted by the yuppies of a new day, perhaps a sack of pretty stones or wonderful marbles would serve just as well to exclaim to the world precisely "where one is at."

In addition to Denny's housemates, there was no dearth of fascinating characters passing through the Kingsley house daily. In fact, colorful characters seemed attracted to Kingsley as butterflies to nectar, or—in some cases—as blow flies to refuse. One evening, for example, a young man who claimed to have stayed for a time at the Manson ranch not long before the bloody outbreak of *Helter-Skelter* paid a visit. "It was okay at first," the fellow with the long, straggly hair explained, "everyone was having fun. Then Charlie started acting real weird, and I decided to bug out."

The fellow seemed pretty weird himself. Bill got bad vibes from him and wished he would make like a cockroach and bug out of the Kingsley house as well.

Then there was Red, the scrawny, amateur porn film star and self-proclaimed official photographer of the Hell's Angels. He claimed the Angels had hired him to ride with them and photograph their cross-country tour planned for the coming summer.

A regular at the Kingsley house was Sanji, a Japanese citizen studying at U.S.C. Bill wondered what Sanji's father, who was financing Sanji's transoceanic education, would think if he knew his son spent most nights stretched out on a Kingsley house sofa with his head wired to an amplified turntable.

A week at the Kingsley house vanished in an instant, and it was time to venture north. Denny had not been to Northern California for awhile and decided to ride along. Bill was happy for the company.

They spent their first night on the road at a house shared by a group of Denny's friends, just north of San Francisco in Mill Valley. In the morning a young lady, the spouse of the head of the house, offered to escort Bill on a tour of nearby Mt. Tamalpais. The young woman was plain and unadorned, but not unpretty. Bill hardly knew how to respond when she explained that her husband had taken zealously to a particular brand of yoga several months previous, and they had been celibate ever since. Bill felt his ears flush crimson beneath the long waves of his hair. Fortunately, the awkwardness lasted but a moment before the subject of their conversation changed.

There was something mystical about this mountain. It was as if some ancient race had walked here, had lived and died and worshiped here. Had sanctified this ground and hallowed it to the observance of their rituals of light and nature. Bill could almost hear the echoes of their living, whispering in the breeze. In the corners of his eyes he thought he saw glimpses in the shadows of the ancient ones.

At a convenient spot, hewn in the mountain's side, was an amphitheater, undoubtedly patterned after one that had served another ancient race in a far distant realm. Bill sat in awe and imagined how it would be to sit here one black summer night, enthralled by the strains of acoustic harmonies and blending voices. These new songs merging with the echoes of ancient singing.

That night, in contrast to the sacred mountain, Bill and Denny made the scene at Fillmore West. Here they experienced the psychedelic enchantment of a modern application of some *dark* and lurid, ancient religion. All the while, on the borders of his consciousness, Bill heard faintly the omming and chanting of ancient priests and whores reciting their pagan rituals.

During the middle of the week, Bill and Denny traveled farther north. It was there in the redwood country where they put to use the expensive 35mm camera Denny had borrowed from Red, the Hell's Angels photographer. The two novices passed the camera back and forth as if it were an instrument of magic, as first one then the other envisioned a remarkable new shot. Time after time the shutter snapped, promising to record photosensitive chemical images of an experience too awesome to reproduce.

Bill had never known greater reverence than he discovered that January morning at the feet of gargantuan timbers—living timbers, whose crowns scraped the very heavens, and whose circumferences reduced the only two humans in attendance to the scale of scampering squirrels on the forest floor. The majesty of the scene, the utter stillness, penetrated to the marrow of one's quivering bones.

It was as if the young men's presence here were an intrusion into sanctity they had no right to disrupt. It was as if their photography threatened to steal the spirit of the forest. Yet they could not withdraw themselves: for in truth, it was the majestic forest that held hostage *their own* helpless souls.

Click, click went the shutter. Fifty shots in two hours time—none of which would ever be developed. Unbeknownst to the hapless photographers, their camera was devoid of film!

By the time they returned to Mill Valley, Bill's compulsion to complete his mission was overwhelming. He had pushed it to the periphery of his consciousness for as long as he could. It was as if two diametrically opposing forces had been battling within him for the past two weeks: one forcing him toward formally and ceremonially acknowledging his cousin's death, the other clinging to the desperate hope that a funeral was premature. After all, Bruce's body had not been found.

Either way Bill knew now, in a manner completely divorced from logic, he could no longer delay the inevitable. He drove to Oakland on Saturday, phoned Jan's home and talked to her mother. Jan was at work, but he could stop by if he wanted. Jan's mom gave him directions.

Bill desperately hoped that Jan's mom would tell him something he didn't already know about Bruce. In fact, within the partition of his mind where fantasies are fondled, he even hoped that she would give him a clue where Bruce was hiding and why. His rational mind simply hoped that she would at least provide some fact that would make sense of the senseless.

Jan's mom did neither. She was sympathetic to Bill's plight, but had very little information to offer. All she could do was share her fondness for Bruce and the trauma his untimely death had been for her family, particularly for Jan. She recalled gazing at Bruce, sitting shirtless on the hood of his car along the curb in front of their home the day before his death, and thinking, *what a beautiful young man he is*. Bruce reminded her of Christ.

That evening Bill returned to the home and met Jan. She seemed excited to meet Bruce's cousin, yet anxious. She too, it seemed, still had a fragile, flickering hope. If so, her hope was vain. They could only share their loss vaguely.

There was so much Bill wanted to talk about with Jan: How close had she been to Bruce? Had they talked of marriage? Where was Bruce's head in the weeks before he died? What happened that day at the beach? Jan, however, was difficult to reach. There was a chasm between them that Bill was unable to span. Her conversation seemed vague and slightly disoriented. She reminded Bill of an injured robin in the hands of a would-be rescuer, skittish and untrusting. Moreover, she could not visit for long; it was Saturday night, and she had a date. Bill departed as unfulfilled as a scorned lover.

Sunday afternoon Bill drove to North Pescadero Beach, *Eleven Miles South of Half Moon Bay*. There he sat in his car for a time, watching strangers go through the motions of life: actors in a low budget flick. He felt strangely alone, yet not. It was as if a part of him did not want to, could not, concede the mortal loss of his cousin. Tearing himself free of his car, as a moth from its protective cocoon, was a sheer act of will. Yet Bill eventually emerged, carrying his offerings with him, and drifted away on the breeze to complete his mission and his metamorphosis.

Bill removed the seed necklace from the car's rearview mirror, slipped it over the dark hair that sprung in bushy ripples nearly to his shoulders, and hung it on his neck. It was the same amulet that had hung on the rearview mirror of Bruce's 1957 Chevy. It felt more powerful even than the gold Buddha chain, also adorning his neck, which John McCullough had worn throughout his Green Beret tour in Nam, then given to Bill before his journey to California. It was as if the power of regeneration surpassed even than the power of incorruptibility.

Bill felt much as a shaman of some primitive tribe must feel when fraternizing with the spirits. Mortal folk flowed past him as apparitions. He saw them, attempted to catch their glances, but could not—they were functioning in another plane. He found himself gliding gently up the beach, feeling his way, sea on his left and cliffs on his right. Eventually he left all mortal apparitions far behind and discovered the solace of solitude.

When he had traveled far enough, when there were no longer tracks in the sand, he stopped. A small stream trickled over the cliff's edge and was reduced to spray in the rushing wind. Like Noah of old, the rainbow that formed where slanting rays of sun met tumbling droplets of mist, seemed to Bill a sign from God.

At the appointed time, he prayed a sobbing prayer, and twenty-four hundred miles away, another prayed as well. The mind's eye of the other, Bill's father, was opened to the scene. The ears of his spirit heard the roaring of the sea. Only Eric forgot his role of ceremonial musician.

Bill approached the awful sea, his growing beard glowing golden in the sun, and proclaimed what he must. His words were a dirge, accompanied by the pounding and roaring of an ancient savage beating furiously on the dried skin of some dead animal stretched over the open end of a hollow log—pounding out the brutal message of mortal loss and wailing his lament. Yet it was only the pounding and roaring of an indifferent ocean: The same ocean whose salty brine pumps through the veins of all living. The same ocean whose icy current sucked the precious life from the lungs of Bruce.

Having spoken his peace, having commended his cousin's spirit into the hands of the Almighty, Bill waded knee deep into the churning ocean. There he poured his bitter tears and the sweet contents of a half-consumed bottle of wine into the salty sea, where they mingled with all the tears of the human family accumulated across the millennia.

Then he cast into the billowing waves the balance of his offering: a Missouri-road-scarred motorcycle helmet and a denim sack bursting at the seams with a fabulous collection of more than a thousand glassy worlds. It was more than just a sack of marbles or a sack of rocks: it was a depiction of where Bill was at, where he had been and where he was going.

The haughty sea rejected the floating helmet instantly, spewing it back at Bill and depositing it on the beach as so much unwanted debris. Bill fetched the offering and tried again, casting it with all his might into the heaving sea. Again the helmet floated. Again the ocean spit it back in his face. Bill weighted the helmet with rocks and tried once more. This time it sank and disappeared, but the greedy sea was unappeased. It tugged at his legs beckoning, cajoling—demanding something greater. It wanted what it could not receive—the ultimate wicked offering.

Bill stood on the sand of North Pescadero Beach until dark. He watched the sun, or was it himself as a sluggish shooting star—slip into the sea in a fiery display, forever changed. As he breathed in the ocean air he entertained a curious notion: perhaps he was inhaling the same air Bruce had exhaled in his last moments of mortality. Perhaps, in this manner, a piece of Bruce would live in him, and he would himself be reborn a new and purer creature.

Perhaps the sea later found a way to once more reject his offerings. Perhaps it cast the weary helmet again upon the shore. Perhaps it tossed there as well an empty green bottle labeled Boone's Farm. Perhaps it even littered the sand with marvelous marbles for some beachcomber to discover, collect and show to others, saying, "This is where I'm at."

Yet if the fickle ocean refused his offering, Bill knew to the core of his soul that his lost cousin accepted it. He was the one who mattered.

Bill groaned within himself, thinking, *It is finished*!

20

OMEGA: The End of the Beginning

In November of 1986, as Aunt Ginny's life was being drained from her withering body by amyotrophic lateral sclerosis (ALS), or Lou Gehrig's disease, Bill penned a poem to her in behalf of his beloved cousin:

They Call Me a Wanderer

When I was small my tiny body
Could scarcely contain my anxious spirit.
Your job then, Mother,
Was nurturing and protecting.
As I grew, I found the rules of school
To be restrictive and was somewhat rebellious.
During those years I required
Your guidance and your counsel.
While yet in youth, my wandering spirit
Carried me to distant places—
Florida, Germany, Vietnam, and California.
Through all these times, Mother, you lent me
Your strength and your support.

I know that I caused you much worry and much grief
During my short walk upon this earth.
The unexpected shortness of my stay with you
Shocked us both,
But when the time for choosing came—
Whether to brave the power of the sea,
Or to remain safely on the sand:
There was no choice to be made.
Did you not teach me, Mother, to reach out always,
And not withhold my hand,
To help the one in need?

And so, in attempting to save a life,
I lost my own.
Yet in losing my life,
I found a better.

They call me a wanderer.
Now I have wandered beyond the veil of mortal tears,
And when your earthly sojourn is ended,
Mother, I eagerly wait to welcome you home.

Virginia L. Stevenson's mortal remains were buried in the northwest corner of the old Harshman Cemetery in the heart of the Village of Riverside, not far from the elementary school bearing her name, nor from the former village hall where she once served as mayor. Her surviving children—Bob, Eric and Louise—had a stone monument placed to mark her grave. It now stands, a silent sentinel, inscribed on the front with her name, her birth and death dates, and a woodland scene, above which appear the words, "TILL WE MEET AGAIN."

Attached to the back, or west face, of the monument is a twelve by twenty-four inch bronze plaque. That plaque, in raised letters, bears this inscription:

Bruce Michael Stevenson

SP 4 US Army

Vietnam

MAR 6 1948 APR 5 1970

No death affected Bill the way Bruce's did before or since. He has struggled to understand why. Maybe it was the unexpected suddenness of Bruce's passing. Maybe it was because Bruce's body was never found, and Bill was denied the closure a traditional funeral provides—the certain visual and tactile knowledge that a loved one is truly gone.

Maybe it had something to do with the flood of unresolved guilt Bill felt after the initial shock of Bruce's death settled into his soul. That torrent of guilt was compounded in his mind because he had not been there when Bruce needed him. His cognitive self recognized his feelings were not rational, but his intuitive self desperately wanted to atone.

Whatever the reason for the profound impact of Bruce's death on Bill's psyche, it prompted him to seek "Truth." He *needed* answers. Somewhere he read, "…seek, and ye shall find; knock and it shall be opened unto you…" and decided to put those words to the test.

Bill pored intensely through every last ounce of his hundred pounds of California books, but did not find the Truth he sought. He engaged every amenable barroom and pool hall philosopher he encountered, but still his search for Truth was frustrated. Then one night, from the opposite side of a bottle of Boone's Farm wine, the most unlikely of voices pointed him in a new direction.

In time, after the sincere exercise of childlike faith and unwavering intent, a new Truth began to reveal itself to his mind. When the image of that Truth became sufficiently clear and focused, he ached to share it with Bruce. That image was the likeness of the Lord Jesus Christ as revealed in His restored Gospel.

Perhaps Bill's intense desire to share what he now considered most valuable with his cousin, and his fear this gift might be rejected, were contributing factors in his recurring dreams. The dreams in which Bruce would return home—alive—without warning for a short period of time, only to leave again despite Bill's best efforts to convince him to stay. The dreams in which Bruce and Bill remained emotionally isolated despite Bill's best efforts to reunite them.

Bill grieved not just for the loss of his cousin, but for his own self-perceived failure to share the Truth with him. Although he had not known, during Bruce's lifetime, the conviction of Truth he now felt, he was painfully aware he had failed to set a living example of that portion of Truth he had known. It was as if he had been appointed from on high to be his cousin's keeper, but had denied his charge.

At last he read somewhere, "Greater love hath no man than this; that a man lay down his life for his friends." This passage spoke hope to Bill's soul: hope that the judge of all would accept Bruce's sacrifice as sufficient to cover a multitude of sins.

Eric now has the three medallions crafted in Missouri by Bruce, Bill and himself. They belong together, for together they symbolize the strength and unity those three shared for a golden moment. The seed necklace Bill wore while fulfilling his mission, *Eleven Miles South of Half Moon Bay*, fell apart with time and was discarded. Bill returned the gold Buddha chain to John McCullough in 1975 at their ten-year high school reunion. By then he had found a greater power—more incorruptible than gold, and more powerful in regeneration than the genetic miracle of a seed. Ironically, that power was symbolized by burial in water and rebirth.

Bill does not dream of Bruce so often any more, at least he seldom remembers the dreams. Perhaps his aching, with the passage of time, has grown dormant. Yet it is there, ever present, in a quiet place within his heart. Occasionally, in a still moment, forgotten images press themselves upon Bill's mind: remnants of hopeless hopes once expressed in the only medium available to them: dreams of the night.

At such moments, Bill sometimes pulls from its yellowed envelope an ancient Polaroid photograph and attempts to revive his fading memory with the photo's fading image. That image—the image of a long-haired young man wearing nothing but cut-off bib overalls and a far away expression, half smile and half smirk; his body blanketed in shadows and his face bathed in a shaft of light filtered through the trees of the Big Sur coast—was a gift from Odus Brown.

Feeling the old familiar stirring of loneliness within his bosom—Bill wonders—will his grieving ever be truly complete?

Eleven Miles South of Half Moon Bay

Since last we talked,
has Eternity passed,
Eleven Miles South
of Half Moon Bay.
Since last we walked,
has Dawn renewed
Half memories
of a future past,
From glory come,
To dust returned,
Eleven Miles South
of Half Moon Bay.

Rest well my friend,
my cousin-prince,
Eleven Miles South
of Half Moon Bay.
The Light of Truth
light your way;
The Truth distil
upon your soul,
Till Breath of Life
your breath refresh;
Eleven Miles South
of Half Moon Bay.
From Heaven's dews,
your cup o'er flows,
Eleven Miles South
of Half Moon Bay.
Until, I trust,
that day when once
again we shall embrace,
And loathsome void
between, shall be
as visions of the night.

Bill married his sweetheart, Donna Marie, March 2, 1971. In June of 1972 they moved, with their infant daughter, Angela, into the old frame house at 4712 Springfield Pike, immediately adjacent to Stevenson's Animal Hospital. They rented it from Bill's Aunt Ginny for ninety dollars a month, which was about what they could afford on Bill's $110.00 a week salary from Dill's Supply.

It was the same house where Bill's cousins and he had played as kids when it had been rented by the Owens and then by the Schulke families. It was here where Bill received his coveted confirmation—that Bruce was indeed okay—through the most peculiar of circumstances, beginning with a simple household project.

When Donna and Bill needed a wardrobe closet for their bedroom, Bill decided to build one. His dad donated a free standing plywood cabinet to the cause, which he had originally built for use in Trader's Haven. Bill had only to dissemble the cabinet, trim its various parts to new dimensions and reassemble it. He also decided to remove the baseboard from one corner of the bedroom to save space and to make it easier to attach the new closet to the wall. When that baseboard was removed, a miracle occurred.

That miracle came in the revelation of a simple and imperfectly formed childhood token. For behind the baseboard lay hidden, among the accumulated dust and cobwebs of decades of living, an object made of thin pressed aluminum, a good luck charm. Bill picked it up breathlessly. Surely it could not be…

It was!

Bill admired Bruce's creation as if it were a rare coin hidden away by some relative years before and newly discovered, or as if it bore an inspired inscription of invaluable portent. The center section of the disk formed a star defined by five small crescents cut clear through the metal. On one side of the center section was embossed a four-leaf clover, on the other an American flag. The outer circumference of the disk was embossed with a ring of dots, like periods. A quarter inch inside the first ring of dots was another, the two rings forming the borders between which Bruce's message appeared on the clover leaf side: "BRUCE STEVESON GOOD LUCK 11."

Noticing the flaw, Bill remembered how Bruce had misspelled his own last name. Yet now the imperfection was endearing. It was as if Bruce were flashing him the peace sign, as he had to Eric in Virginia Beach, or beckoning to him, as he had to Snack in Otway. In fact, Bill could almost see Bruce doing so and smirking his *Ha, ha, I got you last!* smirk.

Bill clutched the token to his chest and wept.

Epilogue

A few brief tributes to Bruce Michael Stevenson are presented here as a fitting epilogue. These tributes come from those who knew and loved him best—his brother, Eric Stevenson, and his friends Ron Martineau, Odus Brown, and Snack Barber. Bruce's brother, Bob, declined to provide a tribute, stating—with a lump in his throat—that it has been too long and he would not know what to say. Their sister, Louise, also struggled to find the words to adequately express her feelings for Bruce, and in the end, decided that she could not.

Eric Stevenson still lives in the home where Bruce and he were reared, although that section of Mad River Township was long since annexed by the Village of Riverside. Eric's tribute is based on his interpretation of his brother's "Poes of Life."

I am the brother of the way-faring stranger. The stranger that sat on the dock "playin" with the rocks, as passers by wondered why. Travel was his name and life was his game. He came to live in the glory of love and the light of beauty, which in his words are reflections of God. He came from a nation as yet to exist for some. He came to say a word, but death prevented him. He ventured into never land, wondering what it was all about. And as he said in a poem of his own: "If death prevents me from speaking my word, then the word will be said tomorrow and tomorrow never leaves a secret in the book of eternity."

Tomorrow is here and his word will be spoken, now by his cousin Bill in his writings. The way-faring stranger, a time ago in his loneliness, met Christ. He had only asked to be free and left to do his own thing, in his own way, in his own time, right or wrong, not to be judged by his fellow man nor to pass judgement on his fellow man. Just a lonely way-faring stranger he was, searching, meaning no harm, not making any laws, and not trying to break any laws. Although many laws he didn't understand, but just the same he tried to live by the laws others thought to be so.

His religion was peace and love of his fellow man; he searched the lands far and wide for his treasure. "Life is what you make of it, so make the best of it," was his story. He walked through the valley of death and had no fear, as he was love of God's love and love lives long after death in each and every man, more in some than in others was his belief. He gave his life for one unknown. Swallowed up by the sea he was, from the sea he came and to the sea he was returned as the Norse blood that cruised through his veins cried to take him home. And now he rests peacefully in God's hands. A man among many from and to a nation yet to exist for some.

And so that is why he was the way he was and why you are the way you are. We are like a blade of grass, a freshly fallen snowflake or a rose petal, we all have certain uniqueness, a certain quality, a certain calling, a certain purpose, a destiny granted to us by God. That shall be done in our own way, in our own time, that is God's plan for us, these are the things that make us different from one another. We are meant to be the same but yet different. We each have our own thing to do, our own word to spread, our own thing to give, in our own way and in our own time. Yes you are one among many and you have a contribution to make, so make it. Dale Carnegie once wrote words to the effect: I shall pass this way but once, therefore any kindness, any goodness I can do or show let me do it now for I may not pass this way again. And in the end our deeds will be judged, not by mans laws, not by fellow human beings, but by God, our judgement day will come and the decision will be based upon the accomplishments of the goals set forth to us, our personal destinies.

Brother Eric

Ron Martineau now lives in Fredericksburg, Virginia with his wife Carol, their son, Troy, and daughter, Angie.

In Remembrance of Bruce

It has been said that, "Who you are now is where you were when." I think that is a true statement. A lot of that truth has to do with the family who raised you, and I am very fortunate to be part of a loving and giving family. But, a lot of that truth also has to do with where you lived during your formative years, and with whom you shared the most memorable experiences of your life. And it is this latter explanation that I wish to reflect on for the purpose of this tribute.

I have very happy memories of my childhood, largely because I grew up in a neighbor-hood rich in adventure and populated by interesting people. To me they are people who truly enjoyed life and appreciated every living creature and thing that God placed on this earth for our experience. Further, the majority of them were, and are still today, outdoorsmen, taking pleasure in game hunting and fishing. I speak of people, who in my youth were good friends, but who in my adult life have become extended family. This extended family includes the Millers, Stevensons, Sullivans, and Tarters; all families in my immediate neighborhood.

I am thankful to God that most of my extended family is still living today. But, as time would have it, some of these beloved people have been called home to be with God. So, today, I can only visit with them in the depths and splendor of my memory. And I do lovingly remember such beloved souls like Dr. Bob and Virginia Stevenson, Grandmother Stevenson, and William "Paps" Miller. These dear ones at least lived the majority of years that we identify as a normal lifetime. But, one such departed soul was taken all too early in his life, very unexpectedly, and before any of us could say goodbye. I speak of Bruce

Stevenson. A drowning accident took Bruce's life in 1970 when he was only twenty-one years old.

I was only five years old when my family moved onto Northcliff Drive, next door to the Stevensons. That would make Bruce about two years old at the time. Naturally, Bruce and his older brother Bobby became my closest friends, along with their cousin Billy Sullivan. It seemed like we did everything together, including tearing down the chicken coop in Bruce and Bobby's back yard. When not doing these more productive chores we were busy playing softball, hide and seek, Mexican hideout, and tag. Fun and games kept us busy for hours, and we played well together. But, for whatever reason Bruce and I got into scraps and arguments early on in our lives. Yes, we were always friends, but we seemed to take out our anger on each other. I can even remember one time when Bruce was about four (and I was probably seven years old) we got into one of our many squabbles. Bruce struck out in anger and hit me in the forehead with a pointed edge of a small metal bucket. The blow gave me a deep gouge right above the bridge of my nose. I guess it was just my youthfulness that prevented me from wearing a scar for the rest of my life. Yes, Bruce and I would fight like cats and dogs, but our friendship never ceased.

I think all the good times we shared overshadow those times of rivalry. And those good times nourished a lasting friendship that I cherish to this day. So many good times, too, like the countless family trips to Lake Cumberland to water-ski, fish, swim, hike, and explore caves. And in 1959 when Bruce went on vacation with me and my family to Washington, D.C., Yorktown, Jamestown, Williamsburg, and the Great Smoky Mountains. Irreplaceable memories of happier times! Plus, who can forget all the Boy Scout outings and camping trips, or the outdoor sleepovers in the field next to Bruce's house?

Bruce made our times together exciting because he liked to live on the edge, so to speak. He liked to take chances and sort of dare danger. One such incident was when he built a hand-made raft when he was fifteen years old or so. Of course, we all knew it wasn't exactly stable because Bruce built it to rather small dimensions, about four to five feet square. But, because it would be necessary to transport the raft from his house to the closest pond or lake, Bruce sacrificed stability for compactness. Even though it was the middle of winter when Bruce completed his masterful creation he was anxious to set out on a christening cruise. So, he mounted his raft on a wobbly dolly and several of us neighbor kids helped him push it to a small pond behind St. Mark's church (on Springfield Street), about a quarter mile away. Upon reaching the pond we discovered it to be almost completely frozen over except for a small area of open water in the middle. Very cautiously, Bruce pushed his nautical masterpiece onto the ice and toward the open water. As he progressed, the ice creaked and groaned a little, but Bruce didn't get alarmed. He persevered and was soon at the edge of the open water. After tying a tether to his raft he proudly launched it and watched as it floated most elegantly. Now it was time for Bruce to step aboard and enjoy the fruits of his labor. With haste, Bruce bounded aboard. The raft was truly sturdy enough to hold Bruce's weight; however, the small dimensions of his maritime trophy caused it to roll like a lopsided guppy. Bruce was in the water in an instant! And we quickly learned that all the movies and lectures we had seen or heard regarding how difficult it is to climb out of water onto ice are all too true. Bruce was clawing at the ice and making no headway. He struggled just to keep his shoulders above the water. The frigid water was taking its toll on Bruce all too quickly. Realizing that Bruce couldn't get himself out of the water, I pulled a small tree from the ground by its roots and crawled onto the ice, extending the tree almost ten feet or so to Bruce's grasp. He grabbed the tree and I was able to pull him from the icy water. We all breathed a sigh of relief when we got Bruce to his feet and escorted him home. The raft, on the other hand, became a permanent fixture in the pond.

It is ironic that Bruce was saved from a watery hazard only to eventually, and tragically, lose his life by drowning later. But, in the latter he bravely sacrificed his life for that of another.

I deeply regret and mourn the loss of my life-long friend. May this book serve as a tribute to Bruce's life. And may this book finally give us the opportunity to say goodbye to an extended family member who we shall long remember.

Ron Martineau

Jack "Snack" Barber now lives in Poplar Branch, North Carolina with his eternal companion, Debbie, and their two daughters, Juliana Grace and Sarah Elizabeth.

It was the time of my youth. I was just 22 years old in 1969 and had already been married and bought a house. Then I lost the house, my marriage, and my little girl, Dawn Renee. It was a hard struggle for me at that time just to make ends meet.

Just about everyone I knew was over in Nam and maybe I thought I was going to be next. I was 4A since October of 1964, but now I was back to 1A and the lottery was on TV every week it seemed. Some were starting to return from Nam and we all would meet at the old hang out, Airway Billiards. I can't remember where I first met Bruce Stevenson when he got back from Nam, but I did remember him from School. He was younger than me. I knew he wasn't like his older brother, a little loud and rough acting. I had just went through a bad experience with a guy I thought I was helping out because he was down and out, but he got me in a lot of trouble. I'm sure Bruce knew all about the trouble I was in but he took me in and gave me a place to stay. It was behind his dad's Vet. office, in a 3 sided old horse barn.

I had 3 army blankets and a rug for warmth; it was 18 degrees in April. One morning there was snow all over me from the wind blowing it in the open space. We both started working for the Laborers International Union down on Third Street, going out on different jobs. Some how we got some lumber and built a wall and a door.

We had us a house to live in, and my brother Bob bought some mattresses from an auction. I put all six of them on the floor. Bruce still had his army cot and he put all of his metals on the wall next to his bed. I never got over on his side and looked at them, or talked too much about them. It seems like I was into his reel-to-reel audio tape. We would listen to them for hours.

We talked a lot about getting it together, me since I had lost everything and Bruce just starting over on the right foot, forgetting Nam and enjoying life. He loved life so much, I remember when he talked he would smile and move his one arm back and forth across his belt buckle. He talked the jive of the time, as we all did.

But Bruce had changed from a red neck to a peace lover, I mean he was for real about it. One day out of the blue he said to me, "Hey snack I'm going to California. Odus Brown is out there."

"Far out," I said, "how are you going?" He said, "I'm riding my 305 Honda." I thought he was crazy, 2500 miles on a 305 Honda. "Sure, go ahead," I said, "have fun."

I can't remember now where I was at but I remember hearing that he made it from Odus's brother Larry. Larry wanted to go so I went with him out to California (Santa Anna). I met up with Bruce again, he had just got a ticket for something on his bike and got a $15 fine. He told me that he couldn't pay it so he was going to have to serve jail time. I said, "too bad." Bruce said, "no its not, it will only be a day and a half, in Orange county." He went in and when he got out I asked him how it was. He said that they had a library and he read the whole time he was there.

We spent a lot of time at Newport Beach, body surfing and looking for food. We were beach bums; that's what we would tell the girls (tourist). We had dark tans and we would tell the girls that we lived on the beach and ask them if they had any peanut butter and bread. Sometimes it worked.

We hooked up with some guy from Pittsburgh and when Odus went to Oakland we hitch hiked up there and stayed with 3 college girls. I slept on the back porch and Bruce and Jeff slept on the floor in the front room, it was a three-bedroom house. I was going to stay there for a while in Oakland. The Mormon temple was just up the hill from where I worked. I got a job pumping gas and so did Bruce.

Some time had passed and I had $100 saved up, and Jeff, the guy from Pittsburgh, had a motor bike and wanted to go back to Pittsburgh. I thought it would be fun to ride on the back of a bike, well wrong move. Anyway we went over to where Bruce was working and said we were leaving, and Bruce said he was staying. I remember thinking that he was getting it together just like we talked about back in Dayton, and off we went up through the Napa Valley. The first week in October I ended up in Otway, Ohio on a farm my parents owned and wished every day that I was back in California and how lucky Bruce was, because he had it together.

All that winter I would think I'm going back out there and see my old friend Bruce when it gets warm, my friend who took me in and gave me a roof over my head and food to eat, but it was never to be. Good Bye Bruce, I'll see you again in the next world.

Your Friend Snack

Odus Brown now lives in Morgantown, West Virginia with his wife Rosanna.

A Tribute to the legacy of Bruce Michael Stevenson

It has now been 30 years since Bruce drowned at Half Moon Bay, California, after repeatedly swimming out and saving other peoples' lives who were caught in rip tides. That was so typical of Bruce, putting others' safety before his own. He was only 22 years old.

Bruce was my best friend and had been for many years. We knew each other since our early teenage years and he and his family helped me when I was young in more ways than I can enumerate here, but suffice to say, those memories will be with me for the rest of my life.

Bruce and I shared many adventures together, although we did not look at them as "adventures"; it was just our lives. We also had the distinction of serving in Vietnam at the same time, although in different units. We were able to spend some time together on one occasion, which was fortunate under the circumstances of war. We both survived without a scratch (at least any visible scars).

Growing up and "becoming men" in the 1960s was, in retrospect, bizarre and enlightening, to say the least. But we faced it head on with all our might. When we are "young" we usually consider ourselves to have many friends, but as we grow older and hopefully wiser we realize we have many acquaintances but very few true friends. A true friend will be there for you no matter what and will accept you and your foibles. And some would say, give their lives for you.

Bruce was just that kind of friend. Bruce was one of the most brave and courageous men I ever knew. While I could cite many instances that he was, the circumstances of his death, saving total strangers over and over until apparent exhaustion took his life, tells it all.

Although as young men we had at times been considered "rowdy," we were not "mean." We just did not take bullying from anyone. Even when significantly outnumbered Bruce would and did stand by your side and "fight to the finish" without hesitation. But that is not the only reason for my undying friendship with Bruce, it was his integrity, loyalty, generosity and honesty. Even to this day if I had to go into battle, of any kind, I would want Bruce by side.

Most of us who had the privilege of knowing Bruce are in our 50s with graying hair, and various professions. I still miss him and think of him often. I know he would be proud of me and I would be proud of him. We would reminisce and reflect on our adventures, be they successes or shortcomings. We would talk about our children, families and friends, as well as our future. I have no doubt Bruce would be (as he was) a great and respected man. He never demanded respect; he earned it.

Neither Bruce nor I were saints, and there are some things we did that I am not proud of, but they were things we did to survive. This is not rationalization or avoiding responsibility for our sometime less than honorable actions, but we lived on the streets using our wit and the will to survive.

Knowing Bruce as well as I did, I know he would not hesitate to again perform his heroic action to save the many people at Half Moon Bay, as he did April 5, 1970. If he had survived, he would have smiled, jumped into his beautiful '57 Chevy and driven away with his girlfriend not expecting or seeking any platitudes or publicity. Instead he made the ultimate sacrifice.

When Bruce's cousin, Bill Sullivan, told me of his desire to write a book about Bruce, I was impressed and supportive. Apparently he is ready to publish his laborious effort. He asked me if I could write something for the epilog, which I feel an honor. I must confess it was not easy but I could do nothing less.

I wish Bill and all his family nothing but the best and I thank him for this opportunity to once again voice my heartfelt love and respect to the memory of the best friend and bravest man I will ever know.

Respectfully,
Odus Brown

Shortly after Bruce's death I jotted down a few short words, or poem if you like, to try and deal with my deep hurt and loss of my best friend:

Truth exists in many different colors
Each itself, one inside the other

Fire warms food and burns the trees away
As bees make honey and sting you when they can
Water quenches thirst and drags along the sand
And be what may takes away A Man

OB 1970

About the Author

Bill Sullivan, a lifelong dweller of the Dayton, Ohio area, is the proverbial "jack of all trades." He graduated from Walter E. Stebbins High School in June of 1965 and enrolled the following January at what would become Wright State University, majoring in *biology*. Fifteen and one half years later—through no fault of his own—he was dismissed due to graduation. His degree was in *English education*.

When Bill refused to attend his college commencement ceremony, the woman whom God had ordained to love, honor and afflict him forever "had a hissy." Bill insisted that by his reckoning one hot June night spent in the midst of a crowd of fidgety folks dressed in sweaty robes and tangled tassels, while well meaning officials drone on and on, should be accounted more than sufficient to atone for the sins of a single lifetime. The woman, though, his eternal sweetheart, the former Miss Donna Marie O'Keefe, predicted dire consequences and eventual overwhelming remorse if he did not relent and attend. Bill thought about it for thirty seconds, then went fishing.

A few of Bill's jobs over the years include live bait catcher, fur trapper, construction grunt, red iron walker, pistol packing pool hall honcho, assembly line robot, supply weenie, uncivil servant, newspaper columnist, and perhaps most daring of all, substitute high school teacher. None of these jobs, however, as well as seven years as a teenager himself and stints as both a Scoutmaster and an Explorer Post Advisor, prepared Bill for what was to become his most challenging vocation—shepherd of his four lively youngsters through their teen years. Somehow, though, Bill and his sweetheart survived those years. Today, four fine young adults, as well as two spouses and three grandchildren, bear witness to their parents' success. Still though, Bill and Donna never seem exactly sure how many children and grandchildren are living with them from one month to the next.

In retrospect, Bill sees the premature death of his cousin, Bruce Michael Stevenson—*Eleven Miles South of Half Moon Bay*—as a turning point in his life. That loss prompted him to question more deeply than he ever had before the meaning of Life and the source of Truth. With his sweetheart and eternal companion by his side, he eventually found that meaning and that source in the restored Gospel of Jesus Christ.

9 780595 09827